Isle Be Seeing You

JoAnn Bassett

Published by Lokelani Publishing
Green Valley, Arizona 85614
http://www.joannbassett.com
* * *

This is a work of fiction. Names, characters, places, and incidents are either the product of the author's imagination or used fictitiously. Any resemblance to actual events, locales, organizations or persons, living or dead, is entirely coincidental and beyond the intent of the author and publisher.

ISBN-13 - 978-1973852360
ISBN-10 - 1973852365

Also by JoAnn Bassett:
"Islands of Aloha Mystery" Series
Maui Widow Waltz
Livin' Lahaina Loca
Lana'i of the Tiger
Kaua'i Me a River
O'ahu Lonesome Tonight?
I'm Kona Love You Forever
Moloka'i Lullaby
Hilo, Goodbye

"The Escape to Maui" Series
Mai Tai Butterfly
Lucky Beach

For Susan Cook-Goodwin, a mainland mom with an aloha heart.

1

In a battle between truth and honor, which should win? Most people would pick truth. After all, from the time we can talk we're scolded for lying. "Don't lie to me," is right up there with, "Eat your vegetables," and "Respect your elders." So, it takes a bit of doing to challenge that mindset. But should truth always prevail? After what happened in late July, I'm not so sure.

My new husband and I were headed home from a clinic next to Maui Memorial Hospital, each of us lost in our own private reverie. I say "new husband" because we'd only been married six months. As far as I was concerned, the honeymoon wasn't over but the clock was definitely ticking.

We turned *mauka,* or inland, off the Hana Highway to the Haleakala Highway. The dark bulk of the mountain loomed before us—a vivid reminder we were but a speck in the natural landscape. The depth of our silence was a pretty clear sign neither of us was ready to accept the news we'd been given, much less talk about it.

Finn flipped the turn signal to make a left onto Hali'imaile Road and I finally spoke up. "When are you due back on O'ahu?"

"Gotta go tomorrow. I was supposed to be there tonight, but..." He downshifted in lieu of finishing.

"Yeah. Well, I appreciate you sticking around."

He nodded.

We went inside and I half-heartedly offered to make dinner, but Finn wisely didn't take me up on it. I'm a lousy cook in the best of circumstances. Given my current attitude, I'd probably poison someone.

"Think I'll sleep upstairs tonight," he said.

"Seriously? Don't you think we should talk about this?"

"What's there to say? You made it clear what you want and I can't cut it. If you want to wipe the slate clean, I understand."

"What's that mean?"

"You can get an annulment for this kind of thing, you know."

"Wait a second. I'll admit this is—"

He cut me off. "Look, Pali. I need some time, okay? It's bad enough as it is. Let's not make it worse by rehashing it all night long."

The next morning Finn crept downstairs before daybreak. I heard the fourth stair creak and hoped he'd come in to say good-bye but then I heard the back door click shut. There were no flights out of Kahului to Honolulu until after seven, so his early departure meant he'd opted for airport coffee over dealing with me. It stung, but I respected his wishes. I like to jump in and get things straightened out. Finn prefers a "time heals all wounds" approach.

Since this was more Finn's problem than mine, I was willing to let him call the shots. We'd both been single far into our adult years and we'd grown accustomed to flying solo. Wrangling things out as a couple often got us bogged down in perceived slights and accusations of "you're not listening." This was clearly not the best time to strain our already precarious communication skills.

I got up at six-thirty and slipped on my usual work attire: cropped pants, plain color t-shirt, and *rubba slippas*. I didn't take a shower. I ran a hand through my hair attempting to fluff out the "bed head" as I made my way to my car. It wasn't like me to go to work grubby, but then it wasn't like me to wallow in self-pity like this, either.

I considered pulling in at my shop, but kept driving. I've been a wedding planner going on four years now. I own my own business, "Let's Get Maui'd," and my shop is smack dab in the center of the über-chic hippie enclave of Pa'ia, Maui. When I first moved to the area, the town was mostly known for simply being the last recognizable town on the road to Hana. It was a place where tourists gassed up and picked up a picnic lunch before heading out on the twisting trek to Maui's nether reaches. Now, it's cheek-to-jowl with high-priced bikini shops, art galleries, and organic cafés that serve stuff like arugula and kale bruschetta. Go figure.

I'm thirty-six years old, born and raised in the islands. I was born on Kaua'i. After my mom died and my dad took off for parts unknown, my guardian, who we called Auntie Mana, moved us to Maui. I've been here ever since except for the four years I went to the University of Hawaii on O'ahu. The U of H now has a satellite campus here on Maui, but that's a recent addition.

I pulled into the alley behind Palace of Pain, the martial arts studio or *guan*, where I work out. A banged-up black Jeep Wrangler signaled that my *sifu*, or head instructor, was already there.

I pushed through the unlocked door. "*Aloha*, Sifu."

"*Aloha,* Pali. How'd it go?"

"Not so good."

When I failed to go on, he narrowed his eyes in what I covertly call his "Vulcan mind meld" look.

"What'd the doc say?"

"It's not looking promising."

He stared, and then raised his palms. "What? Am I gonna need a crowbar to get more than that out of you?"

"Sorry, Sifu, but it's hard for me to talk about."

"You need tea."

He motioned for me to follow him to his office. As I trotted behind him, it occurred to me I'd probably been in that office more times than I'd been in the kitchen of my own house. I'd trained with Doug Kanekoa for over ten years. I'd been in my house in Hali'imaile half that long.

He began his brewing ritual which was as choreographed as a Japanese tea ceremony. Flip the switch on the electric kettle to boil the water, lift the lid from the pottery wish pot that held his proprietary tea blend and then measure a heaping spoonful of tea leaves for each cup he was brewing. I could tell how long he expected me to hang around by how many cups he made. This time he tapped the spoon against the porcelain teapot four times, so I knew this wasn't going to be a quick sip and go. He must've been gearing up for a speech. I hoped he was expecting to do most of the talking, because I was in no mood to delve into my situation.

Sifu Doug's tea is legendary, although it's totally on the down low. Doug only offers it to those in his innermost circle. It was only when I earned my first black belt that he invited me to share a cup.

Rumor has it the blend includes some herbs of questionable origin, but far be it for me to demand the recipe. All I'm willing to say is that I usually finish my cup in a much better mood than I came in with.

"So, let's review," he said. "What exactly did the doctor say?"

"She found what she called 'fertility issues' with Finn."

"But you were kind of expecting that, right? I mean, you told me he'd been a paid guinea pig for a nuclear medicine experiment when he was in college. That kind of stuff can mess you up."

"True. But we were hoping it hadn't."

"Did the doc say that was the for-sure reason?"

"No. She said there's no sure way to know what caused it, but for now, Finn's sperm count is pitiful."

Doug winced at my reference to unmanly-things. "So, now what?"

"I don't know, Sifu. We both avoided talking about it last night, and now Finn's off to O'ahu for the next week or so."

He nodded.

I set my empty cup down on his desk. "Do me a favor and don't tell anyone, okay? Finn's having a hard time. He said maybe we should get an annulment."

"Whoa, that's harsh. But no worries on the talkie-talk. I got marriage problems of my own."

I looked up. "You and Lani? You guys are as reliable as the tide. What's going on?"

Leilani Kanekoa, who everyone calls Lani, was Sifu Doug's wife and the mother of his two early teens *keiki*.

"Seems she's got somethin' goin' on."

We'd switched roles. Now he was the reticent one, and I was the one probing for answers.

"What kind of 'something'? What are you talking about?"

"She's been sneakin' around. Tellin' me she's goin' someplace and then I find out she never showed up. I'm thinkin' she's steppin' out on me."

I blew out a breath. "Okay, look. I'm not sure about much, but I'm a-hundred percent sure that's not true. Lani and you are like mac salad and rice. I mean, plate lunch is no good without both."

"Maybe. But it looks like maybe she's piling on a second helpin' of kalua pig. Maybe I'm not enough man for her."

I laughed. "Then every dude on this island's in trouble. Look, I'm not buying it. You need to talk to her."

"I've tried."

"You need to try again. Don't give up."

"I'm givin' you this strictly on the DL, right? I mean, don' go sayin' nothin' to Farrah or Finn. I jus' needed to tell somebody."

"I'm honored you'd trust me with this, Sifu. And don't worry, I won't tell a soul. But I'm positive you're wrong. Promise you'll call me as soon as you figure out what's going on, okay?"

"Even if she's doin' the deed?"

"Look, you've said yourself I've got great instincts. And my gut tells me there's a perfectly logical explanation that has nothing to do with her cheating on you."

"I hope you're right."

"I *am* right. And now I want you to go home. I'll teach the *keiki* class at two."

"But you don't know what to do."

"Oh, come on, Sifu. It's a bunch of little kids. And their moms. Have a little faith in me."

He shot me a tight smile. "If you insist."

"I do. Now go home and have a heart-to-heart with Lani."

"*Mahalo*, Pali. I owe you."

"Sifu, on the great tally sheet in the sky, I've still got hundreds to go."

Doug left and I rinsed out our cups and wiped out the hot pot. It was only twelve-thirty. Plenty of time for me to grab a bite to eat before the kiddie class showed up.

Seriously. How hard could it be to wrangle some little ankle-biters for an hour?

2

After lunch I went back to the *guan* and saw six cars parked in the alley. That meant I'd be running a class for at least six kids who were hip deep in the throes of the terrible twos and threes, along with their harried mothers. Although an hour earlier I'd brushed it off as a no-brainer, I'd never actually watched one of Doug's "Keiki Kung Fu" classes so I wasn't up to speed on the routine. But how hard could it be? I'd lower my voice an octave, growl at them to stand up, sit down, and then assume an easy form Doug had probably already taught them. It'd be like running a dog obedience class for knee-high humans.

I pushed through the door and was greeted to a roar I'd never heard before at the Palace of Pain. At least a dozen kids chased each other around, shrieking and giggling like they'd just stuffed their faces with Halloween candy and their blood sugar levels were spiking in the red zone. But Halloween was three months away.

The mothers huddled in a far corner on metal folding chairs. They looked like refugees waiting for UN peacekeepers to show up to get the situation under control. Then it hit me: I was the UN.

Doug had a canister air horn he'd been given as a joke when he'd been asked to referee a seniors' martial arts tournament. The horn had actually come in handy as he'd pretty much lost his voice after only a few rounds of officiating at full-volume when the participants kept shouting, "Speak up! Can't hear you." I found the air horn in his office and came back out to the practice room and gave it a toot. The blast was ear-splitting.

The *keiki* screeched to a halt. The mothers' heads snapped up as if they were marionettes and someone had jerked their strings. After a beat of stunned silence a few of the younger-looking kids started to sniffle, then a couple of them burst into full-blown tears. One of the bigger boys gently patted a smaller compadre on the back as if to assure him he'd be okay.

"What the *hell*?" One of the mothers stood up, hands on hips.

In a calm voice I said, "*Aloha*. My name is Sifu Pali, and I'll be conducting class today. Lesson one: each of you will show respect for the *guan* by waiting quietly in a sitting position until your *sifu* directs you to do something."

One little girl kept up the waterworks. She glanced over at her mother as if hoping she'd come over and comfort her. Or more likely, she was waiting for mommy to promise her something if she'd knock it off.

I held up an arm. "Okay, *everybody* on the floor. Cross your legs and fold your arms across your chest." I demonstrated folding my arms but I stayed standing.

The little kids looked from one to the other as if I'd spoken Swahili but I kept my mouth shut. When it dawned on everyone I wasn't going to elaborate, one of the mothers got out of her chair and sat down cross-legged on the floor. She folded her arms.

The other mothers followed suit. One by one, they got out of their chairs and down on the floor with their arms folded. A very pregnant mom had a hard time crossing her legs so she tucked them along one side.

I hadn't meant for the moms to sit on the floor, but now that they'd done it I wasn't about to back down. Not one of them looked like she'd suffer much damage by participating in the class. Besides, it gave me an idea.

The kids drifted over to their mothers and plopped down, legs crossed, arms folded.

"Okay. Good. Second lesson of the day: obey your mother. Watch what she does and do the same thing. Today your mom will be your honorary *sifu*, so learn from her."

For the next twenty minutes we played a kind of "Simon Says" where I barked a simple instruction, then demonstrated it, and the mothers did their best to keep up. The kids watched and copied their moms. Some moms seemed to be in better shape than the others, but I kept the workout easy and nobody fell behind.

When we'd gone through every basic form I could think of, I announced that the first part of the class was over. I told the kids to watch carefully as I demonstrated the correct way to show gratitude to their mothers for acting as their *sifu*. I modeled placing my right fist into the palm of my left hand and lowering my head while keeping my eyes focused forward.

"Look your *sifu* in the eye and say, '*Mahalo, sifu*, for your time and wisdom.'" I made that last part up. At PoP, adult students offer silent respect to their *sifu*, but I felt the kids needed to say something.

The kids solemnly followed suit.

I asked the moms to "take five" while I divided the kids into groups of four and ordered them to run relays from one end of the practice room to the other. They took off and once again the noise level approached deafening as the team members cheered each other on. When the kids started looking sufficiently winded, I gave the air horn a split-second peep and everyone froze.

Thankfully, this time nobody freaked out.

"*Mahalo* for coming today," I said. "Sifu Doug had to deal with an *'ohana* matter, but he'll be back next time."

As moms began herding their offspring out to the alley, one of them came up to me. "That was a really good class. *Mahalo* for stepping in for Doug."

"My pleasure. Kids this age sure have a lot of energy."

She laughed. "Tell about it. It was great for you to run them like that. I'll bet my boy goes down for a nap without a fight for the first time in months."

I locked up and drove to my shop. After a half-hour of puttering I hadn't accomplished much beyond opening the mail and staring blankly at my emails. My thinking kept getting interrupted by thoughts of what was going on with Lani, not to mention my own disappointing news from the day before.

At three-thirty I closed up and went next door to see Farrah Kingston, my long-time best friend. Since earlier that year, she was also my sister-in-law.

"Hey, girl," she said waving at me from the produce section. She was lining up glistening ruby-red tomatoes into neat rows. The sign above them read "Local Tomatoes $5.99/lb."

"Seriously? Six bucks for a pound of tomatoes?"

"They're organic."

"For that price, they should be hallucinogenic."

"These little dudes are from Moonbeam Farms up in Kula. People swear they're the bomb."

"The what?"

"The bomb, you know, the bestest ever."

I picked up a tomato, careful not to squeeze it. "At least that's what they tell you. People who hand over half their paycheck for fancy vegetables probably need to convince themselves it's worth it."

"Did you boogie in here just to dis my glorious vegetable matter, or did you—" She stopped and put a hand over her mouth. "My bad. I spaced about you goin' to the doctor yesterday. What'd you'd find out?"

"It doesn't look good. The doc said we have 'reproductive issues' and it's going to be hard for me to get pregnant."

Farrah squinted. "But she didn't say 'no cigar,' right? I mean, you're tough. I've seen you do heavy lifting when you had to. You'll power through."

"It seems I'm not the one with the problem."

"Oh. Bummer, man."

We fell silent as we both considered the implications of Finn, or any red-blooded male, learning he had fatherhood issues.

"How's he takin' it?" she whispered, although there wasn't anyone within thirty feet who could hear us.

I shrugged. "He left for O'ahu this morning. I tried to talk to him last night but he shut me down. Right now it's pretty much 'don't ask, don't tell.'"

"Like that ever worked before."

"I know. I'm pretty sure he wouldn't be pleased if he knew I was telling you about it."

She crossed her heart. "No prob. Mum's the word."

"What about Ono? I can't ask you to keep secrets from him." Ono was Farrah's husband, and my husband's brother.

"Ha! Again, no prob. With the twins climbin' in our bed every night, he'd be jealous of his little bro's extended honeymoon. I know you guys want *keiki* of your own, but what I'd give for a little alone time with my man, eh?"

"I'm north of thirty-five, Farrah. Not much time left to start a family."

"I hear ya."

"I'd like Finn to be able to tell Ono in his own way. Those two have been competitive from day one."

"True dat. I'll tick a lock." She twisted her bottom lip with a thumb and forefinger. "Not a peep outta me."

"*Mahalo.*"

We let a beat of silence pass before Farrah said, "Oh, I almost forgot. I'm pretty sure our new place is haunted."

"What?"

"Yeah. Total bummer, yeah? In all the craziness over getting the coin to buy it and then moving the *keiki* and everything, we spaced on getting the house blessed. Seems we got a *Night of the Living Dead* thing goin' on. There's a dude in cane worker duds haulin' a big machete around the back yard. You can kinda see through him, like a ghost. "

I shot her a quizzical look.

"No, serious," she said. "Ono and me have both seen him."

"That doesn't sound good."

She shrugged. "He's outside, so for now it's no biggie. But Ono's stressed he could boogie inside. I mean, it's a ghost, right? Those dudes can go through walls. And even if he stays outside he might take a mind to going after the *keiki* when they're playing in the yard."

"What're you going to do?"

"Ono told me not to stress about it. He's hoping it'll just go away, but I'm not so sure. On the sly I've been trying to get in touch with the dude to see what he wants, but so far, *nada.*"

Farrah's sort of a paranormal princess, like a Mystical Barbie. She's got all the accessories needed to contact the dead, as well as the "undead." She claims the undead are souls who've shed their mortal bodies but continue to walk among us. Most are hanging around trying to complete personal unfinished business and are generally harmless. But she acknowledges some harbor darker intentions.

"If you contact this guy but he won't go away, what's your plan B?" I couldn't believe I was talking about this as if contacting the dead was a commonplace chore we all deal with from time to time.

"I s'pose I'll have to hire a *kahu* to do a blessing," she said. "But that will cost moolah, and we're pretty tapped out."

"You know Finn and I are happy to help."

She held up a palm. "No dice. We're already going down for the third time in the money pool. We can't keep moochin' from you guys 'cuz we'll never be able to pay you back."

"You don't have to pay us back. You're family."

She laughed. "'*Ohana* are the worst moochers of all. *Mahalo*, but no. We'll figure this out on our own."

I hugged her, and bought a pre-packaged Greek salad for dinner that night. When I was little, my auntie Mana used to tell me, *"Ipo, you got lots to think about, but nuthin' to worry about."* *Ipo* is a Hawaiian word that's used like the English word, "sweetie."

But, from where I was sitting, it seemed the past two days had dragged up quite a bit to worry about.

3

At ten that night, Finn called from his super-secret location on O'ahu. He'd never told me exactly where it was, or what his specific job entailed, but I knew he worked in military cyber-security. I assumed his office was at Hickam Air Force Base near Pearl Harbor or maybe Schofield Army Barracks in the north-central part of the island.

"How'd your day go?" he asked.

"Not great."

"Me neither. I found out they're sending me overseas."

Alarms went off in my head. "Where? And what for?"

"Can't say. But I'm allowed to tell you I won't be in a hot zone. My boss swears we won't hear bombs falling or bullets flying."

"That's a relief. Can you at least tell me what continent?"

"No can do. In fact, this project's so secret I probably won't be able to call home much. We'll have a satellite phone in case of emergency, but we can't bring our mobiles." After spending the past few years in Australia Finn still called cell phones, mobiles. With the long "i" sound. In the early going I'd corrected him a few times but he shot me stink eye. Definitely not the hill I wanted to die on.

"How about Skype or email?"

"Nope. Just the sat. My assistant here on O'ahu can get a message to me, if necessary, but that's it."

"When are you leaving?"

He blew out a breath. "Tomorrow, early."

"But what about packing? I thought you only kept a week's worth of clothes over there."

"They'll hook us up with the stuff we'll need."

"When will you be coming home?"

"Can't say. They said they'll cut us loose when we get what we came for."

"We need to talk, Finn. And now you'll be gone for who knows how long."

"Sorry." He didn't sound very sorry. He sounded like a guy who'd volunteered to go to who knows where for who knows how long rather than talk about his malfunctioning man parts.

"Bring me back a souvenir, okay? You know, maybe some Russian vodka or a pair of those silk Chinese slippers."

"Nice try, but I swear I don't know have a clue where we're headed."

"I'll miss you," I said.

"You too, *ku'uipo*." He'd used the Hawaiian word for "sweetheart." In the past few months he'd made an effort to learn the local lingo. Usually he used it correctly. Sometimes he didn't. But I was smart enough to know if I wanted him to keep trying, I'd best not nit-pick.

"Love you," I said.

There was a pause. "Love you, too, Pali. I'm sorry things didn't work out."

Before I could respond he went on. "And don't worry. I'm in good hands. They said they'd pull us out at the first sign of trouble."

I didn't like the sound of that. Not any of it.

* * *

The next morning I slept in, but still managed to make it to my shop by nine. I had a ten o'clock appointment with a bride and groom whose wedding was only six days away. I still hadn't met them, which was unusual for me. I normally like to meet clients at least a week before their wedding date, but today's happy couple had had their flight cancelled from the West Coast so they'd arrived a day late. Then, when they got to Honolulu , the airlines managed to lose the bride-to-be's luggage so they'd spent an entire day on O'ahu tracking it down and waiting for it to be delivered to their hotel. It arrived so late they couldn't get a flight to Maui until the next day.

If I viewed life through the same lens as Farrah, I might've been wondering if the universe was trying to tell them something. I'm not superstitious, but still my anxiety level ticked up a notch with every phone call detailing the latest snafu. I'm a wedding planner, with emphasis on the word, "plan." In this business, winging it doesn't pass for playful serendipity, it's a recipe for disaster. Florists run out of flowers, limos are in the shop, and restaurants are too booked up to take a dinner reservation for twelve. In short, I was eager to get things nailed down.

The couple showed up on time looking none the worse for wear in spite of their ordeals. The bride-to-be, whose name was Katrina, but went by Kat, was a tiny woman. She was probably five feet tall if she stood on tiptoe and weighed no more than ninety pounds. Her skin was so fair the pale blue veins at her temple, neck and inner arms looked like an Aloha Airlines interisland route map.

In contrast, Alex, her fiancé, was a *bruddah* of substance. He was at least six feet six, with the shoulder-to-fingertip wingspan of a long-distance swimmer. He was dark-skinned, probably from both parentage and sun exposure and he had jet black hair with thick eyebrows that met in the middle. I always marvel at couples who seem mismatched, whether it's due to disparate age, physical attributes, or education level. How do these people meet? And is it true opposites attract, or was my freshman college roommate right? She used to say, "Opposite attraction only works with magnets." Wouldn't you know, she was a physics major—a rather cynical physics major. If I remember correctly she was from one of those skinny little states on the East Coast like Vermont or New Hampshire.

I invited the wedding couple to sit down and I covertly crossed my fingers as Alex dropped into one of the wicker guest chairs across from my desk. The chairs were sturdy, up to a point. But I had no idea what that point might be—two hundred pounds, two-fifty?

The chair held. He reached a beefy paw out to grip the childlike fingers of his fiancée. She shot him a thin smile. Then she pulled her hand back and crossed her arms. From their body language she appeared to be the one in control. The alpha to his beta.

"Great to finally meet you," I said.

Kat spoke first. "Yeah, it's been a long week. Will we still be able to get married on Tuesday?"

"I don't see a problem. It's good you picked a weekday. We might've run into some problems if you'd chosen a Friday or Saturday, but Tuesday is typically one of the slower days around here. Not as much demand for sunset beach permits or dinner reservations."

A look passed between them and Alex said, "Uh, we don't want to get married at night."

"Ah, so much the better. Afternoon weddings rarely run into conflicts."

Kat locked eyes with me. "Actually, we want to get married *before* afternoon."

I let a beat go by in case they cared to elaborate. They didn't.

"Okay. I'm a little confused. I'm pretty sure on your booking form you said you wanted an outside wedding."

"That's correct," said Kat.

I scanned the page I'd printed of their online reservation. My website includes a checklist of venue choices.

They'd left "church," "beach," and "private location" unchecked.

"But you still want to be married outside, correct?"

"That's right," Kat said again. "But not on a beach."

Alex finally chimed in. "We want to get married on a mountain, close to God."

I leaned back in my chair. "Mount Haleakala?" It was kind of a silly question. Haleakala is pretty much the only named mountain on Maui with public access.

Alex grinned. "Yeah, that one. We want to get married at the top at sunrise."

They shot each other a triumphant grin as if they were the first people on earth to come up with such a clever idea.

"I see. Well, that's certainly an interesting setting. Tell you what, let's go up there tomorrow morning and check it out. I always like my couples to get a feel for where they'll tie the knot. It lessens anxiety and gives you a chance to visualize what things will be like on your big day."

"Can you drive us up there?" Kat said. "We don't want to get lost."

"I'm afraid you'll have to take your own car 'cuz mine's a two-seater."

That was more or less true. My little Mini Cooper technically seats four since it has four seat belts, but the seats in the back are just for show, or *menehune*, the Hawaiian word for leprechauns. Even tiny Kat would've been twisted into a pretzel after the hour-long trek to the summit.

Alex turned to his fiancée. "It's okay. We should take our own car, babe. We might want to stick around and do a little hiking. And Pali probably needs to get back."

I nodded. "True. I have a lot of things to line up before next Tuesday. Let's start by getting some of it handled now."

I pulled out a wedding folder and had them fill in their contact information. Then we spent the next hour going through the checklist: flowers, music, officiant, vows, and so on. I gave them a map of Maui and mentioned that in late July sunrise occurs before six a.m.

"How about we meet at five-fifteen in the upper parking lot near the ranger station?"

Kat nodded. "We'll be there."

Before they left, Alex asked if I'd join them in prayer. I agreed, and we all joined hands. He mumbled an appeal for a blessing on their union, requesting good weather for the wedding day.

As they closed the door behind them, I felt a twinge of remorse over what I'd done, or more precisely, what I *hadn't* done. But after four years in this business I've learned you can't sway prospective brides and grooms from insisting on stupid stuff. I've tried to warn dozens of couples away from unwise decisions and it never works. If the least little thing goes wrong they claim everything would've been *perfect* if I'd simply allowed them to do things their way.

Now, I'm all about hands-on learning. I say little but allow my clients to experience the full impact of their illogical ideas. With any luck, they figure out their folly prior to the actual wedding day. This keeps my "I told you so's" to a minimum while giving them the opportunity to save face. But sadly, even in the face of certain calamity, I've had clients insist on staying the course.

When that happens I paste a smile on my face and allow things to unfold as they will. I haven't seen it all, but I've seen plenty: beachside weddings in the pouring rain because the couple poo-pooed the offer of a canopy; or a screaming kid who drowned out the wedding ceremony (and the audio on a seven-hundred-dollar video) because the bride's matron of honor insisted on holding her four-month-old in her arms, even though the little dude had cried and carried on throughout the rehearsal. Or how about the bacon and blue cheese wedding cake with chocolate buttercream frosting? The couple figured their favorite burger and candy flavors would translate nicely to a three-tiered sugary confection. And yes, it tasted as bizarre as it sounds.

But who knows? Maybe Alex and Kat will enjoy getting up at two-thirty a.m. and clawing their way up a pitch-black mountain road in a long line of other sunrise watchers. Hopefully, they'll arrive before the upper parking lot is full and park rangers block it off and make the latecomers return to a lower lot and hike back up. Possibly their idea of a good time is standing around in a whipping wind with temperatures only a few degrees above freezing. And perhaps they'll be cheery even if the cloud cover is so thick it's impossible to see more than a faint glow from the rising sun and not the brilliant explosion of light and color detailed in Maui travel books.

It was out of my hands. I'd said little, but reminded them they'd need to make a reservation with the Park Service before four o'clock that afternoon. The reservation system was relatively new and some visitors hadn't heard about it.

They assured me they'd paid the fee and were ready to go. I kept the smile going until they closed the door behind them, all the while hoping that after our little scouting trip in the cold and dark they'd be willing to listen to reason.

4

At noon, I locked up the shop and made my way down to the Palace of Pain. I was anxious to hear how things had gone with Lani. Doug's Jeep was parked in the alley, but when I went inside, the practice room was empty and the lights were off. This wasn't Doug's style at all. He and I maintained an ongoing tiff over the annoying fluorescent lights. He insisted on keeping them blazing, and I preferred working out in the cozy gloom of a cinderblock room with light coming solely from a row of grimy clerestory windows.

I called out, "Sifu?"

"In here, Pali." The voice came from his office.

I made my way across the dimly-lit room, careful to not trip over the practice mats, and stood in the doorway. I could barely make out his form behind his battered Formica desk.

"Why are you sitting in the dark?"

"First you rag on me about turning on the lights, and now you're on my back 'cuz I don't? Looks like I can't win."

It wasn't like Sifu Doug to be grumpy. I didn't say anything for a few seconds waiting to see if he'd explain his sour mood.

"Sorry, Pali. It's been a rough morning."

"You want to talk? Maybe we should have some tea."

He considered my suggestion, and said, "You mind making it? I'm tapped out."

I couldn't remember a time when Doug had sounded so down. The guy had always been my go-to cheerleader no matter how lousy things were in his own life. But now it appeared the tables had turned and I needed to pull out my imaginary pom-poms.

I flicked on the overhead light and the overhead fixture buzzed for a couple of seconds before blazing to light. He blinked and winced as his eyes adjusted to the bluish glare.

"Sorry, Sifu."

He didn't respond.

I slipped behind him and took a metal tea canister down from the shelf behind his desk. I popped the lid and found it empty, with only a few green flakes scattered across the bottom.

"Seems you're out of tea."

"Looks like I'll need to get some."

I fully expected that meant we wouldn't be having tea, but instead, he reached into his pocket and pulled out a keyring with about a dozen keys on it. He flipped through his keys until he came to one with a neon pink plastic cap. I'd seen key caps like that at hardware store check-out counters. The impulse purchase display said the caps make it easier to identify which key is which.

He used the key to unlock the bottom drawer of his desk. "Don't tell, but I keep the important stuff in here, away from snoopy eyes and sticky fingers."

He rifled through a jumble of papers and pulled out a gallon-size zip-lock bag of dried vegetable matter. Then he dumped about a third of the contents into the tea container, throwing off the unmistakable aroma of illicit herbs.

I pointed to the bag. "Wow. That looks like enough to last you a year."

Doug made a popping sound with his lips. "The way things are goin' lately, this won't last 'til the end of the month."

I'd agreed to make the tea so I got to work. I carefully measured two small scoops of leaves into a tea strainer. Then I checked the little hot pot to make sure it had enough water and plugged it in. Within a minute the water was bubbling. I dropped the strainer into the pot and after a few minutes filled two handleless cups. First one, then the other, making sure each was filled to one-half-inch of the brim.

Doug remained silent throughout the process. I felt nearly as nervous as when I'd first trained with him. He'd scrutinize my every move and then rattle off a long list of mistakes. Daunting, but valuable.

I handed him his cup. "Did you get a chance to talk to Lani?"

"'Fraid so. And she's stickin' to her lies."

There wasn't much I could add to that, so I changed the subject. "It's nearly one o'clock. Don't you have a class coming in?"

He glanced at the clock. "Not 'til two. I canceled my morning classes. I'd like to blow off this next one, too, but we've got a promotion ceremony next weekend."

We sat in silence, each of taking a sip of tea from time to time. My mind wandered to Alex and Kat's ridiculous choice of venue. If after going to the summit tomorrow they still insisted on getting married at sunrise, I'd be faced with logistical problems I'd never encountered before. For starters, I was pretty sure I wouldn't be able to snag a limo driver who'd be willing to navigate a costly twenty-eight foot long vehicle up the narrow twisting road in the dark. And music? Maui has a pantheon of local musicians who'd go to great lengths to book a gig, but I doubted even the most desperate wannabe-Iz would be willing to get up at three a.m.

Doug interrupted my reverie by leaning across his desk, teacup in hand. "You know what I'm gonna have to do, don't ya?"

I shook my head.

Lani was definitely Doug's equal when it came to pluck. She'd been the first female black belt he'd trained at Palace of Pain, and although she'd drifted away from martial arts when the kids were born, everyone knew she was willing and able to go toe-to-toe with him if necessary. If the two of them were warring, I wanted no part of it. Too much chance of becoming collateral damage.

"I'm gonna follow her."

"Like that's going to work," I said. "Lani will spot your Jeep a half-mile away."

"Not gonna use the Jeep. I'm borrowing my cousin Piko's truck."

"Let me guess. It's a silver Toyota Tacoma."

"You got it."

Gray metallic Toyota pick-ups are one of the most common vehicles on the upcountry roads where Doug and Lani live. If Sifu Doug swapped his Jeep for his cousin's truck, Lani would have no reason to scrutinize the driver in her rearview mirror.

"And check this out." He reached under his desk and hauled up a brown paper grocery bag. He pulled out a blond furry object the size of a dinner plate. In one deft motion he stretched it out and fitted it over his closely-cropped dark hair.

"You look like that chef, Guy Fieri," I said. I had to give him credit, though. The pale spikey tufts radically changed his appearance.

"Yeah? Whaddaya think?"

"I think you look goofy, but it might work."

"Next time Lani gives me some song and dance about helping at the school all morning, or running to Kahului to pick up something, I'll be right behind her."

"What about your classes?"

"I was hoping you and a few of the other black belts could fill in. I don't think it's gonna take long to figure out what she's up to."

"I'm happy to help. But you know it could be she's working on some kind of surprise for you."

"Not hardly. My birthday was two months ago and Christmas is five months away."

"How about your anniversary?"

"What about it? It was in June."

"Still, there may be a perfectly reasonable explanation."

"If there is, you'll be the first to know."

There wasn't much more to be said on that subject so I stood. "You want me to teach your two o'clock today?"

"*Mahalo*, but I'm good. I got a couple kids going for their brown belt and they're kinda nervous. Besides, if Lani's planning to disappear today, she's probably already gone. I'll start surveillance tomorrow morning."

"Be careful, Sifu. You know this kind of sneaky stuff can blow a relationship right out of the water."

"Oh, yeah? Seems I'm not the one you should be tellin' that to."

His steely voice and narrowed eyes gave me pause. Doug was capable of snapping a person's neck with his bare hands. Why on earth would Lani provoke him?

5

After my troubled conversation with Sifu Doug I didn't feel like going back to work. I stopped by the Gadda to pick up something for dinner and check on Farrah's attempts to contact her ghost.

I grabbed a bottle of white wine and snagged the last quinoa-mushroom burrito from the hot case in the deli. When Finn's away I never cook. To be honest, I hardly ever cook when he's home, either. It's okay because he likes to do it and I'm a lost cause in the kitchen.

When I'm alone it's easier to grab something from the Gadda than eat out, but I often get stuck with a wilted salad or something from the freezer made with soy-protein fake chicken. Her hot deli items come from a local organic restaurant but they sell out quickly. Farrah's a vegan, so she doesn't stock many items that include meat or animal products.

It's amusing to be at the store when tourists show up asking for hamburger. Farrah never lets on. She leads them to the freezer case and points to the black bean or textured soy burgers. I can see from the look on her face she's struggling against the urge to break into a tirade about "living simply so others can simply live" and not eating "things with a face." But she usually manages to keep it to herself.

I especially enjoy watching her deal with customers who request hot dogs. She takes them to the canned food aisle and pulls down a can of pale-pink soy meal "haute dawgs." I've tried them, and I can say without a doubt I'd prefer to go hungry than eat one of those flesh-colored tubes of mush.

As she rang up my purchase I unfolded my reusable bag. "How're you doing with getting in touch with the walking dead?"

Farrah motioned to the man waiting behind me. "Would you mind taking your purchase to the deli? I'm closing up here."

The guy scowled as if he did mind, but he loped off without comment.

She came leaned in. "Our cane cutter dude is way shy. I've tried a bunch of times to talk story with him, but he's never in a chatty mood."

"Huh. But if he's trying to tie up loose ends, you'd think he'd welcome your help."

"Bingo. I mean, think about it. If you were undead and wanted to boogie on, wouldn't you be stoked if a live person offered to lend a hand?"

I nodded, pondering what such an offer might entail, but not willing to ask.

She went on. "And another thing. What's with the machete? I mean, I get that he prob'ly thinks he needs it for personal safety, but it's a bummer having a dude in my back yard waving a thing like that around. Ya know?"

Again, I was at a loss to add much to the conversation, so I just nodded.

"I mean, I got *keiki* to think about here. This isn't about me, eh?"

I couldn't help but ponder if Farrah would find it perfectly acceptable to have a machete-wielding apparition floating around outside her back door if she didn't have kids.

She reached across the counter and touched my arm. "What I'm sayin' is, I may want to take you up on your offer."

It took me a second to recall whether I'd proposed joining her in her "Ghostbusters" operation, but then it hit me.

"Oh, you mean giving you money for the *kahu*?" I said.

"'Fraid so. I'll check into trackin' one down and I'll let you know how much. I'm totally bummed we gotta hit you guys up again. I pinky-swear when we get a few bucks ahead we'll pay back every nickel."

"No worries. You can't put a price on feeling safe in your own home."

"You're the best. Now go home and nuke this bitchin' burrito. You're gonna sleep good tonight knowing you didn't chow down on somethin' with a mother."

That night as I washed my plate and fork in the kitchen sink, I glimpsed something shiny off to the right. I reached out and picked it up, clenching it so tightly it left a mark in my palm.

* * *

I went to bed early in anticipation of getting up at oh-dark-thirty to make the trek up to the rim of Haleakala Crater. I'd been up there many times so I wasn't worried about getting lost in the dark, but on Sunday mornings locals often join the tourists making the journey to the top. Besides, although the guidebooks say to allow a couple of hours, it can take longer if a car leading the pack slows to a crawl on the twisting two-lane road. I went online to get a reservation. It's a relatively new thing, reserving a spot with the National Park Service to view the sunrise, but if you don't do it, you're likely to be turned away.

I checked my phone one last time before turning out the light. No messages. I'd hoped to hear from Finn, but so far, nothing. I imagined him on a jet high above an ocean. I'd done a stint with the Federal Air Marshal Service and had spent the better part of four months flying back and forth to Taipei in the Republic of China. I found it rough duty and I managed to self-sabotage my way out of the job by snoozing when I should've been keeping a steely eye out for onboard shenanigans. In my defense, most of my fellow passengers were also asleep, but then, they weren't being paid not to.

I snuggled up to Finn's pillow and his scent helped me drift asleep. The next thing I knew my phone was shimmying across the nightstand, pulling me from sleep with an ever-louder disembodied female voice saying, "Rise and shine. Time to get up."

They say it's darkest right before the dawn and they aren't kidding. As I made my way out to my car, I looked up at a dense smattering of stars glistening against an ink-black sky. The moon was a timid curve of light, like a thin paring from a stubby fingernail. I looked *mauka*, or inland, toward the mountain and although it was still too dark for me to be certain, I was pretty sure I saw a bank of clouds obscuring the summit.

A thin layer of clouds is good because they reflect light, intensifying the sunrise colors. But a thick cloud cover reduces the dawn to merely a gradual shifting from night to day. No awe-inspiring golden disk rising over the crater rim, no shooting rays of golden light, no eye-popping change from shades of gray to Technicolor.

I drove out Hali'imaile Road and took a left on Haleakala Highway. From there, it's a pretty steady incline to the upcountry town of Kula. Just past Kula the Park Service has stationed a lighted reader board warning visitors that they must have a reservation to enter the park before seven a.m. After a few miles of twisting two-lane road through stands of eucalyptus, jacaranda and native *ohia* trees, I had to slow down. There was a line of cars waiting to clear the gate at the Haleakala National Park entrance.

From the gate the road opens out onto wide meadows, twisting and turning along the path to the summit. In daytime the views are spectacular, but in the predawn gloom all I could see out my side window was a never-ending blackness punctuated by the hazy street lights of Wailea and Kihei far below.

The stream of taillights ahead of me played hide and seek through dense clouds hugging the road. I'd go through thick sections where all I could see were the two rear lights of the car directly in front of me and then the clouds would part and I'd see a long chain of ruby-colored lights, zigzagging up the mountain.

I arrived at the uppermost parking area at five-ten and the lot was nearly full. I hadn't thought to ask Alex and Kat what kind of rental car they were driving, but it probably wouldn't have mattered anyway as many rentals are the same make, model and color. I made my way over to the ranger station to see if I could spot them in the huddled mass of humanity eagerly awaiting an awe-inspiring experience.

It was cold. Frigid, really. I'd dressed in layers, starting with tights I'd gotten for a Halloween costume a couple of years ago. Then I'd put on my only pair of jeans. On top I wore a long-sleeved t-shirt, a sweatshirt, and a down vest I'd bought for air marshal training in New Jersey. I'd left my *rubba slippahs* at home. Instead, I was wearing two pairs of socks and sneakers I'd gotten when I thought I'd try jogging. I figured it could be my go-to exercise regimen on days I couldn't get down to the *guan* to work out.

The jogging had been short-lived. When I tried running near my house, my neighbors would stop and offer me a ride. I'd tell them I was trying to get some exercise and that would lead to a fifteen-minute discussion of the health and welfare of their various 'ohana members.

"My bruddah tried getting in shape one time. He dropped a barbell on his toe. Mashed it so bad they had to cut it off. He don' do that no more. Uh-uh. You be careful, Pali. That healthy stuff can be dangerous."

"My dad should've done a little exercise. He had that heart attack, remember? 'Bout two years ago now. He's only fifty and he hasn't been the same since. You smart to keep yourself in shape, eh?"

After I realized running in my neighborhood was going to be a non-starter, I tried running at the beach. Getting to the nearest beach meant driving through town, past the *guan*, and out to Baldwin Beach Park. Once I got there, I had to find a parking space and lock up the car and make my way to the hard-packed sand at the water's edge. Sometimes the tide would be in and I'd have to bob and weave to avoid getting my shoes wet. The beach run took more time and more gas than going to the *guan*, so in the end I hung up my sneakers and went back to simply kicking and punching my way to a healthy lifestyle.

It was still pretty dark as I made my way to the ranger station. People were milling around, most of them looking sleep-deprived and shocked by the bitter cold and biting wind. The rangers had helpfully placed a large digital display outside the station showing the time and temperature. It read, 5:18 and 36 F. degrees. Four degrees above freezing. I stuffed my hands into the pockets of my cozy vest and wished I'd thought to bring a hat.

I scanned the crowd. Many of the people were in t-shirts and shorts, wrapped in nothing more substantial than beach towels and sheets. They looked forlorn, like victims at a house fire. I didn't see my wedding couple among them. By now there were only a few more open spots in the upper parking area. If the rangers closed it and began directing late-comers to the lower lot, it could take Alex and Kat another ten minutes to trudge back up. If they arrived any later than that they'd most likely miss the sunrise.

My view across the crater was limited by the gathering crowd and the dusky predawn gloom. Clouds shrouded the area, making it appear like a misty moonscape. It was hard to tell whether the cloud cover would stick around or drift up and provide a dramatic backdrop for the rising sun. Only time would tell.

Behind me, a male voice yelled, "Pali!"

I turned, thinking Alex had finally arrived, but instead it was my friend and former roommate, Steve Rathburn. Steve's a creature comforts kind of guy which makes him one of the last people I'd expect to see at a Mt. Haleakala sunrise in the brutal cold. He was decked out in a puffy blue ski jacket and navy and white striped knit cap but even in the near-darkness I noticed his nose had turned bright red.

"What are you doing here?" I said.

His teeth chattered as he gave me a quick hug. "I could ask you the same thing."

"I've got clients who want to get married up here next week."

"At dawn? It's colder than a well-digger's ass and there's no place to park. Why didn't you tell them it's better at sunset?"

"I figured we'd discuss it after they'd had the occasion to experience facial freezer burn up close and personal."

"You're diabolical, you know it?"

"Not really. I just know what I can and can't tell people. If I'd told them what's it's like up here they might feel the need to stick to their guns. This way, they'll yell at me for not warning them and then we can quickly move on to Plan B."

He looked around. "Where are they?"

"I'm still looking. I figure now that the sun's up it'll be easier to make out faces."

He yawned.

I crooked my arm through his and leaned in to his puffy coat. My getting chummy had as much to do with keeping warm as to exhibit how pleased I was to see him, but it had been at least two months since we'd last met up.

I looked around. "So tell me, what brings you up here? And where's Allen?" Allen was Steve's significant other. For the past seven months they'd been like peanut butter and jelly. Outside of working hours, you never saw one without the other.

"The Twitter post on Allen is he needs some space."

"Uh-oh."

He rolled his eyes. "Yeah. Now I'm just waiting for the 'It's not you, it's me' speech."

"I'm sorry, Steve. But maybe once he spends a little time alone he'll reconsider."

"Maybe, but not likely."

"So why are you here? Leaving an offering to Pele for intervention in your love life?"

Steve laughed. "Not hardly. I'm shooting some downhill bikers."

As ominous as that sounds, Steve wasn't in a murderous frame of mind. He's a professional photographer who specializes in taking pictures of visitors for various tourist-driven businesses. He's my go-to guy for wedding photography, but his real bread and butter comes from tourism concerns like the local zip-line company and the charter boats docked in Lahaina Harbor. He takes everyone's picture as they fly overhead or are about to board a vessel and then sells them the finished photos when they're finished.

"Wow! I didn't realize that zipline was so far up! I need to show this to my pansy brother-in-law."

Or,

"Look, Larry. You look so cute in that little captain's hat. Let's buy it, honey. It's only twenty bucks."

The sun had peeked over the lip of the crater, so we said *aloha* and I went back to searching for Alex and Kat. If they'd decided to sleep in, I'd have to do some deep breathing before calling them. And, I'd scrap the hands-on teaching model and simply demand they come up with something other than a sunrise wedding in a freezing twenty-knot wind or get themselves another wedding planner.

The downhill bikers took off as soon as the sun was completely up and over the rim. The crowd thinned as people made their way back to their cars. As I was about to give up and return to my car I spotted Alex and Kat huddled against the ranger cabin. Alex had thrown a beefy arm around his diminutive fiancée who clung to him like a nervous monkey. They wore shorts and sandals with a beach blanket draped over their heads. Their faces were slack, dazed by the cold.

I trotted over and touched Kat's shoulder. She flinched.

Teeth chattering, she said, "Why didn't you tell us it'd be so freakin' cold?"

"Sorry. I thought you'd researched the conditions up here."

"Well, you can forget about us doing the wedding here. No way."

"Yeah," added Alex. "We'd rather live in mortal sin and suffer the consequences. At least we'll be warm in hell."

I hid a self-satisfied smile. "Let's meet tomorrow morning and discuss other venues."

"No cold places," said Kat.

Alex weighed in. "But nothing in the blazing sun, either. I don't want to sweat through my shirt. It's silk so it has to be dry-cleaned. "

"No worries. Maui offers lots of options."

6

By ten o'clock I was back in my shop. I'd made a full pot of coffee, sucked down half of it, and checked and returned all my email messages. At eleven the carrier brought in the snail mail and it didn't contain a single overdue bill or bit of bad news. I figured I was on a roll, so I took a victory lap by spending the next couple of hours updating my website. It isn't something I enjoy, so it takes a certain frame of mind to get me to do it.

At one-thirty my stomach reminded me I hadn't eaten, but my mind was elsewhere. I needed to get to the Palace of Pain and check when I'd been slotted to cover Sifu Doug's classes. I didn't want to mess up by not being at the right place at the right time. Also, after barely pulling off my seat-of-the-pants *keiki* class on Wednesday, I figured it wouldn't hurt to prepare a little.

I expected the alley to be empty, or to spot the silver Toyota truck in Doug's reserved space. But there was my *sifu*'s black Wrangler. Had his cousin backed out on switching? Maybe the guy needed his truck for the weekend ahead and wasn't willing to trade until Monday.

"*Aloha, Sifu,*" I said, as I came through the door.

Doug leaned against his office doorway, arms crossed as if expecting me.

"Hey, Pali. How's it hangin'?" His voice sounded downright chipper, which was in sharp contrast to our conversation only the day before.

"I see you didn't trade rides with your cousin yet."

"I'm rethinking it. It's prob'ly a stupid idea."

I held his gaze, fully expecting him to enlighten me regarding his change of heart.

"You here to work out?" he said.

"No, I came by to check the class schedule and see when you'll need me."

"My bad. I should've called. Looks like I won't be needing help after all."

Okay. Again, I waited for a clue as to what was going on.

"What happened? You and Lani work things out?"

"Sort of."

When Doug didn't feel like talking, it was tough duty trying to wring something out of him.

"So, it's all good?"

"As good as can be expected."

"Okay, great. Then I guess I'll head back to the shop."

He crossed the room. "How'd it go up on the mountain this morning? Your clients have a change of heart?"

Oh, sure. He plays Mr. Mysterious and he wants me to spill? I don't think so.

I shrugged. "Went great."

We locked eyes, as if we were each nursing a private grudge. It wasn't standard operating procedure for us to refuse to confide in each other, but he'd started it.

I hooked a thumb toward the door. "Guess I better head out."

"Okay. See you around."

I got in my car and looked back at the *guan*. What the heck was going on?

* * *

I went back to my shop and worked the phones for half-an-hour on behalf of Alex and Kat. Steve had given me an idea for a venue, but I wanted to check availability before getting the wedding couple excited about it.

Things were clicking along nicely when my stomach rumbled again, reminding me it was now seriously past the lunch hour. I walked over to the Gadda and found Farrah replenishing canned goods at the back of the store. Soup cans flew from a large cardboard box onto the shelf as if she were a nimble juggler practicing her craft.

"Hey," I said.

She glanced up at me but didn't slow down. "Hey, yourself. You hear from Finn yet?"

I shook my head. I'd been able to avoid fretting over my marriage problems while dealing with a looming wedding deadline with no venue and worrying over whatever was going on with Sifu Doug and Lani, but with Farrah's inquiry, it came roaring back.

"He told me before he left it might be some time before I heard from him."

"Where do you think he's gone?"

"No idea. But I've got a bad feeling they're probably messing with one of those 'Axis of Evil' countries."

"Huh?" Farrah wasn't big on following the news so even if my reference hadn't been fifteen years old she probably wouldn't have gotten it anyway.

"It's an old phrase from back in the President Bush years. The younger Bush, not the first one. He was talking about countries that don't like us. Ones that give us major grief. Back then it was Iraq, Iran and North Korea, but in the past couple of years we've managed to add a few more players to the team."

"Wait a sec. There were *two* President Bushes?"

Like I said, she isn't big on current events.

I gave her the Cliff's Notes version of Presidents Forty-One and Forty-Three and then changed the subject.

"Finn didn't take his wedding ring."

"How do you know? I thought you said he hasn't called."

"He left it by the kitchen sink."

"Probably just forgot it."

"I wish I could believe that."

"They prob'ly told him not to take any valuables. You know, no jewelry and like that. The military industrial establishment's harsh on rule breakers."

"When he left, he didn't know he was being sent overseas. He thought it was just a normal work week."

"Huh. Well, there's nothing normal about the weirdness going on at my house," she said.

She probably changed the subject because there really wasn't much more to say about Finn ditching his wedding band. I welcomed the shift in focus.

"What now?"

"Last night I had a rap session with the scary dude in my back yard."

"You talked to him?"

She nodded. "Yep. I got in touch through my Ouija board, and he started talking story like, nonstop. It was like a totally rad séance, you know? After a while I had to shut it down quick because Ono came looking for me. He's sportin' a bummer attitude about me dealing with the dude. But before that I found out some pretty heavy stuff."

"Like?"

"Okay, he started out mellow. Said his name's 'Ling'— not sure if that's his first name or last—and he cut cane right where our house is now. Said the company shafted him on his final paycheck, but that wasn't the worst of it."

"Yeah?" It annoys me when Farrah drags out a story, but since that's her preferred method of imparting information, I've learned to roll with it.

"Uh-huh. Seems his *keiki* daughter was killed right there, in our back yard. Mowed down by a cane wagon. He's sticking around to make things right. Said something like 'eye for an eye.' Freaked me out."

"What's he mean? *You* didn't kill his little girl."

"Yeah, that's what I said. I told him I was totally bummed about his baby girl, but he hung tough. Said it must be avenged."

"Avenged? That sounds like a threat. What're you going to do?"

"That's where you come in. 'Member when I said I wasn't hip to borrowing money for the *kahu*? Well, now I gotta rethink that. If that dude hurts my Hatchie, I'll die."

Hatchie was Farrah's nearly year-old daughter, Hatshepsut. She has a twin brother, Plácido. No Jennifers, Jacobs, or even a Leilani for Farrah; she went with hard-to-pronounce foreign names that will bedevil those kids for the rest of their lives.

"Of course the money's yours. When will the *kahu* be able to do it?"

"Don't know yet. I rang up a dude on the Big Island, but I haven't heard back." She pulled a folded page from her apron pocket and handed it to me. It was a print-out from a web site offering the services of a dark-skinned, balding, sixty-ish guy wearing a string of *maile* leaves around his neck and a red and yellow *pareo* tied to form a kind of skirt. Something about his countenance hit me as off. As my auntie's boyfriend used to say, "Don't look like I guy I'd buy a used car from."

I looked up. "Seems to me the two of you shouldn't need phones. I mean, since you both hang out in woo-woo world, you should be able to communicate telepathically."

She glared and snatched back the paper. "This is mega-serious, Pali."

"I know, sorry. It's just I wonder if this guy can do anything that you couldn't do yourself. You've got all the hardware."

Farrah has a small fortune invested in Tarot cards, Ouija boards, sacred stones, crystals, you name it. It seemed hard to imagine that a Hawaiian *kahu* would have any greater access to the mystical world than she did.

"It's not about 'hardware,' as you call it. It's about technique. I've never learned the righteous way to do a blessing like this. And I don't have time to screw around getting up to speed."

"Okay. So, where do we go from here?"

"The bank."

We trudged across the street and up two blocks to the Bank of Hawaii. For years I maintained an iffy relationship with them. Being self-employed meant my checking account often teetered on the brink of non-sufficient funds, sometimes actually going over the cliff. But after my father died, I used the bank's trust department to set up monthly stipends to my seven half-brothers and sisters. The fees and interest the bank enjoys from the trust account flipped me from "deadbeat" to "valued customer" status. Valued customers don't worry about bounced checks or annoying fees, everything's discretely handled by the back office. It's yet another example of the one-percenters taking care of their own.

"*Aloha*, Pali," chirped the female bank manager as Farrah and I cleared the door. She always seems to have her radar tuned to high alert whenever a high-net worth client walks in. I wouldn't be surprised if the woman scans the security cameras every few seconds to ensure we never have to stand in line.

"How can I help you today?" She looked me up and down as if hoping I'd brought her another multi-million-dollar account. I'd never let on, but I'm pretty certain my days of stumbling into a seven-figure windfall are forever in my rearview mirror.

"I need to make a withdrawal."

I turned to Farrah and whispered. "How much, exactly?"

"Ten Bennies."

It took me a few beats to do the math. I leaned in and kept up the whispering. "A Benjamin is a hundred dollars, right?"

She nodded.

"So, ten of them would be a thousand."

Farrah appeared peeved. "Well, duh."

I asked the bank manager to excuse us for a moment. I cupped Farrah's elbow and steered her outside.

"Are you kidding me? A thousand bucks?"

She crossed her arms. "That's right."

"Farrah, that's a fortune for a few minutes of chanting. Are you sure you heard him correctly?"

"I talked to his assistant and she was straight up. A house blessing costs seven hundred to a thousand. And he only will come if he gets the money in advance. No credit cards or phony stuff like checks."

"It's a ridiculous amount."

"My baby girl's life is in danger."

"Yes, but it's ... you know."

"No, I don't know. Are you saying Hatchie's not worth it?"

"I'm not saying that at all. But it's a lot of money for something that's kind of dodgy. How do you even know this guy is for real?"

Farrah's eyes grew shiny and her lip trembled. "I dig this seems 'dodgy' to you because you're not a believer, but to me it's life and death."

I pulled her into a hug. "Okay. Sorry for doubting you. I'll get you the thousand bucks, but I sure hope this guy turns out to be real deal."

"Don't worry, he is."

We went inside and I sent a wire transfer to the *kahu's* bank account on the Big Island. It galled me the guy refused to accept a cashier's check and he'd demanded payment in advance. But I figured it was worth it if it meant Farrah would sleep well. She'd been through more than her share of trials and tribulations in the twenty-five years I'd known her, but this latest scare over the safety of her children seemed to be taking an especially heavy toll.

As we left the bank, I handed her the receipt for the wire transfer.

"You won't regret this, Pali," she said.

In my experience when someone says, "No disrespect meant," or "I'm only saying this because I love you," or "You won't regret this," it often turns out to be quite the opposite.

7

I walked back to my shop rifling through my beach bag purse in search of my cell phone. I couldn't find it. I was about to dump out the entire contents on my desk when I spied the phone where I'd left it—acting as a paperweight on the Alex and Kat wedding folder.

I tapped in my code and a little "2" popped up on the voicemail icon. I called for messages, hoping to receive a go-ahead from the winery about holding the wedding there. The wedding was less than four days away and I'm never comfortable leaving things to the last minute. In my world, folks who claim they "perform better under pressure" are simply rationalizing sloppy work habits.

The first message was, indeed, from Bobby Fielding, an acquaintance of Steve's and the manager at Maui Winery. In a chilly voice he told me they don't normally host private events, but things were slow at the moment so he'd consider making an exception. This one time. Don't make a habit of asking, and so on. I didn't take umbrage at his tone. I'd probably have done the same thing under the circumstances.

I hung up and went to the second message. It stopped me cold.

"Hey, Pali, it's me. I just have a minute. I had plenty of time to think on the plane and I can't do this. But don't worry, I'll handle everything." A static-filled pause went on so long I thought Finn had hung up, but then he said in a husky voice, "Okay, I better go. Take care of yourself."

I was about to delete the voicemail, then decided to save it. Maybe I'd misunderstood. Maybe when Farrah heard the message she'd offer a different take on what I thought I'd just heard.

I blew out a breath and called Bobby at the winery. I wasn't sure if his relationship with Steve included any awkward history, so after I name-dropped how I'd heard about him I didn't press for details.

I got to the point. "Will you be in tomorrow?"

"Saturdays are my day off," he said in the same cool tone he'd used in the voicemail. "And as I said in my message, we're a winery, not a wedding chapel. We don't normally host things like this."

"I realize this is a big ask, but my wedding clients have already had quite a few set-backs. Their mainland flight got cancelled, and then the airlines lost their luggage. If anyone deserves a little 'aloha,' it's them."

I could practically feel his eye-roll coming through the phone.

"Okay. I'll come in tomorrow, say eight o'clock. I've got a thing at ten so don't show up late. You said six people? The couple, two witnesses, a minister and photographer."

"I'll also be there, which will make it seven. We'll go elsewhere for dinner."

"You better, because as I said, we're a working winery. If you want to eat you'll need to go across the street."

"Is there a restaurant?"

"In a manner of speaking."

I let that hang. I wasn't about to quiz a guy who was doing me a favor, regardless of his snarky attitude.

After a couple of beats, he went on. "It's the 'Ulupalakua Ranch Store. Their food operation isn't fancy, but people seem to like it. Especially the burgers."

"Do you know when they stop serving?"

"You'll have to ask them, but we close at five-thirty. Your party must be off the premises by then."

"May I ask how much you'll charge?"

"Will you be buying wine from us?"

"Absolutely. I'll get some for the wedding dinner and I'll buy some for the newlyweds to take home."

"Are we talking at least a case?"

"A case is twelve bottles, right?"

"That's correct."

"Okay, I'll buy a case."

"Then there won't be a charge."

"*Mahalo*, Bobby. I really appreciate you bending the rules. I wouldn't be asking if the situation wasn't desperate. I definitely owe you one."

"Ms. Moon? Make sure you allow enough time to get here tomorrow morning. Highway 37 can be slow-going if it's foggy or you get stuck behind a cattle truck." He seemed to be warming up a bit. I've learned most people actually like helping out as long as they get credit for it.

"I'll see you at eight sharp."

We hung up and I immediately called Kat.

I triumphantly crowed, "Great news! I've found a wonderful venue."

"Okay. Where?"

"I had to pull a few strings, but I was able to talk Maui Winery into letting us hold your ceremony there."

She barked a dry cough. "Nice try, Pali, but I'm sure by now you've figured out Alex is hard-core Christian. He doesn't smoke, swear or drink."

"You don't have to drink. It's a gorgeous up-country setting and they've agreed to let us hold the wedding there even though it's not something they normally allow."

"He still may not go along with it. I'm pretty sure he won't like the idea of supporting the liquor industry."

"You won't be *supporting* anything. They're allowing us to use their beautiful grounds for free, no strings attached. The photos will be spectacular." Okay, I'd fudged a bit on that one. First, I was going to have to buy a case of wine, so there were strings, and second, I hadn't been to Maui Winery since they'd changed management several years ago. I mentally crossed my fingers that the grounds and gardens were as lush and manicured as I remembered.

After obtaining Kat's grudging promise to do her best to persuade Alex, I clicked off and replayed Finn's message.

Sadly, it sounded even more depressing the second time around.

* * *

I got to bed early Friday night since the next day I'd once again be up before dawn. The winery was in an area of the island called 'Ulupalakua, where Highway 37 (aka the Haleakala Highway) becomes Highway 31. At that point the road heads east along the extreme south side of Maui. If you choose to stick it out after mile marker twenty-five, it becomes a rough narrow roadway that will take you all the way to Kaupo. After Kaupo the road widens a bit, with less brain-jarring ruts and holes. If you keep going, the road leads to Hana.

The south side approach is definitely not the usual, nor the easiest, route to Hana and rental car companies threaten everything short of bodily harm to deter visitors from attempting the journey. My little Mini Cooper, with its low-slung suspension and go-kart size tires would probably never make it in one piece and I have no reason to try. Besides, locals in that part of the island value their peace and quiet. I'm pretty sure that's one reason the state has been reluctant to improve the road.

The next morning I only had to make it to 'Ulupalakua, deep in the heart of Maui cattle country. Most visitors would be surprised to learn that Maui is home to some of the largest cattle ranches in the state. Everyone thinks all of the big ranches are on the Big Island, but Maui includes more than fifty thousand square acres of pasture. Our little corner of paradise raises thousands of cattle, providing a substantial percentage of the beef consumed locally.

In 1793, explorer Captain George Vancouver presented a gift of a few mainland cattle to King Kamehameha on the island of Hawaii. The cattle did so well that by 1820, with their numbers multiplied many times over, they became a nuisance: over-grazing the king's lands and menacing the local population by tearing up cultivated food crops and charging at unsuspecting people who got in their way. In time, some of those cattle were brought to Maui and became the root stock of the current cattle population.

Maui's pastures aren't flat prairie like Texas. They're on the hilly, sometimes steep, flanks of Haleakala where grass grows as tall and thick as a cane field. Rounding up the wandering cattle was a problem for the king, so he brought in Spanish-Mexican *vaqueros* to teach the locals what they needed to know. The result is the modern-day Hawaiian cowboy, or *paniolo. Paniolos* dress pretty much like their mainland cousins—blue jeans, wide-brimmed cowboy hats, big belt buckles and leather boots.

I occasionally see *paniolos* in the upcountry town of Makawao driving dusty pick-ups blasting country music and I can't help but marvel at how they could be plunked down on a ranch in Midland, Texas and they'd blend right in.

* * *

On Saturday I awoke at four-thirty and couldn't get back to sleep. I got up, showered and did a load of laundry. I planned to head out at about six. Since it was the weekend, there wouldn't be as much truck traffic as on a weekday, but you never know. From Kula, Highway 37 becomes a twisting, two-lane road with little or no shoulder. If there's an accident or a vehicle breaks down, the back-up can stretch far down the mountain and stay that way until a tow truck is summoned from Kula or even as far away as Kahului.

The predawn sky sparkled with a splash of stars so bright they seemed within reach. It's the best time of my day. Nothing but balmy silence. No one demanding the impossible or insisting I resolve a problem I didn't cause.

I pulled onto Hali'imaile Road and made my way along the rise and fall of the roadway as it winds through the cane fields to the Haleakala Highway. At the light, I turned left and joined a smattering of traffic—no doubt people headed to the crater. I checked the clock. Five-fifty-seven. Sorry, folks. Too late to make it for the sunrise.

A few miles beyond Pukalani I peeled off to the right to continue on Highway 37 while others took Highway 377, the access to Haleakala National Park.

The breeze through the open car windows became cooler as I made the steady ascent. At the junction of Lower Kula Road a sign alerted me to the elevation: 3,208. From sea level to over three thousand feet in twelve miles. No wonder my ears were popping.

Beyond Kula, signs of civilization—houses, businesses and cars—dwindled to a few here and there. The emerald green vegetation along the roadside grew thick and tall. As the roadway narrowed, shoulders and turn-outs became non-existent. I smoothly took the turns, marveling at the jaw-dropping views of Ma'alaea Bay and the West Maui Mountains. From this perspective, the island I'd called home for almost thirty years seemed strangely unfamiliar, as if I was viewing it standing on my head or in a funhouse mirror.

Small clusters of cattle huddled by the fence line. The grass was so tall only their heads poked above it. Their beseeching brown eyes made me wish I'd joined Farrah in embracing a vegan diet. I avoided eye contact, but the hairpin twists were now coming closer together so I really didn't have time to get emotional over their fate anyway.

I pulled into the parking area at Maui Winery a few minutes after seven, nearly an hour early. The gate to the main walkway was open, so I trudged up the path. The tasting room, which they call "The King's Cottage," is a solidly-built white cottage with green shutters and an open porch extending across the front and around the right side. In front of the cottage is a wide, grassy *lanai*, with a ring of tall wooden figures carved to portray the human form.

A sign provided clues to the history of this serene property. In the late-1800's, Captain James Makee built the cottage as part of his expansive ranch in 'Ulupalakua. He hosted elaborate parties at the estate, and invited prestigious guests such as King David Kalakaua, Hawaii's "Merrie Monarch." King Kalakaua had rescinded the missionary-inspired ban on practicing hula in the islands so when the king visited, Makee made sure a group of the most skilled dancers were on hand to provide entertainment.

In Kalakaua's day, the grassy lanai used by the hula dancers was surrounded by a ring of ironwood trees. When the trees were felled decades later, the enormous stumps were carved into figures depicting those long-ago dancers.

The lush grounds were tidy and ablaze with color. As I inspected a two-foot long string of aqua-colored blooms on a plant I didn't recognize, a deep voice behind me said, "That's jade vine. It's beautiful, don't you think?"

"I thought jade plants were succulents with oval-shaped leaves."

He smiled. "They are. This is jade *vine*. The devil's in the details."

"Don't I know?" I stuck out my hand. "Pali Moon, wedding planner."

"Ah yes, weddings. Then I guess you *would* know." I looked him over as we shook hands.

He was about five-ten, tanned, with a shock of bleach-blond hair that hung over one eye. Too bad, because his gray-green eyes were shocking both in color and intensity. My husband's a handsome man, and I'm not the only one who thinks so, but this guy was disarmingly attractive. The kind of dude who'd probably been a beautiful child and was used to having his looks work to his advantage. I made a note to chide Steve about not mentioning the guy looked like a Greek god.

"I'm Bobby. We spoke on the phone." His penetrating gaze was unsettling. "I trust you didn't run into any problems on the way up."

"No problems."

"Good. Well, if it's okay with you I'd like to get this wrapped up and get out of here. Tell me about your wedding couple. Do you think they'd enjoy a short tour of our wine operation before the ceremony?"

How could I tell this guy the groom would start spouting Scripture in support of the Eighteenth Amendment, the one that established prohibition, if he caught even a whiff of the wine-making operation?

"Uh, no. *Mahalo* for the offer, but it seems the wedding couple has alcohol issues."

"Understood. It's good when people know their limits, don't you think? I've got a close friend in AA, and I'm in complete support of his recovery."

I left it at that.

He gestured for me to join him. "Why don't we walk the property and you can decide where you'd like to hold the ceremony. I have two or three places I think might work."

At the far edge of the property I looked across the road to the ocean. "Is that Kaho'olawe?"

"Good eye, Ms. Moon."

Kaho'olawe is the uninhabited island off the south-west coast of Maui. At forty-five square miles it's big enough to support life, but its grim history has left it a literal wasteland. In early times it had a few fishing villages and was home to ancient Hawaiian religious sites. In the middle 1800's sheep and cattle were brought to the island and allowed to overgraze its sparse vegetation to the point that it became a barren, windswept desert. After the attack at Pearl Harbor, the U.S. Navy began using it as a bombing range. They dropped tons of ordnance. Most of the bombs exploded, but countless numbers didn't.

After decades of protests, the military finally stopped the bombing in 2003, and ownership of the island was transferred to the State of Hawaii. The still-live munitions are being cleared and new vegetation is being planted by volunteers but no one really knows if the island will ever fully recover.

Bobby walked me to a tiny cottage on the property with a sign that read, "The Old Jail."

"This was the original owner's office, but at one time it was used to lock up locals who'd partied a bit too hard."

"Not a great visual for a wedding," I said, pointing to the sign.

He squinted in confusion.

I went on. "You know, *the ol' ball and chain. No more freedom for him*—that sort of thing."

"We could drape something over the sign."

"I think they'd like to be outside. With so few people we won't need chairs or even a roof over our heads. And the view is spectacular."

"Okay. What time are we talking about?"

I didn't have the heart to admit I hadn't heard back from Kat whether it was a go or not, so I winged it.

"Four o'clock. Plenty of time for photos and the ceremony and still be finished before you close."

"Excellent," he said. "Let's head up to the tasting room so you can select your wine."

* * *

Before leaving, I dashed across the street to check out the 'Ulupalakua Ranch Store but it didn't open until nine. I peeked through the windows and saw what appeared to be more gift store than ranch supply store. I circled around the ancient plank porch and came upon a huge grill and smoker, along with a series of picnic tables. As Bobby had said, not fancy but homey. If Alex and Kat didn't like it they'd have to drive down to the Kula Lodge for somewhat fancier fare.

During the ride down from 'Ulupalakua I sent up a silent prayer that Kat and Alex would agree to get married at the winery. I didn't have a Plan B, and anyway this was already Plan B after their disastrous choice of sunrise at the crater. The wedding was now just three days away, meaning I didn't even have time to get a beach permit, let alone try to book a private location.

I parked in the alley behind my shop. I was eager to find out what they'd decided but first I needed something to eat. I find it easier to wheedle and cajole on a full stomach.

Farrah was at the front counter at the Gadda. "Hey, girl. Where've you been? I went over to see you."

My antennae went up. Farrah rarely left the store during business hours.

"What's up?"

She held up a finger as if to say, "Give me a minute," as she waited on a woman buying a gallon of milk. When the shopper cleared the door, she plunked down a sign directing customers to pay at the deli counter.

"C'mon," she said, steering me to the back.

"What's with the cloak and dagger?"

She leaned in. "Your *sifu's* the talk of the town."

"What's going on?" I said.

Farrah knew Doug, but they weren't close. Lani Kanekoa shopped at the Gadda so Farrah knew her better.

"Seems Doug and Lani went nuclear at Chico's last night," Farrah said in a whispery voice. "The bartender even called the cops."

"That's crazy." I recalled Doug's easygoing attitude at the *guan* the day before. What could Lani have said or done to rile him?

"Nah, it's true. Seems they came in early and ordered a couple burgers. Bartender said Doug had one beer, maybe two. By ten o'clock Lani was totally freaking out. Screaming, throwin' stuff. She picked up a chair and tried to deck him, and that's when they called the cops."

"Lani threw a chair?"

"Yeah. Totally out of it. They had to cuff her to get her to mellow out."

I'd never seen any evidence of Lani being anything but sweet and kind. At Sifu Doug's tournaments I'd seen him transform from my laid-back instructor into a bone-breaking combatant but Lani didn't practice martial arts anymore. In fact, in the whole time I've known her, I've never seen her exhibit even a hint of anger or frustration.

"Where is she now?"

"The cops let her go. Doug said she'd had a bummer day and she just needed to catch some zz's. But from the story people are tellin', seems more was goin' on there than lack of sleep."

"Poor Doug."

"Yeah, well I figured you'd want to know. You been to the Palace yet?"

"No, I got up early and went to the winery at 'Ulupalakua."

"Kinda early to be hittin' the sauce, don't you think?"

"It's for my wedding on Tuesday. The couple had this lame notion about getting married at the crater at sunrise but that was a non-starter."

Farrah crossed her arms tightly. "Brr, total bummer."

"Yeah. Steve gave me the idea about the winery. It's a gorgeous place, but the groom's got a thing about drinking so I'm not sure they'll go along."

Farrah made a fist with an extended thumb and touched it to her lips. "Lush, huh?"

"Quite the opposite. Seems drinking alcohol is against his religion."

"Muslim?"

"No, super-Christian."

"Whoa. Even the J-man drank wine. Heck, he *made* wine, right?"

I wasn't about to debate religion with a woman who was an ordained minister of the über-liberal Church of Spirit and Light as well as a loyal advocate of several voodoo practices, so I changed the subject.

"How are things with your backyard ghost?"

"The kahu lives on the Big Island but he's willing to fly over here for the blessing. Have juju, will travel."

"Sounds promising."

Just then, a knot of bare-chested kite-surfer types banged through the front door.

"Gotta run before they steal me blind," said Farrah. But we both knew they'd probably be her best deli customers all day. After a morning out on the water, those guys can wolf down two thousand calories and still claim to be hungry.

I left, but a half-minute later it hit me. I'd forgotten to mention the call from Finn.

8

On Sunday morning I woke at six-thirty and basked in a moment of bliss before the bubble popped. Kat and Alex would be at the shop at eight o'clock. I'd promised to make it quick so they could make it to nine-thirty church service. I hopped out of bed and into the shower. On my way out the door I grabbed a stale half bagel and munched on it as I careened down Baldwin Avenue.

I got to town with fifteen minutes to spare so I kept going, pulling into the alley behind Palace of Pain. Sifu Doug's Jeep wasn't there, but a shiny red Camaro was. It belonged to Luke, a newly-minted black belt. We rarely trained together so I didn't know him well, but I'd been a judge at his promotion ceremony so I'd seen Doug hand him a key to the *guan*. It was an honor our *sifu* bestowed on every new black belt.

"*Aloha*, Luke," I said as I came inside. It's customary to announce your presence when you intrude on someone else's workout. Training brings out a combat frame of mind and sneaking in can have unintended, and sometimes bruising, consequences.

"*Aloha*, Pali. Good to see you. Don't you usually work out earlier than this?"

"Yeah, I slept in. I was hoping to catch *sifu*."

"You know about what went down at Chico's Friday night?"

"A little. What'd you hear?"

"I wasn't there but I heard things got ugly. Sifu's wife went full-on Rambo."

"That's not like her at all."

"Yeah. I'm pretty new here, but she seemed nice. Hard to imagine her tossing furniture around. Especially on *sifu's* head."

We mentally chewed on that image for a beat before he went on. "Oh yeah, and read this. *Sifu* left a note."

He handed me a ruled piece of paper with a jaggedly torn left edge. Sifu Doug's training journal had paper like that, but I'd never seen him rip a page out of it.

I read the short note. *Black belts—Won't be around for a while. Pls cover classes. Call if necessary—DK*

"He made a schedule." Luke handed me another page apparently ripped from the same source. Sifu Doug had listed his classes by day and time and had assigned each of the six black belts at PoP three or four sessions per week.

I pointed to a morning class on Tuesday with my name next to it. "I can't do this one. I've got a work thing on Tuesday."

"Yeah, I got some that won't work for me neither."

"Can we switch?"

"Don't know. *Sifu* didn't say."

One of the irrefutable aspects of martial arts is the *sifu* is king. You don't ask why, you don't argue, and you certainly don't mess around with a direct request without seeking and receiving permission.

I blew out a breath. "I'm the senior black belt, so I'll talk to him."

Luke looked relieved.

I handed back the schedule. "Make a note of the classes you need to switch and I'll see what I can do. Tell the others to come in and do the same."

"*Mahalo*, Pali. I didn't wanna...well, you know. I'm the lowest guy on the totem pole 'round here."

I nodded. I can always tell mainland-raised people by the way they talk. Totem pole order doesn't hold much meaning for us locals.

I checked the clock. "Uh-oh. Gotta run. I've got clients this morning."

"You in real estate?"

"No, I'm a wedding planner."

"Seriously?"

"Yep. Got my own shop and everything."

"Hey, good for you. I might be talkin' to you one of these days. My girlfriend's got ideas, you know? Now that we got the kid and all, she's thinking we need to make it legal."

I didn't have the time or the inclination to offer up a lecture on the moral responsibilities of fatherhood, so I clapped him on the shoulder. "Give me a call anytime. I give a discount to *kama'aina*, and an even bigger discount to fellow black belts."

I went in the back entrance of my shop and hurriedly looked out the window before unlocking the front door. Kat and Alex were across the street, waiting for traffic to clear. I rushed to the back and began making a pot of coffee, hoping the cheerful aroma of freshly-brewed Kona coffee would put Alex in a receptive mood.

"*Aloha*," I sang out as they came through the door.

Alex glowered. "What's this about us getting married in a place of sin?"

C'mon coffee, I silently begged.

"Before you make a decision, let me show you some photos. I plugged my phone into my computer and began downloading pictures I'd taken at the winery.

"This setting is now a winery, but it's got a wonderful history. I proceeded to give them a thumbnail account of the story of Captain Makee and his famous upcountry cattle ranch. I mentioned King Kalakaua's visits but left out the part about Christian missionaries banning hula and the king bringing it back.

"It's truly a magical place," I said. "The grounds and views are better than anywhere else on Maui."

Okay, so I fudged a little there. The 'Ulupalakua property is beautiful, and even special, but everyone's who's been to Maui could argue there are even more spectacular settings elsewhere on the island. Trouble was, Alex and Kat's wedding date was two days away so we were pretty much down to 'Ulupalakua or the courthouse, and the courthouse definitely wasn't going to cut it.

"Will there be drinking going on?" Alex demanded.

"Not outside. Only in the tasting room. And even there, visitors are given only small amounts so they can decide if they want to buy some."

He crossed his arms. "Can we get them to close the drinking area while we're there?"

It took a great deal of self-control to keep the shrill out of my voice. "Alex, they're allowing us to use their beautiful property for free, as a favor to a friend of mine. It's not like we can make demands."

At that moment I made a mental note to get there early on Tuesday so I could stash the case of wine in my car before Alex and Kat showed up.

Alex looked at Kat. "I don't know. It feels sinful. I don't want to start our life together like Adam and Eve, sinning in the eyes of the Lord."

"Darling, we won't be sinning. No matter where we go we'll encounter sin in one form or another. Pali says it's gorgeous and our wedding photos will be stunning."

I hadn't promised "stunning" photos but this wasn't a time to quibble. Besides, her reasoning was sound.

Alex stood. "I've got an idea. Why don't Kat and I drive up there right after church and check it out? If it turns out to be something we can live with, we'll call."

I forced a sunny smile. "Great. Do me a favor? Call me either way. If this doesn't work for you, well..." I let it hang, putting them on notice I had no Plan C. And, more to the point, I felt under no obligation to come up with one.

* * *

I was putting final touches on a long email to a client who'd booked a September wedding when the front door creaked open. I glanced at the clock. It'd been less than two hours since Alex and Kat left. Had they managed to fit in a church service and a trip up to 'Ulupalakua that fast?

It was Steve.

"Hey, Pali. I went to your house but you weren't there so I thought I'd try here. I'm surprised to see you working on a Sunday."

"I've got that wedding on Tuesday. Have a seat."

He sat in the chair recently vacated by Alex. "Yeah, the one up at Maui Winery."

"Hopefully. They can't decide."

"What's to decide? It's a gorgeous setting. I promised Bobby I'd shoot his kid's baby pics for free if he'd let you do it there."

"Seriously? He hit me up to buy a case of wine."

"Give the guy credit. He knows how to negotiate. So, what's the problem with your wedding couple?"

"The guy's full-on religious. He thinks drinking's a sin."

"Okay. So it'll be a dry wedding. It's not like that's something we haven't encountered before."

"He thinks having his ceremony at the vineyard would be supporting the liquor industry."

Steve clamped his hands on his head. "Are you kidding? That's nuts."

"Anyway, they've gone up there to check it out. I hope to hear from them any time now."

"What'll you do if they say 'no'?"

"I'll give them back their deposit and steer them to the courthouse."

He absentmindedly scratched behind his right ear. That was one of Steve's "tells." It signaled he was about to ask a favor.

"Uh, I got something to run by you," he said.

"Shoot."

"Remember I said me and Allen were having issues?"

I nodded.

"Well, it seems we've gone from bickering over little stuff to full-blown fighting over just about everything."

"Sorry to hear that." I wanted to commiserate by launching into my own sob story about Finn but kept quiet to allow him to finish.

"Yeah, well, here's the deal. Can I couch surf at your place for a few nights? Tell Finn I promise to totally stay out of you guy's way. I put a notice on the Gadda message board, but who knows how long it'll be before something pops? Going back to Allen's is *not* an option."

"You're more than welcome. Finn's off-island this week so it'll just be me and you."

"*Mahalo*, Pali. I wouldn't ask, but the guys I windsurf with have their hands full with kids and dogs and *'ohana* coming and going."

Most likely he hadn't really talked to the guys he regularly surfs with at Ho'okipa, but I didn't push it. Steve prefers to keep his lifestyle choice and fussy personal hygiene regime hush-hush except with close friends.

"No worries at all. I enjoy your company."

"So, Finn's on O'ahu?"

"Last I heard."

My voice must've provided Steve with a "tell" I was unaware of, because he lifted his eyebrows.

"Do I detect trouble in paradise?"

"Have you eaten lunch? I'm starving. Let's grab a fish sandwich."

On the short walk to the Pa'ia Fish Market I pondered how much I was willing to divulge about recent events in my marriage.

After getting our food, we joined a table of college-aged kids who seemed much too absorbed in checking their phones and recalling the previous night's pool party to listen to us. I chowed down my mahi-mahi burger, alternately swallowing and talking.

"Finn's wounded," said Steve. "Guys like him don't deal with bad news well. And when it's manhood stuff … Well, you don't need me to tell you how ugly that can get."

I pulled out my phone and handed it to him so he could listen to Finn's voicemail. He held it to his ear, his face taut with concentration, and then wordlessly he handed it back to me.

We sat in silence, the lunch hour din swirling around us like the roar of pounding surf.

After half a minute he got up from the table. "Let's talk later. I'll make dinner."

I followed him out and turned to walk back up to my shop. After about a block, I remembered I'd promised Luke I'd talk to Sifu Doug about the black belts switching classes. Hopefully, he'd had time to talk to the others and see who needed to make changes. I crossed Baldwin and headed for the *guan*.

Doug's Jeep wasn't out back, but I hadn't expected it to be. When I looked up after pulling out my keys, I noticed a sign taped to the door.

"No Classes Until Further Notice"

It wasn't like Doug to shut things down like that. He seldom cancelled classes, and he'd gone to all the trouble of making a schedule of how he wanted the classes handled. What was going on?

Halfway back to my shop, my cell phone chimed. It was Kat.

"We're back."

"What did you think?" My hand trembled, either from still thinking about Doug or fretting over Alex and Kat's decision—maybe both.

"You're right, the place is beautiful. But…"

I hate that word. "But" is the bane of wedding planners everywhere. I didn't say anything, waiting for her to finish.

"Alex wants you to promise there won't be a single picture that shows we were married at a winery. He says his mom will go ballistic."

I was tempted to quote that line from the Bible where a man leaves his father and his mother and cleaves to his wife, but figured this was one of those times when biting back a snarky comment was probably in order. Besides, he could counter with the commandment about honoring your father and mother, and if we got into a Bible verse slap-down, I'd most certainly lose. No amount of Vacation Bible School could make up for every Sunday, rain or shine.

"No problem. My photographer's the best. He can edit or crop shots if necessary."

I pressed on. "So, let's say a four o'clock ceremony? Will that work for you? The manager said there will be fewer visitors then."

She must've put her phone to her chest and consulted Alex, because I heard a series of thumping and scratching sounds before she came back on.

"Yeah, that'll work."

"Great. If you have any questions, call me. Otherwise, I'll meet you at the ..." I balked at calling it a winery, so instead said, "...at the 'Ulupalakua location at four on Tuesday."

Steve made spaghetti with chicken Italian sausage that night, one of my favorite comfort foods. He'd stopped by the Pa'ia Bakery and emptied his wallet for a loaf of their chewy olive bread. I set the table and he pulled a beautiful tossed salad of arugula and mango out of the refrigerator. Aside from the carb overload it was a perfect meal.

As I forked spaghetti into my mouth, I kept saying, "I really shouldn't be eating so much of this."

"Why not? Worried about losing your girlish figure? From what I can see you look like you've lost five or six pounds since I moved out."

"You should talk. I've never seen you so skinny. Did Allen keep the refrigerator padlocked or something? I wouldn't be surprised. He looks like the type."

We went on like that, dishing compliments to each other while throwing down trash talk about our respective significant others. After dinner, we veered much too close to boo-hoo land when we began reminiscing about how happy we'd been earlier that year when I'd hastily married Finn and Steve had set up housekeeping in Allen's swanky Kapalua townhouse.

We went out on the front porch and watched the evening sky shift from cerulean to deep violet as we sat in silence on the rickety wicker chairs. After a few minutes we both said, "I miss him," at the same time.

Steve went upstairs to sleep on the sofa bed in the guest room since his old room had been turned into an office for Finn.

I got into bed but tossed and turned, mentally replaying every recent conversation I'd had with my husband. How had our relationship blown apart so fast? "For better or for worse, in sickness and in health?" Didn't our vows mean anything to him?

As I pondered the mystery of my easy come, easy go marriage, it hit me. What about Doug's marriage? He and

Lani had been tight for more than fifteen years. And now she's hurling chairs at him?

Being in a relationship is like building an elaborate sand castle. It's a ton of work easily swept away by a rogue wave. For Finn and me, it seems our first unexpected wave—finding out we couldn't have kids—was about to do in our sand castle before we even got the turrets up. But what had been Sifu Doug and Lani's wave? After a decade and a half, wouldn't it take more than one strong surge to pull down all they'd built?

I went to sleep determined to track down Doug and get some answers.

9

I was in the shower when he called. If he'd dialed the landline I'm sure Steve would've picked it up. But he didn't. Finn called my cell.

At least he left a message. In a weary voice, he said, "Hey. Sorry you're not answering my calls, but this may be the last one. To say I'm in a safe place would require you to believe in the Tooth Fairy, Santa Claus and most of what comes out of Vladamir Putin's mouth."

He paused. When he resumed, his tone sounded even more fatigued. "But believe this. I'm sorry, Pali. For everything. I would've come clean about my medical issues before, but I forgot all about those college experiments. Besides, they told us it was safe." He barked a throaty laugh. "Maybe one of these days I'll stop being so gullible. Anyway, again, I'm sorry. Neither of us has time for false starts. Bye."

I held the phone up to my ear for what seemed like minutes but was probably just a few seconds, hoping he'd tack on an "I Love you," or "Miss you" postscript. But there was only static.

I called to Steve from the bottom of the stairs, but got no answer. In the kitchen I found a note from him saying he'd be back in a little while and asking me to wait.

At eight-twenty he banged through the back door carrying a white bakery bag in one hand and his car keys in the other. He had a glazed donut clamped between his teeth. He put the bag on the counter and took the donut out of his mouth.

"I brought us consolation calories."

I unfolded the bag and the aroma of warm, sugary dough wafted into my nostrils.

I shook my head. "You know how bad these things are for you?"

"Not if you're grieving," he said. "Look, there's the regular food pyramid and then there's the break-up pyramid. Regular pyramid is vegetables, grains, milk, that kind of stuff. Break up pyramid's got Ben & Jerry's, fresh-baked donuts, and all-you-can-eat fish and chips night at Cisco's."

I bit into the soft, sweet confection while Steve went on. "Oh yeah, and speaking of Cisco's, sit down because I heard something bad at the donut shop in Pukalani."

"I already know about Doug and Lani having a fight there last Friday."

He looked crestfallen. Steve does not like to be the bearer of old news.

"Okay, but there's more."

I sat down and finished the donut in four bites.

He reached in the bag and handed me another. "Well, seems things didn't improve over the weekend."

"What'd you hear?"

"Doug's neighbor was ahead of me in line and I heard her tell the clerk there were two cop cars at the Kanekoa's house this morning."

"Seriously?"

"Yeah. She was pretty sure Lani called them because Doug's car wasn't in the driveway where he leaves it."

"What about the kids?"

"She thinks they're at Lani's sister's. Seems Doug tried to pawn the kids off at another neighbor's but she had *'ohana* visiting from the mainland."

"Who was the woman you were eavesdropping on?"

He flinched at the accusation. "I didn't have to share this with you, you know."

I mumbled an apology, but it was about as heartfelt as his feigned irritation.

"Don't know. I was being *très* discreet, but I heard the clerk call her 'Keoni.' Not sure if that's her name or just one of those 'hey, girl' kind of Hawaiian words."

"It's a name," I said. I absentmindedly wolfed down the second donut.

"Anyway, I thought you'd want to know."

"*Mahalo.* I've been trying to reach Doug since yesterday. Oh, and guess who finally called me this morning?"

Steve grinned. "I thought you weren't fond of guessing games."

"Sorry, you're right. Anyway, it was Finn. He said they're not in a safe place, after all. He didn't sound good." I wasn't ready to share the rest of the message.

"Did you ask when he'd be home?"

"I didn't get to talk to him. He called while I was in the shower."

Steve shoved the donut bag across the table. "Go ahead. You deserve another one."

* * *

I called Doug's cell and home number at least ten times. The first few times I left detailed messages about how worried I was and how I much I needed to talk to him, but after call number five I simply hung up.

At around nine-thirty I drove to the PoP and was startled to see a police car parked in front. The curb outside the *guan* is painted red, which means "No parking— ever," but I suppose cops don't worry about stuff like that.

I pulled around to the alley and was surprised again by yellow crime scene tape crisscrossed on the jamb to the back door. The door was open, so I parked and walked over.

A uniformed Maui Police officer stood just inside, playing doorman.

"Good morning, Officer."

"Mornin', Miss. I'm afraid you can't go in."

"My name's Pali Moon and this is where I train. I'm a black belt level student of Doug Kanekoa."

The guy shot me stink eye that seemed to say, *"Goody for you, but you're still not going in."*

"Is Doug okay?"

"I'm not at liberty to say."

"Oh, come on. I'm a local. I own a business just up the street from here. Tell me what's going on with my *sifu*."

"The detective in charge is inside, but I got word they're gettin' ready to leave," he said. "You can wait out here for him if you want."

After a couple of minutes, a plain clothes guy I'd never seen before ducked under the tape and began heading down the alley. The doorman cop nodded as he passed by.

"That the guy?" I whispered.

He nodded again.

I hurried to catch up with the detective, practicing my most ingratiating smile as I went.

I stuck out a hand. "*Aloha*, Detective. Pali Moon here. I train here at Palace of Pain and I'm a good friend of Doug Kanekoa's. I'd be happy to answer any questions I can."

The cop looked way too young and green to be a lead detective, but I figured it made sense for the police department to send out the rookies on small-time stuff like minor domestic disputes.

The guy shook my hand. "Oh, yeah? Well, here's a question for you. Why do you think your so-called 'good friend' took off after calling in his wife's murder?"

* * *

I staggered back to my car, barely conscious of the short ride back to my shop. It's a good thing I always park in the same spot because I was totally running on auto-pilot. Before even checking in at my shop I went next door to the Gadda.

Farrah rushed the door as I came in. "Did you hear?" She'd said it so quickly it came out sounding like, "Da chair."

"Yeah," I said. "I'm dumbfounded."

She leaned in and said, "Lani's gone? I can't believe it."

I nodded, unable to say anything without choking up.

"Have you seen Doug?"

"I've called and called. But he's not picking up. The police said he called them, but now he's missing."

Farrah wrung her hands. "Okay, sure, they had that little rumble at Cisco's the other night, but it didn't sound like nothin' nuclear. This is, like, blowing everyone's mind."

"I can't imagine what happened."

She blew out a breath. "Like, I wasn't tight with Doug like you are, but he always seemed to be a totally right-eous dude. Never heard of him losin' it. And from what everybody said about last Friday, when Lani was comin' unglued at Cisco's he kept the Zen goin'. Never yelled or nuthin'."

I kept quiet but I agreed. In all the time I'd known Doug, I'd seen him angry, but I'd never seen him lose his temper and extract physical vengeance beyond the con-fines of the *guan*. In martial arts, we call it, "leaving it on the mat," and Doug had been adamant that people who trained with him had to do just that.

Finally I said, "What've you heard?"

If anyone knew what the locals were saying, it'd be Farrah. The Gadda served as the best place in town to find something to chew on, both literally and figuratively.

"Everyone's saying that after Doug and Lani duked it out at Cisco's he must've just lost it. Weird thing is, a guy claims he saw Doug's car at the Palace of Pain this morning. The cops went there looking for him, but he's in the wind."

I hated to ask, because I was pretty sure I didn't want to hear the answer, but I went ahead anyway. "How did she die?"

Farrah pointed a finger at her temple. "Shot. In the noggin'."

I leaned in and we collapsed into a long hug.

"It's so horrible," I said when we finally stepped back.

"Yeah. Totally."

"I have to find Doug."

"When you do, tell him to turn himself in, Pali. It's getting' gnarly."

After a few beats, Farrah suddenly perked up. "Hey, on a groovier level, guess what?"

Farrah was big on guessing games, even when there was absolutely no way I could've figured out the answer. But after thirty years of friendship I'd given up hope of side-stepping the guess-a-thons, so I played along.

"You're selling the store and moving to Thailand?"

"Not even close."

"Okay, how about Ono found a big sack of diamonds and when he turned it in the owner gave him a million-dollar reward."

"No, but that'd be way cool."

"Last one. You traced your genealogy and you're a third cousin, once-removed to Princess Kate of England."

"Nah. But that'd be way groovy, too. Do you think that would make me a princess-once-removed?"

My patience was being profoundly tested and Farrah must've sensed it, because she hurriedly continued.

"Anyhow, I talked to the *kahu* and he's coming over this week to do the blessing." She beamed as if Ono really had found a sack of diamonds.

"That sounds promising. And you're sure the guy's legit?"

"For sure. He's got all kinds of far out testimonials on his website, and when I talked to him, he seemed ultra-psyched to help."

"When's he coming?"

"Not completely sure, but probably Friday. Can you make it?"

"After the wedding on Tuesday I don't have anything booked until next month. So, yeah. If you want me there, I'll be there."

"Cool." She gave me another hug, this one just a quick body squeeze. "I can't tell you how blissed out I'm gonna feel when this is *pau*, you know, over. I've been, like, a jumpy cat every night since that dude showed up with his gnarly face and that freaky blade."

"I can't imagine," I said.

And honestly, I couldn't.

I trotted back to my shop considering my options. I had to find Sifu Doug and see what I could do to help, but I also had a wedding to put on the next day. I didn't know how long it would take to find Doug, but I could line up everything needed for the wedding pretty quickly. So, first things first. I vowed to set aside thoughts of the Doug and Lani situation and focus on finalizing the plans for Tuesday's ceremony.

As I waited on hold for Bobby from Maui Winery to check inventory and make sure the wine I'd agreed to buy was in stock, my mind drifted to wondering how Doug's kids were doing. The two kids, a boy and a girl, were in their early teens, a rough time in life as it is. Now they were motherless. And, I'd gotten a strong sense from Detective Ho he had their father at the top of the list of suspects.

A click signaled Bobby was back on the line. "We have everything, but we can only sell you two bottles of the Lehua. It's one of our most popular wines so we limit it to two per customer."

I waited to hear what he'd suggest in place of the other three bottles of Lehua I'd requested.

"Sorry about that. Would you like to stick with your order, which would make it just nine bottles, or do are you want to add some others?"

"Can I only order nine?"

"Certainly. The one-case minimum is merely a recommendation. For your small party a lesser amount is sufficient."

When he toted up the charges, it was a relief I was only on the hook for nine bottles. The total was close to two-hundred-and-fifty dollars. I'd have a nice collection of wines to pick from when Finn made us a special dinner, but it'd wipe out my entire commission for the Alex and Kat wedding.

That thought stopped me cold. Not the lost commission, but the point about Finn making dinner. Was he even going to be around? Or was I reading more doom and gloom into his messages than was warranted? After all, he was far from home doing military skullduggery I'm not at liberty to know about. That had to be a factor in his despondent attitude.

I spent the next hour pushing back thoughts of Doug and Lani as I finalized plans for the ceremony. Farrah used to officiate at my weddings but since she'd had the twins she'd taken a leave of absence. The guy I'd gotten to take her place was a tidy fifty-something guy who looked like he'd been in insurance on the mainland. I wasn't sure what his principle means of support was now that he'd moved to Maui, but figured it best not to pry.

I called and clued him in on the couple's religious views and he offered to throw in a few appropriate Bible verses and end the ceremony with a windy blessing and an extended prayer.

"No additional charge," he said.

I continued with my checklist. The couple had agreed to drive themselves to the venue so I didn't have to bother finding a limo, and they'd agreed to hosting a casual wedding dinner of burgers and salad at the 'Ulupalakua Ranch Store across the street.

I called Steve to confirm the time and to see if he'd mind driving the two of us up there a bit early so we could stash the wine in his trunk.

"It'll cost you," he said.

"Okay, I'll tack another half-hour onto your bill."

"No, don't worry about that. What I mean is, I'll take it out in wine. Last Saturday I told a guy at the Ball and Chain I was shooting a wedding at the winery and he got positively dewy-eyed over their pineapple bubbly. It'll give me a good reason to call him."

"You're already back on the market? You and Allen only broke up a week ago."

"Hey, I don't want to give Allen the satisfaction of thinking I'm pouty and miserable. And besides, can't you hear it?"

"Hear what?"

"The *tick-tock*. Neither of us is getting any younger, you know."

He'd come perilously close to Finn's final line on his message that morning.

"Fine," I said. "You're more than welcome to a bottle of the sparkling wine. That stuff gives me a headache anyway."

"Uh-oh. Sounds like you've started without me."

"Started what?"

"Your pity party." He went on in a falsetto voice, 'Ms. Pity, party of one.'"

"Look, I've gotta go."

"You coming home for dinner? I'm thinking of making my specialty."

"After I finish here at the shop I'm heading to Doug's place. I should be home by seven. Dare I ask what's your specialty?"

"You can ask, but I won't know 'til I make it. Dinner's at seven. Don't be late."

We hung up and I made two more phone calls, one to the Ranch Store and one final call to Doug's cell. I'd crossed off everything on my wedding checklist and it was only four-thirty.

I locked up, confident I'd be home for dinner with time to spare.

10

I turned onto Doug and Lani's street in Pukalani but only got a few houses down before coming to a police barricade. A uniformed cop took his time sidling over to my driver's side window.

"Your license, please."

"My license? What'd I do wrong, Officer?"

"Nuthin'. But this road's closed to people who don' live here, so we're checking licenses."

"I live in Hali'imaile. I came to help a friend who lives here."

"Sorry. Nobody but residents."

I did a three-point turn and drove back the way I came. I parked on a street two blocks away and zigged and zagged through unfenced yards until I came out a few houses down from Doug's. The Kanekoa residence was a beehive of activity.

The garage door was open and a canopy was set up in the driveway. Uniformed police guarded the perimeter of the property. A sweaty *ali'i*-size cop standing near the canopy looked like he'd been there a while. His vacant expression, slumped shoulders, and mouth pulled down in a fatigued frown gave me an idea.

I trotted back through the neighbors' yards and drove to the supermarket on Pukalani Street. I grabbed a couple of sports drinks out of the cooler and got three hot dogs and packets of various condiments from the hot foods section. In the candy aisle I picked up a couple of king-size Snickers bars, and I swung by the produce section for some apple bananas.

I returned to my former parking spot and retraced my path to Doug's house. The big cop was still standing guard, his back to me. As I approached, he whirled around as I noisily stomped through the gravel.

"Stop right there."

I held out the grocery bag while reading the name tag above his pocket. "Officer Puno. Thought you might've missed lunch."

He shot me a guarded look.

"It's nothing big. Just a couple hot dogs and snacks. Also some Gatorade. It's good to stay hydrated, you know."

The cop warily reached for the bag. He looked around as if checking to see if anyone was watching, then dug out the foil-wrapped hot dogs.

"They supposed to relieve me hours ago," he said. "Been here all day."

"There's ketchup and mustard in there."

"*Mahalo*, but I take 'em plain." He unwrapped a hot dog and pushed half of it into his mouth.

While he munched, I talked. "Pretty weird what went down here, eh?"

He swallowed. "Yeah. Poor lady. Looks like some low-life broke in."

"I heard they were lookin' at the husband."

"Don' know 'bout that, but the window in back's busted out. When we first got here I did the initial recon and saw the busted window."

I pointed to the canopy. "What's going on in there?"

He'd shoved the rest of the hot dog in his mouth so I waited while he chewed.

"That's where they found her. Took all day for forensics to show up. I guess they called in the big guns from Honolulu."

"You think they'll be finishing up soon?"

He shrugged. "Hard to say. They don' tell guys like me much." He reached in and retrieved another hot dog.

"What about the other people in the house? I heard they've got a couple of kids."

"Not sure 'bout that, but last I heard there's still no sign of the husband."

"Is he a suspect?"

"What's with it with you? You a reporter or somethin'? We're not s'posed to talk to reporters."

"I'm not a reporter, I'm a concerned neighbor. You know, Neighborhood Watch. This is a safe neighborhood so people are asking."

Okay, there was a smidgen of truth there. I'm a member of my local Neighborhood Watch in Hali'imaile, and I was sure the people on Doug's block were all dying to know what was going down at the Kanekoa place.

"All's I know is the lady of the house got shot this morning and the husband called it in."

"Was he here when it happened?"

"Don't know. He a friend of yours?"

I heard the sound of crunching gravel. When I turned, Detective Glen Wong of the Maui Police Department was about thirty feet away and closing the gap quickly. Detective Wong and I go way back, some of it good, most times not so good.

Officer Puno thrust the grocery bag at me and I took it without comment.

"Ms. Moon, it pains me to acknowledge I was almost expecting to see you here," said Wong.

I shot him my most winsome smile and stuck out my hand. "Detective Wong, good to see you again. I was shopping in the neighborhood when I heard the news." I hoisted the grocery bag to corroborate my fib.

"Nice try, but we both know this crime scene is also the home of your martial arts instructor. Detective Ho advised us he found you prying into police business earlier in the day."

I grinned at Wong as if conceding his clever hypothesis. "True. So you can imagine why I'm concerned about what's happened."

"As we all are, Ms. Moon. Do you have information I need to know?"

"Not really. But maybe if I knew what you know, I'd be able to fill in some blanks."

He shook his head. "Your never-ending meddling never ceases to amaze me. Look at me, Ms. Moon. Do you see a rookie fresh out of the academy?"

"No, sir. I certainly do not."

He glared at the implied dig, then turned to Officer Puno. "I hope I won't learn you've been engaging with this citizen in exchanges that could be construed as unprofessional."

Puno's face clouded. I couldn't tell if he thought Wong was accusing him of some kind of carnal shenanigans or if he was simply distressed by his use of the word, "unprofessional."

I broke in. "Far from it, Detective. I'll admit I attempted to extract information from this officer, but it didn't work. He's a pretty closed-mouth guy."

Wong pointedly looked from me to Puno and then back to me. "As I said, I better not hear otherwise. Officer Puno, isn't your shift nearly over? When are you supposed to be relieved?"

"Three hours ago."

"Check out with your supervisor. I'll take over for a while."

Officer Puno slunk away as if he'd been dismissed for dereliction of duty. Wong watched him go, muttering, "They bitch about paying overtime and then they wonder why turnover's so high."

He seemed surprised to realize he'd said it out loud, adding, "Not that it's any of my business, of course."

I jumped at his lapse and pointed at the canopy. "What can you tell me about what's going on in there?"

"Nothing."

"Oh come on, Detective, I know this *'ohana*. I might be able to help."

"I'm not lead on this. Besides, everything has to go through the Public Information Officer."

"Okay, how about I tell you what I've pieced together so far and you confirm or deny?"

"Why would I do that? You've got no jurisdiction, no credentials, no possible reason to be concerned with police business." He pointed at the grocery bag. "I suggest you take your little bait sack and head on home."

I felt a jolt of wonder at Wong figuring out my bribery scheme. Then I remembered he was pretty good at his job.

"Look, Detective, Doug Kanekoa is more than just my martial arts *sifu*. He's also one of my best friends. It's killing me that he's lost his wife and his kids are now motherless. How am I supposed to sleep, knowing my friend is missing and some nut job killer is still at large?"

"Could be one and the same."

"You can't possibly think that. Why would Doug call the police if he'd done it?"

"You said he's your friend, so you tell me."

* * *

I was nearly home when my cell chimed. It was Farrah's home number. I took the call and was surprised when Ono answered.

"What's up, Ono?"

"That's what I'd like to know." He sounded cranky.

Okay. I mentally scrambled to figure out what I may have said or done to upset him.

"Is something wrong?"

"What's this I hear about you loaning my wife money?"

"Ah, that. Well, actually it's not a loan. I told her I'd give her what she needed to get your house blessed. She's been really stressed about that apparition in the back yard." I'd chosen my words carefully. I didn't know how onboard Ono was with the whole ghost thing.

"Don't you think that's something you should have brought me in on? It's my house, my family, my so-called apparition. I don't appreciate being kept in the dark."

It never occurred to me that Farrah hadn't discussed hiring the *kahu* with Ono before asking for the money. I wasn't about to throw her under the bus, though. She had way more to lose than I did.

"I'm sorry. It's my fault. I convinced Farrah to hire that guy and I paid before she had time to talk to you. Don't blame her."

The line went quiet for a few seconds and I wondered if he'd hung up.

"Ono?"

"I'm here. I was just thinking of how to put this, but I guess there's just no good way to say it. Don't you think it's bad enough my wife is scheming behind my back without you lying to me about it? I thought we were friends."

And with that, he did hang up.

I drove right past the turn-off to Hali'imaile and kept going.

When I pulled into Farrah and Ono's place in Haiku it was nearly six. I'd be late for dinner, but there was no way I could let this squabble fester.

I knocked and kicked off my *rubba slippas* while I waited for someone to answer the door. After a minute, I knocked again—louder this time. When it became clear no one was coming, I slipped my footwear back on and headed around the side of the house.

Farrah and Ono were sitting outside on the cracked concrete lanai that served as their backyard gathering place. Farrah's face was splotchy and her hair more tangled than usual. She looked up and saw me approach, then swiped the back of her hand across her eyes.

Ono leaned back, arms crossed. His eyes were mere slits. A person didn't need to be clairvoyant to figure out neither of them was happy to see me.

"Sorry to intrude."

"Then why are you?" Ono snarled.

"I had to come by and see if we could work this out. I feel bad about what's happened."

Farrah looked at me with a mixture of anger and sympathy. "Not a good time, Pali. I'm not sayin' you're not always welcome here, but right now you're not."

I tried to decode that one and gave up after a few seconds.

"Look, guys. I've had a lot going on lately and the last thing I meant was to cause a problem." I directed my next remark to Farrah. "You didn't tell me Ono was against the blessing."

"He's not. He's against you giving me money."

"Wrong!" Ono bellowed. "I'm against all of it—this smarmy voo-doo guy, the outrageous cost, and the two of you plotting behind my back. I'm the man of the house here and keeping my family safe is *my* job, not yours."

I felt a tug to point out the obvious sexism, but thought better of it.

He gathered steam. "You know how it makes me feel for my wife to be paying huge bucks to some con man so she can sleep at night?"

I looked toward the back door.

Farrah must've picked up on my discomfort. "It's cool. The *keiki* are at the store with Auntie Bea. Ono and me will get 'em after we've kissed and made up."

From where I was sitting, it seemed Auntie Bea had better be prepared to feed those kids dinner and get them ready for bed.

* * *

When I finally got home it was almost seven-thirty. Steve wasn't in the kitchen and when I called for him, he didn't answer. I couldn't remember a time I'd felt more desolate. My husband was threatening to end our marriage, my best friend and her husband were feuding over something I'd inadvertently meddled in, and my *sifu* had disappeared after his loving wife of sixteen years had been found shot to death in their home. Although I felt a twinge of guilt for not making it home in time for dinner, it paled in comparison to everything else swirling around me.

Steve had left a note on the stairs.

Gone out. Dinner in oven. C U when I C U –S.

11

Steve's "specialty" turned out to be a spicy chicken stir fry that had devolved into a mass of unappetizing glop in the oven. But who was I to complain? My culinary skills stop at salad-from-a-bag. And I wasn't hungry anyway.

I toyed with the bowl of gunk, picking out the still-recognizable veggies like broccoli stems and chunks of carrot, while considering what I knew about Lani's murder. I didn't have much, and nothing had been corroborated by solid sources, so it was a pitiful mash—much like the stuff in the bowl in front of me.

She'd been killed in their garage, presumably on Monday morning, shot in the head (how many times?), and a window in the back door of the house was broken. Doug had alerted the police and then vanished.

Where was he? Had the killer taken him hostage? Maybe he'd seen the killer and he was now in hot pursuit. Or, painful as it was to even consider, maybe he'd had something to do with Lani's death and had gone into hiding.

That was so unlike the *sifu* I knew, I quickly dismissed it. He was much more likely to be breaking the law via vigilante justice than cowardly eluding capture. And since he never fully briefed me on what he'd discovered when he followed Lani, I was pretty certain her death would be linked in some way to what had been going on these past few weeks.

I threw the rest of the glop in the garbage and hid it under a strategically placed paper napkin. Steve wasn't above checking the garbage and launching into a lecture on hungry people on Maui, and in my present state of mind I wasn't certain I could rein in my urge to punch someone.

I flopped down on the sofa and clicked on the TV. Nothing but inane reality shows and silly sitcoms I didn't find funny. The laugh track roared, leaving me wondering if Steve was right about time marching on. Had I become so tired and shopworn that even contemporary humor had passed me by?

There's something about lolling in a prone position in the flickering blue light of a television that brings on the munchies. I wasn't hungry. In fact, every decent thing I considered—celery sticks, string cheese, air-popped popcorn—didn't inspire me to get up. What did? The two humongous Snicker bars still out in my car.

I'd pondered the healthy options available for minutes without taking action but as soon as I remembered the Snickers I was up and off the sofa like a shot.

I'd parked out back. Steve had dibs on the one-car garage, so I rarely even checked to see if it was available. My car was at the end of the driveway about thirty feet from the back door. I tucked my feet into my *rubba slippas* to avoid stepping on something in the dark and made my way to the Mini. The weak interior light came on, providing barely enough illumination to see my hand in front of my face. I manually searched the cluttered back area—you can't really call it a trunk since the tiny car isn't big enough for such an extravagance—until my fingers detected the fake fabric of a reusable grocery bag. I pulled out the bag and jogged back to the house with the anticipation of a kid coming home after trick or treating.

As the back door slammed behind me I heard a faint *ping*. I raced to the living room and snatched up my phone. The screen showed I'd missed a call two minutes earlier.

I can barely recall what life was like before cellphones, but I'm pretty sure it was easier. I resent being tied to a device that can malfunction, run out of juice or be out of range, and costs as much as my electric bill. Owning a cellphone implies a pledge to be immediately available to whoever calls you, twenty-four seven. Not answering is akin to putting your hands over your ears and droning, "nah-nah-nah-nah" when someone's trying to talk to you. I think it's anti-*aloha* to require such an invasion of my personal time and space.

Once again I'd missed a call from Finn, and once again he left a voicemail chastising me for refusing to take his calls. Worse yet, his short message left me little hope he'd changed his stance on working things out.

I called Doug's cell one more time before turning in, but the call went immediately to voicemail. I was brushing my teeth when I got a call back. I spit in the sink, wiped my mouth with the back of my hand and grabbed the phone in less time than it takes to sneeze and say "bless you."

It wasn't Doug. And it certainly wasn't Finn. It was Ono.

"Hey, Pali. Sorry about today."

"I understand. I'm sorry I didn't get Farrah's pinky swear that she'd talked to you about it."

"Nah, I'm sorry for jumping all over you. I'm actually mad at Farrah, not you, but I didn't want to go there, you know?"

"I do."

"Speaking of not wanting to go there, I got a weird call from Finn tonight. Can you tell me what's going on with him?"

I paused. How much did I want to divulge to my husband's brother? "Uh, he called when I was outside and I couldn't get to the phone in time."

"Huh. He said something about you not taking his calls."

"That's not it. I'd love to talk, but every time he calls, I miss it."

"Okay. Just checking. He sounded bummed out."

"What'd he say?"

"I guess things are pretty rough. I thought I heard an explosion but when I asked, he said they'd cut him off if he said too much. I'm kinda worried, you know?"

"Me too. If he calls again, tell him I love him and to please keep trying to call me."

"Will do."

A beat of dead air went by before Ono went on. "Yeah, well once again I'm sorry about today. It's just hard for a guy like me to not be able to give my wife what she wants, you know? Makes me feel like a loser."

"I get it. But cut yourself some slack. Sometimes Farrah wants some pretty bizarre stuff."

"Like this Hawaiian witch doctor."

I didn't agree with him calling the *kahu* a witch doctor, but our truce was fragile so I let it slide. "But don't you agree if blessing the house will make her feel safe it's a good thing?"

"It better. For a thousand bucks I could buy a pretty nice shotgun."

How being armed with a "nice gun" could protect his family from a malevolent ghost was a mystery to me, but again, I didn't argue.

* * *

I got up Tuesday morning determined to embrace the serenity prayer as much as possible for the rest of the day. Especially the part about "accepting the things I cannot change." I'm not good at letting things go, which is strange since I've had to let so much go in my life: my parents, my longtime boyfriend who chose his career over me, my dream of being "wedding planner to the stars." Okay, that last one was short-lived and pretty iffy from the get-go, but still.

Steve was heading out to go windsurfing when I banged into the kitchen.

"I see you finally got home and retrieved your dinner," he said.

"Yeah, sorry about being late. I got in the middle of a dust-up between Farrah and Ono and I wanted to stick around until things settled down."

"They're having problems, too? What's up with relationships lately? Bad moon rising?"

"They're okay now. I gave Farrah money to get their house blessed and Ono didn't know about it. He got worked up and I apologized."

"Sounds to me like Farrah should be the one apologizing."

"Yeah, I took one for the team."

He grabbed his gear bag. "We still on for 'Ulupalakua this afternoon?"

"Yep, ceremony's at four, so we should get there by three-fifteen. Can you give me a ride?"

"Can't. I've got a dinner date in Wailea at six and I'm going there right after the wedding."

"I've got to hand it to you. You sure don't let any grass grow under your social life feet."

"*Tick-tock,* Pali."

Steve left and I hurried down to the shop to make sure everything was still on schedule. I'd ordered a tiny cake from my cake baker in Kula which I'd pick up on my way up the mountain. For small weddings I usually ordered flowers from the Gadda, and Farrah had promised they'd be ready by noon.

It had been a few days since I'd worked out and my body was becoming peevish. The Snickers attack hadn't scored me any points, either. I dashed next door, vowing to find something healthy to make up for my slothfulness. I was dithering between Greek or regular yogurt when Farrah sidled over to me.

"Totally frown-face over getting you jammed up with Ono," she said. "Buds?" She put out a fist for me to bump and I did.

"No worries. Better that he's mad at me than you."

"Yeah, but the thing is, he's still kinda mad at me, too."

"What's going on?"

"He's not cool with coming to the blessing 'cuz he thinks it's bogus, but he said I don't have to call the dude and cancel. So, that's groovy."

"Would you like me to be there?"

She perked up. "That'd be rad. I didn't wanna ask, 'cuz, like I thought maybe you were not cool with it, either. I mean, stuff like this is kinda not how you roll."

"It's fine. Tell me the when the guy's showing up and I'll be there."

We hugged and I returned to my shop, spooning yogurt into my mouth as I walked. It went down cool and creamy, but let's face it. When it comes to pure eating pleasure, cultured dairy products are a far cry from a Snickers bar.

At two-thirty, Steve pushed through the door of my shop. His giddy facial expression reminded me of my little brother racing into the house to tattle to our auntie. I stood to greet him.

"Guess what?" he said, panting as if he'd run the whole way.

"What?"

He blew out a ragged breath. "The police found Doug Kanekoa."

"What a relief. Then I guess he's okay."

"Not really."

"He's *not* okay?"

"He's fine, but he's under arrest."

"For what? Going missing?"

"Nope. Murder."

I sank back down into my chair. "Wait a second. Where'd you hear this?"

"It's all over town. Besides, everybody knows the spouse is always the prime suspect."

"That's ridiculous. Doug loved Lani. He'd never hurt her. And besides, the police don't arrest someone without probable cause. What're the—."

Steve cut me off. "My source tells me he'll be arraigned tomorrow morning."

I knew better than to ask Steve to reveal his source, and anyway it wasn't necessary. He was good friends with

Glen Wong and although the by-the-book detective probably wasn't the snitch, someone in his inner circle undoubtedly was.

I looked at the clock. "We've got to go in a few minutes, and I still need to pick up the flowers."

"I know. I wasn't going to say anything about it until after the wedding 'cuz I didn't want you to worry and mess up. But I figured you'd be even madder if I didn't tell you."

I'm not sure where he got the idea I'd "mess up." After five years I've put on so many weddings I could probably do it sleepwalking. The hard part of this job is dealing with the bad behavior that weddings seem to bring out in people. I've seen fairy tale weddings devolve into mai tai-fueled cat fights over bridesmaids vying for the eye of a particularly handsome groomsman. I've witnessed moms and stepmoms sparring over who stands next to the father-of-the-bride in the "parents-of" photo. In one mom vs. stepmom showdown over the seating arrangement at the rehearsal dinner, both women were wearing Spanx so tight they could barely sit, let alone eat. I've poured gallons of coffee down hung-over grooms—and even a few brides—and provided innumerable bottles of Visine to conceal bloodshot eyes at the photo shoot.

I balk at admitting I'm jaded, but there you have it. Been there, done that, and teetering far too close to the abyss of my own failed marriage to be worried about "messing up" Alex and Kat's simple two-hour event.

Steve was rearranging photography gear in the trunk of his car when I came back from the Gadda with the flowers.

"You sure you're gonna be okay?" he said. "I'm sorry about dumping bad news on you right before show time."

"I'm not going to think about it until I can talk to Doug. The police are simply doing their job, but I'm sure once the facts come out, Doug will be released."

He opened his driver door and slid inside. "See you top side."

I'd put on a good face for Steve, but as I got underway I ran through a long list of what-ifs concerning Doug and Lani. As much as I wanted to believe my *sifu* lacked the motive, means or opportunity to be responsible for his wife's death, events of the past week niggled at the edge of certainty.

Had I completely misread this man I'd known and believed in for ten years? First Hatch, then Finn and now Doug? My confidence in trusting the males of my species was at an all-time low. And with good reason. My current standing was pretty much zero for three.

12

As luck would have it, I got behind a school bus going through Kula. High school kids, who never seem to be in much of a hurry for fear of appearing "uncool," sauntered down the steps of the bus, and then milled about waiting for malingering friends to make their way out. Finally, the door closed and the bus trundled a few blocks further down the road. Red flashing lights came on, the brakes *whooshed* to a halt, and the whole process began again.

I kept checking the time. Each bus stop burned at least three or four minutes. Mercifully, at last the bus turned left and I was able to get back up to speed. I was sailing through the curves a few miles from 'Ulupalakua when my Bluetooth went off.

"*Aloha*," I said.

"Don't you 'aloha' me, Pali Moon." It was Farrah.

"What's wrong?"

"Ono told me what you said last night."

"Okay." I scrambled to come up with whatever I may have said that I'd have to apologize for.

"I don't dig you calling me names behind my back."

I couldn't recall any name-calling.

"What names?"

"Ono said you called me weird."

In high school, Farrah had worked hard to be accepted into the Goth crowd, a weird bunch if there ever was one. Now she's offended?

"I think Ono misunderstood. I simply said the *kahu* thing might be a little weird."

"You don't dig it? Because if you saw the dude's website you'd totally get that he's for real."

"Farrah, I'm on my way to a wedding. Can we talk about this later? "

"Now you're ditching me? Great. See ya around, Pali." The line went dead.

I arrived at the winery at a quarter to four and Steve was already deep into photo shoot mode. He'd posed the couple under a towering tree at the center of the garden area and was instructing Alex in the finer points of exactly how his hands should be placed on the bride's shoulder. Off to the side, the officiant was chatting with Bobby. I breathed a sigh of relief as everything looked delightfully under control.

Bobby beckoned me over.

"Any problems?" I nodded toward Alex, who was starting to look a bit shopworn with Steve's fussing.

Bobby said, "None that I know of." He looked over at the officiant who shrugged his agreement.

"I'm afraid the groom had a small issue with holding the ceremony here," I said. "I'm glad to see he's gotten over it."

"Issue?"

I waved it away. "Nothing major. His religion forbids alcohol, so there was some concern over this being a winery."

The two men exchanged a glance, and Bobby spoke up. "Seems he's experienced a religious epiphany."

The officiant smiled. "Yes, facing down matrimony can do that to a man."

"I'm not following," I said.

Bobby reached over and picked up an empty champagne flute from a nearby table. "Your teetotaler groom has already enjoyed two glasses of our Lokelani sparkling wine. And his blushing bride has guzzled at least three."

"What?"

"Yes. Looks like they'll have to repent tomorrow."

The officiant excused himself so he could get the ceremony under way.

I dug through my purse. "I brought payment for the wines I'll be buying."

"Good. But you're already more than covered. The bridal couple ordered a case shipped home."

"Did they pay for it?"

"On his Visa card."

"Go figure."

The ceremony went off without a hitch. Steve snapped away while the couple exchanged rings and vows, and the witnesses—a couple Kat and Alex had recruited from their hotel—beamed at the wedding couple as if they'd been close friends for years.

"Now, by the power vested in me by the State of Hawaii, I pronounce you husband and wife," intoned the officiant. "You may kiss the bride."

At this point, both couples—Alex and Kat, and the two witnesses—locked lips as if the men were about to go off to war.

Bobby nudged me and nodded at the witnesses who were still enjoying a lingering lip lock. "Is that customary?"

"Not that I know of."

At that point, the male witness came up for air. "We had a no-frills courthouse ceremony back home, so we're pretending this is our wedding, too. We're hoping to upload a few shots to Facebook."

Kat reached up and pulled the flower wreath and attached veil from her head. She hugged the other woman before carefully setting the veil in place. "There you go. Now take some snaps that'll make your friends jealous."

Just when I go getting jaded about putting on weddings, someone does something that reminds me Hawaii can bring out the *aloha* in anyone.

* * *

We went across the street for brisket sandwiches and cake and everyone was fed and getting back in their cars by six o'clock. I'd left my phone in my car and checked it as soon as I climbed in.

The screen showed I had three voicemails. I figured the calls were probably from Farrah, anxious to make things right.

I was wrong. All the calls were from the same number, but it wasn't Farrah. It was James Kanekoa, Doug's brother and the family lawyer. In the first call, James was circumspect, only saying he needed to talk to me. In the second message, he added a bit more context. His brother was in jail and had asked James to get in touch with me. By voicemail number three he was sounding anxious.

"Pali, sorry to bother you again but I really need to talk to you. I don't like to discuss sensitive information on cell calls, but you need to know this is serious. My brother's threatening to confess and I'm desperate to hear from you. Call as soon as you get this."

Confess? Doug was going to tell the police he killed Lani?

It took much less time to go down the mountain than it had taken me to go up. And it wasn't just because there was no school bus.

As I pulled in my driveway I called James. I hadn't wanted to risk Bluetooth coverage on the mountain, and I wanted to hear the whole story without interruption.

"James, it's me, Pali Moon."

"Thank God you've called. I was beginning to think you didn't want to get involved."

Tell that to Detective Wong, I thought. He accuses me of meddling when I simply ask, "How are you?"

"I'm sorry I couldn't call sooner but I was at a wedding up in 'Ulupalakua."

"No problem. Are you in a place where you won't be overheard?"

I'd planned to sit outside and enjoy the sunset, but went inside. "Yep, I'm inside my house. Nobody here. My roommate may come in soon, but for now I'm alone."

"I'd rather discuss this in person, but I don't want to come to your house if you're expecting your roommate to show up. Douglas is being arraigned tomorrow and he wants to plead 'guilty'"

"Okay. I appreciate the heads-up, but I don't understand why you're telling me this."

"Because I can't allow him to do it. If he pleads 'guilty' or even 'nolo contendre' it's over. He'll have no shot at providing a defense, no chance to tell his side of things."

"I still don't understand where I fit in."

"Here's the deal. I don't want to discuss this on the phone. Can I ask you to come to my office in Wailuku?"

"Now? It's after seven. It'd be close to eight o'clock before I could get there."

"I know it's late, but my brother's life is at stake."

"Would you mind meeting me at my shop in Pa'ia? It's about halfway between us."

He agreed and we hung up. He still hadn't answered my question about why he thought I could make a difference, but I was flattered he'd asked.

I got to my shop in record time since there's never much traffic on Baldwin after dark on a Tuesday night.

Never many speed traps, either. James arrived a few minutes after I'd turned on the lights.

I let him in and headed for the back room. "Would you like tea?"

"Love some. I don't suppose you have any of Doug's famous blend?"

I stopped in my tracks and turned around. "You know about that?"

"Doesn't everybody?"

"But you're a lawyer."

"All the more reason I should know. How do you think my brother's managed to stay out of jail all these years?"

I filled the electric kettle. "Well, he's in jail now."

"Yeah. And I appreciate you meeting me so late. If I can't talk sense into him before his arraignment tomorrow, he'll be shipped off to Halawa before the ink dries on the warrant."

Halawa, Hawaii's maximum security prison, is on O'ahu. This makes it difficult for family and friends from the neighbor islands to visit inmates since the only way to get there is by air. Visitors without family on O'ahu usually have to come and go the same day since prices for rental cars and hotel rooms are geared to well-heeled vacationers, not local people with loved ones in prison.

I pulled out two cups, teabags, and sugar. Steam rolled out the spout of the teapot. As I reached for the pot my hand slipped, sending a stream of boiling water onto my bare foot.

"Ow, ow, ow." I hopped around for a few seconds, then hoisted my burned foot into the sink and turned on the tap. The tepid water didn't help much.

"You should get some ice on that," James said.

"My mini-fridge gave out about a year ago."

"Then I'll make this fast so you can get home."

James filled me in on how Sifu Doug had shown up at the main police station in Wailuku and turning himself in. "It was nuts. He walked in and said they could stop looking for whoever killed his wife. I've been doing criminal law for ten years and I've never heard anything that stupid."

"Did he do it?"

"Who knows? When he called from the jail he told me he and Lani had had a fight and when she went out to the garage he followed her."

I screwed up my face, contemplating this implausible scenario. "So? That doesn't mean he killed her."

"I know, but that's how he phrased it."

"None of this sounds like Doug, does it?"

"No. And here's where you come in. He said you'd be able to back him up."

"Me?"

"Yeah. He said he was counting on you to corroborate his story."

My foot was throbbing, making it hard for me to think. "I need to get some ice on this. But before I go, I need you to know I won't be supporting Doug's story.

How can I? I wasn't there, and he never said anything to me about planning something like this."

"Are you willing to say that to his face?"

"Of course."

"Then come with me to the jail in the morning. We can get in to see him until after eight. I'll tell them you're my paralegal."

"When is the arraignment?"

"The judge usually rolls in around ten."

"That gives us plenty of time to get Doug to change his story."

He smiled. "No wonder Doug thinks so highly of you."

We shook hands. I limped out to my car, hoping I'd remembered to flip the little wire thing up in the ice-maker. Then I remembered Steve was staying with me. One of the great things about sharing space with a fussy roommate is you can always count on there being ice.

Needless to say, I didn't sleep well. Work was going fine, even though I didn't have another wedding for a couple of weeks, but my personal life was up in flames like a divorcée torching her ex's midlife crisis sports car. My best friend was fuming over me calling her "weird," even though I'd given her a thousand bucks for something that had "woo-woo" written all over it. My husband hadn't called back, so I hadn't had a chance to explain why I'd been unable to take his calls earlier, and I was worried about his safety. Leave it to the military to sugar-coat a dangerous mission and then leave the family back home agonizing.

Worst of all, a good friend was in jail for a capital crime I was hoping he didn't commit, but was admitting he had. Why would Doug say that? And what about that shattered window in the back door? Had it been smashed during the fight, or had an intruder actually broken in? And if there was an intruder, why was Doug taking the fall?

I hate it when there are a dozen questions and not even a handful of answers. And I really hate it when it keeps me up at night so I'm drowsy and dull-witted the next day.

At four, I got up and called it a night. No sense staying in bed if I wasn't going to sleep. I had four hours until James picked me up to go to the Wailuku jail. If things went right, James would convince Doug to plead "not guilty." Then the police would have to get back to work finding Lani's killer. If things went wrong, my *sifu* would probably spend the rest of his life in prison.

Regardless of which way Doug chose to go, there was no way I could wrap my head around him killing his beloved wife, not even by accident. He was a man of integrity. And that left me wondering, if he didn't do it, why would he lie?

13

At six a.m. the sun still wasn't up. I paced the kitchen floor, not looking forward to wearing footwear on my burned foot. James had instructed me to dress as if I worked in a law office which I assumed meant wearing something other than my usual crop pants, t-shirt and *rubba slippas*. I'd put on a black knit A-line dress and tried on a pair of strappy sandals but the burn on the bridge of my foot had begun to blister. I bandaged the wound and when I tried on the sandals again they were too tight. I dug in the back of my tiny closet for a pair of flats I couldn't remember the last time I'd worn, and slipped them on before going out to my car.

When I got to the Gadda, Farrah still hadn't flipped the "closed" sign to "open" but my relentless banging brought her out from the back. I'd gone to the front door since the back door doesn't have a window and she's still spooked from the time a guy broke in and attacked her. Things were already tense between us; no use making it worse by creating unnecessary anxiety.

"It's you," she said, stepping back without even so much as a pat on the arm. Farrah's a hugger, so when she failed to make physical contact I was pretty certain the chip on her shoulder was still firmly in place.

"I called but you didn't pick up," I said, explaining my hammering on the door.

"Duh. Maybe you shoulda taken the hint."

She pointed at my feet and snorted, "What's with the mainland shoes? You expecting snow?"

I explained I'd burned my foot and was attending a meeting that morning. I didn't go into specifics about going to the jail because I didn't want to be a source of potential gossip.

"What're you doing here, Pali? You want your money back?"

"C'mon, Farrah. This is crazy. We've been friends forever. If you want me to say I'm sorry, then I'm sorry."

She turned and walked behind the counter. "Yeah, so you said last night."

"But you're still mad."

"It was so uncool to dis me to my man. After all the crap-o-la we've been through, I thought you were the one girl I could count on."

"You're right, I was totally out of line. And I'm really sorry. Ono was mad at me for giving you the money so I just said what I thought he wanted to hear."

"You think he wanted to hear you call me a weird-o?"

"No, I thought he wanted me to agree with him that a thousand bucks is a lot of money for something he doesn't believe in."

"Okay, so he doesn't dig it. But I do. And I know this *kahu* is gonna make things right for our family."

"Well, tell that to your husband, because he jumped all over me about it. But I'm not here to argue my case. I'm here to make up with you."

She quickly trotted around the counter. I wasn't quite sure what would come next. Farrah and I have been friends for decades, but I still find her outlook on life a mystery. She's been known to pout or fume over the smallest slight, but other times she's done some pretty heavy lifting on my behalf and shrugged it off as if it were nothing.

Her scowl remained as she leaned in and grabbed me in a tight hug. "No way I can be mad at my bestie for long," she said. "And besides, I'm feeling real bummed about something."

"You mean about Doug and Lani?" I hoped Doug's confession hadn't been leaked, but I knew if it had, Farrah would be among the first to hear about it.

"No, about you."

Just then, Ono came out from the back. "Well, look who's here. Miz Money-bags. You come to pick up your first payment on the loan?"

"Of course not." Why on earth were these two people, both self-described "free spirits," so obsessed with money?

Farrah stepped back. "Wait a sec. I thought you said the moolah was gift, not a loan. You pullin' a switch-a-roo on us?"

I wanted to shriek that I was tired of talking about the money and I wished I'd never offered to help. But instead I patiently explained that it was indeed a gift. "As god-mother to Hatchie, I insist on you getting your house blessed. It's for her safety. So the money is a gift to my god-daughter."

Ono crossed his arms. "Oh, yeah? Well, what if she'd rather put it in her college fund instead of giving it to a witch doctor?"

"Don't go there," Farrah muttered.

I broke in to ward off another spat. "Look, this is important to me. I want you to get your home blessed. We can talk about college when the kids are old enough for kindergarten."

Farrah brightened. "Will you be coming to the blessing?"

"I'd love to. When is it?"

"He said he could come on Friday."

Ono wheeled around and headed to the back room. Over his shoulder he said, "Don't expect to see me there. I think this whole thing's a scam. That dude looks like a time-share huckster."

After Ono was out of earshot, Farrah said, "Ono's just sayin' that 'cuz the *kahu's* a babe. Big muscles, groovy bod. I think my man's jealous."

I didn't want to weigh in on that so I asked her to call me after she'd confirmed the date and time of the blessing.

"Will do."

I was almost out the door when she called me back. "Well, duh. I almost forgot what I was gonna tell you."

As I walked toward her, she crooked a finger indicating she wanted me to come closer. "Don't want big ears and even bigger mouths to hear this." Since there were no customers I figured what she meant was she didn't want her husband to hear.

"Remember I tol' you Finn called Ono the other night?"

"Yeah."

"Ono doesn't know it, but I heard what they said. Walls in our place are super-model thin."

"Okay."

"Your man asked my man if he knew a lawyer."

"What? Is Finn in trouble?"

"Don't think so. I heard Ono say, 'what kind of lawyer,' and then he kinda yelled, '*A divorce*?' Then there was a pause, like Finn said something.' Before he hung up, Ono said, 'I'll ask around and get you a name.'"

I stumbled out of the Gadda as if I'd been sampling the wares in the liquor aisle. Finn was looking to hire a divorce lawyer? I had to force air into my lungs as I walked back to my shop. In ten minutes James would be arriving for our trip to the jail.

James pulled up in front of the shop and honked his horn a few minutes later. I usually take offence at guys honking and expecting me to skip outside, but then again, this wasn't a date.

"Sorry about not coming in," he said as I slid into the passenger seat of his fancy Mercedes. "There's never any parking around here."

"You can park in the alley."

"The sign says it's private property and I'll get towed."

"Since when do attorneys follow rules? Isn't that what they teach you in law school—always try to get away with everything you can?"

He shot me a stern look. "Do you have any idea how sick I am of people putting down lawyers?"

I mumbled an apology and told him he was welcome to park in the alley anytime he wanted. It seemed everyone in my life had suddenly become incredibly thin-skinned. Or had I somehow lost my *aloha*?

We rode in silence for a few minutes, allowing the sting of the squabble to pass, and then I asked, "Can you bring me up to speed on what you hope to accomplish this morning?"

"I want to get my stubborn brother to retract his confession and plead 'not guilty' at the arraignment."

"And why did you ask me to come along?" I was fully prepared for him to say something churlish like, "*I'm sorry I did,*" but he surprised me.

"Because you're his closest confidant. He trusts you. If anyone can get him to talk about what really happened in that garage, it's you. "

Whoa. I wasn't expecting such a vote of confidence. I couldn't help but wonder what my *sifu* had told James that gave him the notion we were such close friends. Sure, we shared hush-hush tea now and then, and I'd been training at the PoP longer than any other black belt, but didn't Doug have a guy friend higher up the pecking order?

"Do you know if the police went after Doug because he's the spouse or is there more?"

"Unfortunately, there seems to be a lot more. The cops found a recently fired handgun at the scene and it has my brother's fingerprints all over it. "

"Where would Doug get a gun?"

"It's an M9 Berretta, the service weapon issued to Army Rangers. Doug must've got it when he was in Special Forces."

"They get to keep their guns?"

"No, they're supposed to turn them in, but since Doug stayed on in the reserves, it probably fell through the cracks."

We turned into the jail parking lot and James found a spot right away. Without saying anything, he opened the console between our seats and took out a small white box the size of a fat stick of butter. He ripped the box open, shook out a roll of gauze and began wrapping his right hand like a boxer getting ready to put on the gloves.

"What're you doing?"

"Hang on, you'll see."

With his hand completely swathed in gauze, he gestured to the back seat. "You mind carrying my briefcase? I'm kinda laid up here."

We got out and I opened the back door and pulled out an expensive-looking calfskin briefcase. It was starting to dawn on me what he was doing, but I held off saying anything since I was pretty sure the jail not only had surveillance cameras but maybe even sensitive listening equipment, as well.

He took long strides and I had to hustle to keep up, especially since I was favoring my burned foot. When we got to the door, he leaned in. "I'll do the talking."

We stood there as if waiting for the door to magically open before James said, "Mind getting the door?"

I pulled the door open and waited as James entered first. Although I firmly believe in women's rights and the new world order, it felt odd to stand aside and hold the door open for a guy my own age. Especially one with a fake injury.

James approached a plate glass window with a uniformed guard sitting behind it. He leaned down to speak into a round metal piece in the glass. "I'm James Kanekoa, attorney for Douglas Kanekoa. I'm here to see my client before his arraignment hearing this morning."

The guard said something I couldn't hear and pointed at me. James went on, "This is Pali Moon, my paralegal." He held up his bandaged hand. "I've banged myself up a little and she'll be taking notes for me."

James' little fib slipped from his tongue like honey dripping off a hot spoon. I couldn't help but wonder why he'd taken such offense at me chastising him about the reputation of the legal profession when he was already planning this audacious bit of playacting. But then again, truth often bites deeper than fiction.

The guard looked wary as he asked for my ID. I slid my driver's license through the slot in the window and he peered at it as if trying to decide if it was fake.

"What'd you say your name was?"

I sighed. My name is an ongoing point of contention. My legal name is a long jumble of astronomical gibberish my parents foisted on me at birth. They're both deceased, but their *pakalolo*-fueled hippie legacy lives on.

"That's my birth name, but I go by Pali for short."

He pointed at the license. "What kinda language is that? Russian?"

"No, actually I think it's Greek."

"You're Greek? Like the yogurt?"

I looked at James, hoping he'd jump in and stop the inane discussion of my name, but he appeared amused rather than eager to help out.

"I never knew you had a classy Greek name." He motioned to the guard to return the license. "Let me see that."

"It's not 'classy.' I was named for a group of stars."

He stared at my license. "Ah, the Pleiades. I remember studying the Seven Sisters in astronomy."

I shot him my most winsome look. "Mr. Kanekoa, I think our client is waiting."

"True."

After leaving our cell phones and "weapons" (which in my case was a tiny Swiss Army knife I carry for wedding emergencies) at the jail entrance, we were led to a ten-foot-square room with a metal table and two straight-backed metal chairs bolted to the floor. The guard asked if we needed another chair.

James declined. "We won't be long."

When the guard left, James said, "Have a seat. Does your foot still hurt?"

"Probably a lot more than your hand."

"Point taken. Anyway, I want you sitting since you'll be the one taking notes. And, be prepared, Doug will be shackled."

I sat down and stiffened my spine as Doug was led into the room. His head was down and he was dressed in a baggy orange jumpsuit that hung on his body like a kid wearing his dad's pajamas. James had told me to be prepared. Unfortunately, there was no way to prepare for what Doug was about to ask me to do.

14

"Why'd you bring her here?" Sifu Doug demanded right off the bat. "I specifically told you I didn't want visitors."

James shot a furtive look at the guard outside the glass door. "Keep it down. She's my paralegal." He held up his bogus-bandaged hand. "I brought her along to help me take notes."

Doug's eyes bore into me with the same intensity he reserves for final tournament matches. I'd never been on the receiving end of his "you're a dead man walking" glare, and I have to admit it's exceedingly effective.

"Your arraignment is this morning," I said by way of attempting to focus on the task at hand.

"You don't think I know that?"

"We don't want you to plead guilty."

Doug looked up at James. "I can't think straight with the both of you here."

I began to stand up.

"No, you stay. I want my brother to leave."

James leaned on the table and spoke in a whispered but urgent voice. "I'm your lawyer. The only reason we have this private room is because of that fact. You kick me out and she's nothing more than a jailhouse visitor, like *that*." He snapped his fingers. "No more privacy, no more unlimited time. So, if you want me to leave, I'll leave. But we leave together."

Doug glowered at James. "You're a friend of the court, right?"

"No, I'm an *officer* of the court. Big difference."

"But you're sworn to uphold the law. If I say something incriminating, you'll be forced to tell them."

"Okay, *brudda*, that's not how it works. First of all, you've already confessed so there's not much more you could say that would make things worse for you. And second, I'm your attorney. We have attorney/client privilege which means I can't be forced to disclose what you say to me while I'm representing you."

James hooked a thumb my way. "Which is more than you have with Pali. She *can* be forced to testify against you."

Doug leveled his gaze at me. "But she wouldn't."

I squirmed. The clock on the wall ticked like a count-down to Armageddon.

After about six ticks of the clock, Doug went on, "Okay, how about this? I'm going to ask Pali to do something for me. I want her to write it down and follow it exactly as I say it. Meanwhile, I want you to back off. Don't ask her what it means, and don't badger her about it later. Understood?"

I was glad I was on the receiving end of the secret request because it would've killed me to have been in James' shoes. I'm not good with letting sleeping dogs lie. In fact, I've been known to kick a metaphorical sleeping pit bull in the private parts even though there was no doubt in my mind that the resulting bite was going to hurt—a lot.

"You ready?" Doug said.

I poised pen to paper like a mid-century secretary about to launch into shorthand.

"Tea stash at *guan*. Pink key. Empty it."

"Pinkie?" James echoed.

Doug shook his head. "Pali knows what it means."

I wrote it down even though there was no chance I'd forget those eight words. I looked up and said, "Okay, but what about your arraignment?"

"What about it?"

I looked up at the clock. "It's in a little more than an hour."

"Yeah."

James chimed in. "Are you willing to plead 'not guilty'?"

"I've already confessed. Isn't it a little late to go claiming I'm innocent?"

"No, because it's always smart to keep 'em guessing. If you plead 'not guilty,' we have a shot at getting the confession thrown out."

"I'm not going to change my mind."

"Fine. But let's not burn any bridges, okay? Will you let me enter a 'not guilty' plea?"

Doug blew out a breath. "It's your show." He turned to me, "In the meantime, do what I said. You'll understand once you see what's in there."

I promised I would. I reached across to give Doug's hand a squeeze, but James gripped my forearm to stop me. "Don't touch the client."

I checked out the guard, who was seemingly catching a few winks as he leaned against the thick glass window outside. "Like he'd notice."

James nodded toward the upper corner of the room where a steady red light about the size of a pencil eraser glowed almost undetectable against the dark metal corner beam.

"I thought you said this was a private meeting," I said.

"Private, but they watch on video. They don't record voices but they keep a close eye on everything that goes on."

"So, then it's not private, is it? I mean, if they're watching your every move."

"Welcome to the Alice in Wonderland world of American criminal justice."

* * *

James dropped me off at my shop obviously peeved Doug had trusted me, rather than him, with vital information.

"You know, clients are sometimes their own worst enemy. I'd like a call when you find what he sent you for."

I didn't respond.

As I slid into the driver's seat of my own car it dawned on me it was fortunate my *sifu* had been arrested at work rather than at his home because the house had been sealed by the police. Breaking into a crime scene is a big-deal offense.

I pulled into the alley behind the PoP. The notice cancelling all classes was still on the door but thankfully the door wasn't sealed. I used my pass key to get in. The place had been locked up for more than three days making the aroma of sweaty feet and disinfectant more pungent than ever.

I went straight to my *sifu's* office hoping he'd left his keys on the desk. I sifted through a clutter of bills, equipment receipts and martial arts newsletters hoping to hear the clink of metal on metal, but no luck.

Then it occurred to me. He must've hidden his key ring. What had he been thinking in those last moments before he'd been whisked off to jail? They'd processed the scene after he'd been arrested, so maybe they'd taken the keys as evidence. But evidence of what? It wasn't a crime to have keys to your own home and business, even if you'd just confessed to a heinous act.

Tea stash, pink key. Just for the heck of it I tried opening the bottom desk drawer but, as expected, it was locked. I started rifling through the file cabinet when I heard someone at the back door.

"*Aloha*, anybody here?"

I shoved the file drawer shut and entered the practice room to see who'd come in. I couldn't immediately put a name to the face, but I recognized the woman as one of the mothers from the *keiki* class I'd taught the week before.

"*Aloha*, can I help you?"

"Do you know when Sifu Doug will start up classes again?"

I was about to say something snide, like, "*You want a wife killer to teach your kid martial arts?*" but then realized not only would that be rude, it didn't ring true. I didn't believe Doug killed Lani, but I had a hunch he knew who did. And he was protecting them. The thorny question was: who? Which led to an even thornier question: why?

I held out hope I'd be able to answer both questions once I found that bright pink key.

15

After a few minutes of reassuring the *keiki* class mom that everything would be back to normal in a week or two, she left and I got down to the serious task of tearing the *guan* apart. I emptied drawers, upended trash cans, and rolled up the practice room mats checking to see if Doug had deliberately hidden his keys from the cops.

Once I was certain the keys weren't in the practice room, I turned off the lights and headed back to the office. Forget the keys. I'd try jimmying the flimsy drawer lock. I began digging through my beach bag purse trying to find a screwdriver, letter opener or any other tool capable of picking a lock. As I dug, a memory flashed to mind like one of Doug's annoying fluorescent tubes sparking to life after a half-dozen flickers and sputters.

The metal coffee can on the back shelf.

Doug's main stash was in the drawer, but he always kept a ready supply of tea in that can.

I pulled the coffee can off the back shelf, shook it, and was rewarded by a metallic clink. I snapped off the plastic lid and retrieved the wad of keys hidden under a layer of pungent vegetable matter.

"Doug's *pakalolo* tea always calms me down," I whispered to myself. "I hope whatever's in that locked drawer can do the same."

I flipped through the keys until I located the one with the bright pink plastic cap. I peeked out into the dark practice room just to be sure another black belt hadn't quietly slipped in while I was muttering to myself.

I unlocked the bottom drawer and fished around for the plastic bag containing the *pakalolo*. It didn't seem reasonable that, under the circumstances, Doug was all that worried about the police finding his marijuana stash but it was a good place to start. I dug out a jumbled mess that included crusted plastic containers still holding remnants of lunches brought from home, a bag of brightly-colored mouth guards, and a stack of equipment catalogs. The bag of pot was tucked at the very back of the drawer. There were also two manila envelopes. I was about to take them out and see what was in them when I heard someone at the back door.

Even though the sun was blazing outside, the concrete-block walls of the practice room made the area cool and shadowy. I slipped behind the office door jam and peered out as the exterior door creaked open.

It was Detective Ho. He entered alone, closing and locking the door behind him. His hand hovered over the bank of light switches near the door, but he didn't flip them on. I considered my options: call out my presence or wait and let him find me. I chose the latter. After all, the Palace of Pain hadn't been sealed as a crime scene and as a key-holding member of the *guan* I had every right to be there.

He stood in the quiet stillness of the practice room, apparently allowing his eyes to adjust. Then he started heading toward the office. I had only a few seconds to lock the open drawer and frame an explanation of why I was there.

I stepped into the doorway just as Detective Ho got there. He skidded to a stop.

"You startled me," he said in a voice an octave higher than when we'd talked on Monday. "What are you doing here?"

"I could ask you the same thing."

"I asked first," he said in the petulant voice of a schoolyard tough. "And besides, I'm police. I can go anywhere I want during an on-going investigation."

He looked around the office, seeming to take in the general upheaval. "Were you looking for something? And how'd you get in? I made sure the door was locked when we left the other day."

"Look, detective, this is my home *guan*. I was given a key when I reached black belt status."

His eyes narrowed. "I heard you were at Douglas Kanekoa's pre-appearance conference this morning."

"Seems boring news travels fast."

"It's a small island, Ms. Moon. Not much goes on that we don't hear about." That's the same line Detective Glen Wong used to give me. They must offer a class in platitudes at the police academy.

He went on, "Is your being here a result of something you discussed with the accused?"

"Are you questioning me? If so, I think you should read me my rights."

"You watch too many cop shows, Ms. Moon. This is not a formal interview. I'm just trying to ascertain why you're in a confessed killer's office. Not to mention this place looks like it's been tossed."

"Obviously you don't know Doug Kanekoa. He's not exactly Martha Stewart when it comes to housekeeping."

"We processed this scene two days ago and this office was orderly. Now it's not. I'm going to ask you one more time what you're doing here. If you dodge the question or lie to me I'm going recommend charges of obstruction of justice. Am I clear?"

"Crystal." I'd always wanted to use that famous Tom Cruise line.

We silently faced off for a few seconds. Then Ho folded his arms and said, "I'm waiting."

I mentally scrambled for a good fib. I'm not good with lying on the fly, so I went with something closer to the truth. "Doug asked me to locate a very small amount of *pakalolo* he kept here in the office. It bothered him that it might come out that an illegal substance was found at his place of business."

Detective Ho snorted. "Right. As if the court gives a rat's ass about that when he's facing murder charges."

"He's a mentor to dozens of kids who train here and he's got two teenagers of his own. Like I said, he seemed concerned about being branded a drug user."

"He's a freakin' murderer. He's admitted to killing the mother of his kids. If the guy's thinkin' insanity plea you can tell him this fixation with a few ounces of weed isn't gonna cut it."

I shrugged. It looked like Ho was buying, so I stopped selling.

Ho looked around the room. "You find it?"

"Not yet." I shot him a tentative smile.

"Where do you think it might be?"

"Give me some credit, Detective. I'm not about to a help a cop locate contraband owned by a friend of mine."

"Fine, but let me be abundantly clear. I don't care one iota about Kanekoa's drug use unless it's materially significant to either the motive or commission of the crime he's been charged with."

"I swear it isn't."

"Then I'll make you a deal. You trot on out of here and if I stumble over it I'll turn a blind eye. But that only holds if you agree to not come back. I've got a capital case on my hands and I don't want some looky-loo screwing up the evidence.'"

I held up a palm. "Okay, I'm outta here."

"And you won't be back?"

"No reason to now."

"Good. Now get out of here. I've got work to do."

I was nearly to the door when Ho said, "You know, Detective Wong warned me about you."

"I'm sure he did. Did he also tell you I've helped solve at least four murder cases here in Maui County?"

He scowled as if I'd insulted his mother. When it was pretty clear he wasn't going to comment further I went outside, closing the door behind me.

I didn't want to go far, fearing if I didn't retrieve whatever was in those manila envelopes there was a good chance Ho would stumble onto it sooner or later. I got in my car and headed out of the alley. It wouldn't do to leave my Mini Cooper sitting there like a red flag. From what I'd observed, Ho wasn't the detective that Wong was, but he'd surely figure out I was lying in wait if I didn't even bother to move my car.

I went around the corner to the Pa'ia Fish Market. It was nearly lunchtime and I'd skipped breakfast so a mahi sandwich sounded like a great way to pass the time waiting for Ho to leave. I perched on the end of one of the back benches and waited for my order to be called. The place was filling up but I still had the table to myself.

My curiosity over the contents of the drawer pecked at me like a parrot working over a stale cracker. What was I supposed to find? And why had Doug been so circumspect in his instructions? It was hard to imagine he'd be concerned about a bag of pot when a life sentence was on the line.

"Order fifty-seven."

I grabbed my sandwich and then wished I'd ordered it to go. I'd been away from the PoP for almost twenty minutes. Surely Ho had found what he'd come for and I'd be able to slip in and empty the drawer before anyone else came by. I wolfed down the fish sandwich, thankful there were no other diners on the other side of the table observing my complete lack of table manners.

I was halfway back to the *guan* when I realized I'd forgotten to ask James about divorce laws in Hawaii. Could Finn just hire a lawyer and do away with our marriage without my consent? And what about our vows? Finn had pledged to stick with me "for better, for worse" and "'til death do we part." Didn't that mean anything?

I cruised past the entrance to the alley behand the PoP and Ho's plain white cop car was nowhere in sight. Just to be sure, I parked on Baldwin. No use throwing up a red flag in case Ho was still lurking around.

Then I saw it. Ho had sealed the door with a crime scene sticker. A really big sticker. I looked up and down the alley to confirm I was alone and then started picking at the edge of it, but it was no use. The adhesive had bonded to the paint like white on rice.

I fisted my hands in frustration. Why had Detective Ho waited three days before securing the *guan*? Was it possible he'd listened to a recording of the pre-arraignment meeting?

I drove over to James Kanekoa's law office. The receptionist was out. Through a glass partition I saw him munching on a sandwich at his desk.

I waved and his head snapped up. He hastily wrapped up the rest of the sandwich as if I'd caught him in a shameful act and waved me in.

"Sorry about that," he said. "My girl took a long lunch today. Something about it being a friend's birthday."

I let the reference to his forty-something receptionist as a "girl" slide but only because I was about to ask him for free legal advice.

He gestured toward a guest chair and invited me to sit. "I'm hoping you've got some information for me."

"Sorry, I ran into a snag."

His eyes narrowed.

"I went to the Palace of Pain but it's been sealed as a crime scene."

"What? I was just down there yesterday. When do you think they sealed it?"

"Hard to tell. I just came from there and there's a big sticker on the door. Do you think there's a chance they listened in on our meeting this morning? Doug mentioned the *guan*."

"If they did listen in, it's a clear violation of the law."

"But you said yourself the jail watches. Maybe they used a lip reader?"

James made a *pfft* sound. "That's ridiculous."

"But still, don't you think it's pretty coincidental? I mean, your client mentions his place of work and then the next thing you know the place is sealed?" I squirmed under the scrutiny of his stare. But there was no way I'd admit to being the reason Ho had sealed the door.

"I don't believe in coincidences, Ms. Moon."

"Neither do I."

I gazed around the office seemingly taking in the gilt-framed diplomas on the wall. I was scrambling to come up with a good way to change the subject but came up short.

"On different topic, would you mind me asking you a legal question?"

"Sure."

"It doesn't have anything to do with Doug. It's me."

"Okay, fire away."

"Can someone divorce you without your consent?"

He screwed up his face as if the question had come from so far out of left field he'd lost sight of the ball.

"May I ask why you're asking?"

"It's just speculative. I'm wondering, strictly hypo-thetically, if Hawaii law provides for divorce if only one person wants it."

"Ah, I see. Is one of your wedding clients trying to toss out the old before tying the knot with the new?"

Why didn't I think of that? "Yeah, something like that. I was just curious."

"Technically, divorce is a type of lawsuit. And the law requires both parties in a claim to be notified and allowed to respond. I don't generally handle that type of case but I'm pretty sure it needs to be worked out between the two parties. It's not like in those countries where a guy can just divorce a woman willy-nilly by saying, 'Get lost' three times or whatever."

"So, they need to agree?"

"Not necessarily agree. But they each get a chance to respond. In some sticky cases it goes before a judge, but judges don't like to get in the middle of stuff like that unless all other avenues have been exhausted."

James went on, "Sorry, but you're gonna have to tell your client they need to clean up their old mess before getting themselves in a new mess." He laughed and I smiled along with him, even though I was as sick of hearing "ball and chain" humor about being a wedding planner as he was of "shark" jokes about lawyers.

I walked back to my car and drove to my shop. It was too early to call it a day but I sure wanted to. I fussed around on the computer for a few minutes before giving up and wandering over to the Gadda.

As usual, Farrah was at the front counter. "Any oosnay from in-Fay?"

High on the list of Farrah's quirks that make me grind my teeth is her use of Pig Latin. It's right under her love of Twenty Questions. If I'm in a good mood, I play along. But unfortunately, I was about a hundred-and-eighty degrees from a good mood.

"Farrah, would you just speak English? If you haven't noticed, we're not wearing training bras anymore."

She looked down at her billowy *mu'u mu'u* which was making a valiant effort at camouflaging her ample bosom. "Like trying to train these gigantic girls ever did me much good."

I chose not to pursue the matter. "And no, I haven't heard from Finn since I saw you this morning."

"No worries. I bet I didn't hear it right. I mean, maybe he didn't say 'divorce,' but, 'duh horse.' Like maybe he's thinkin' of buying a pony for Hatchie. You know, we could totally groove on that. We've got that humongous pasture out back and the *keiki* would love having a pet they could ride on."

What with worrying about how I was going to get my hands on whatever was in Doug's bottom drawer, along with stressing over Finn's request for a divorce lawyer, my heart wasn't in the mood to parse Farrah's half-baked effort at walking back what she'd said that morning.

"Let's talk later," I said. "I just came by to make sure we're still good."

"No sweat. It's gonna take more than a little trash talk to make me stay mad at you. So, I heard you went to the ale-jay this morning. Did you see Doug? Was he wearing an orange jumpsuit? Ya know, if a person's got an orange aura, they've got issues, uh, down there." She made a vague gesture toward her groin.

"What?"

"Yeah, totally bad color for prison clothes, right?"

I let it slide. "Is Ono around? I want to ask him something."

"He went down to the boat a few hours ago." She nodded toward the Felix the Cat clock on the wall. "He should be boogeying back soon."

"Would you ask him to call me?"

She nodded. A customer came up to pay for their purchases so I leaned over the counter and gave her a hug before leaving.

16

At dinner that night I dropped the bomb about Finn asking Ono to recommend a divorce attorney. Steve, bless him, reacted by appearing suitably appalled.

"That rat. He may be gorgeous, and God knows the man's a specimen, but to go behind your back like that is nothing short of an impeachable offense."

"I think he's hoping for impeachment. That's the point."

"Well, don't give him the pleasure. You force him to throw you under the bus and then make him back up and run all over you again. If you can't win, at least go out with the pity vote on your side. That's how to get a big alimony award."

The conversation wasn't going quite the way I'd hoped. "I don't care about alimony. I want to save our marriage."

"I know you do, sweetie. And I want what you want. But if you change your mind, just say the word. I know a guy who knows a guy, if you know what I mean."

I had no idea what he meant, but thought it best to move on. "On another note, I have a big dilemma in the Doug situation."

"Really? Word on the street is he confessed. Doesn't that sort of render 'dilemmas' moot?"

"This morning he pleaded 'not guilty.' It'll probably be on the news tonight."

"How can you confess and then plead not guilty? Is he going for an insanity plea? Or a crime of passion or something?"

Steve rambled on about how he'd be so flattered if one of the guys in his life committed a crime of passion over him, but I'd stopped listening. Had Doug discovered Lani in a compromising position? He'd followed her and then acted as if it'd simply been a misunderstanding. Maybe instead of being relieved at what he'd learned he was just biding his time while he plotted revenge.

But that was so unlike Doug. I'd seen the man battered and bruised by illegal moves and cheap shots more than once and he always took the high road. "*The guy had to take me down any way he could,*" he'd say. "*'Cuz he knew I was about to clean his clock.*"

I'd never once seen him exact payback or protest a call. And I'd watched as clueless, or perhaps biased, tournament referees turned a blind eye to blatant cheating. How could Doug remain disciplined and magnanimous in battle and lose his cool in the worst way possible with the mother of his children? It didn't make sense.

Which brought me back to the dilemma at hand.

"All that aside," I said as Steve took a breath. "Here's my problem." I outlined my jailhouse visit with and Doug's puzzling request. I explained about getting into the drawer but then having to leave everything behind when Ho kicked me out.

"Why didn't you just shove the stuff in your purse? Heaven knows there's enough room in there to stash a body."

Bad analogy, I thought. But I kept quiet.

"I had no reason to believe Detective Ho would seal the door. I didn't say anything to tip him off."

Steve shot me a withering look. "Oh, honey, I'd love to play poker with you. He knew you were up to something. Your face is about as simple to read as 'The Cat in the Hat.'"

"Fair enough. But I was under pressure."

"So now what? You trying to figure out a way to get inside without breaking the law?"

"No way to do that now. But I'd settle for getting inside without getting caught."

"If you end up in jail, you're gonna need someone to watch this house."

"What?"

"I'm just saying it's not a good idea to leave this place empty. What with Finn gone and you in jail, who's gonna water the plants and make sure your ancient refrigerator doesn't give up the ghost?"

"I have a feeling this is leading somewhere, but I'm not sure where."

Steve hung his head. "I haven't heard word one from the notice I put up at the Gadda."

"Nobody's looking for a roommate? In this economy? That's hard to believe."

"I think anyone who's willing to share is going with Airbnb. More money and less commitment."

"So, in your usual round-about way, you're asking if you can move back in here?"

"For just a little longer. No more than a few weeks, six at the most. If I don't find something by the end of August I'll have to rethink staying here on Maui."

"But where would you go?"

"My mom's got an extra room at her place in LA."

"I thought she disowned you when you came out."

"Not disowned, exactly. More like she put me on the prayer list at her church, permanently."

"You can't go back there. And besides, with the way things are going with my marriage, I may have to start looking for a roommate myself."

We sat in companionable silence for a long minute before Steve put a hand on my shoulder. "I don't want to get in the way of you guys working things out."

I was surprised to feel tears building in my eyes and swiped away one that threatened to break free and head down my cheek.

"You're not in the way, Steve. In fact, there's nothing I'd like better than having you here. I don't want to go through this alone."

That night I didn't sleep much. I spent equal time wondering how I could get past the sticker on the Palace of Pain door and fretting over Finn's shocking conversation with Ono about finding a divorce lawyer. There wasn't much I could do about my marriage until my husband came home, but I was determined to obey my *sifu's* request and get my hands on the contents of that drawer.

In an ironic twist, I recalled something Sifu Doug had said to me at a tournament where I faced a formidable foe. "Balance what you can control against what you can't and then use your mind to tip the scales in your favor." At first I thought he was encouraging me to cheat, but Doug would never suggest that. Then I got it. Focus on what is possible and disregard the impossible.

It was time to focus.

* * *

I hopped out of bed with new resolve. Even though I couldn't immediately get my hands on the contents of the bottom drawer, there were other avenues to explore. Doug and Lani's kids had been in the house watching everything that led up to their mother's death. Maybe they'd be willing to talk. I wasn't close to the kids, but I'd been around them enough as they were growing up to be considered a friend of the family.

Douglas Jr., who was called "DJ," was fourteen. Well, maybe he was fifteen. I wasn't exactly sure whether his birthday was in June or September. His younger sister, Maia, was thirteen. I remembered her birthday because

Lani had thrown her a "come one, come all" blowout party when she'd become a teenager in March.

I was pretty sure the kids were staying at Lani's sister's place in Haiku, but I didn't want to show up there without being certain. I drove to the Gadda to confirm my hunch.

"Yeah, they're hangin' out at Kaili's," Farrah said. "Bummed out, for sure. They came in yesterday and I gave 'em a cookie like I do with small-kid *keiki*. The girl was as pale as the ghost in my back yard. Speakin' of which, you still coming tomorrow?"

I mentally scrambled to recall the date and what I'd offered to do. "Tomorrow's Friday, right?"

"Uh-huh. You said you'd be there."

"Of course. What time?"

"Two o'clock. And not island time, *real* time. The *kahu* wants to catch the four o'clock back to the Big Island."

Ah, yes, the house blessing. "I'll be there."

We hugged and I headed over to my shop to call Lani's sister, Kaili. I practiced a few lines before I made the call, hoping to avoid coming across as ghoulish or snoopy.

She answered on the second ring.

"*Aloha*, Kaili. This is Pali Moon." I'd decided I wouldn't tack on "...*a friend of Doug's*" since I wasn't sure of Kaili's stance on her brother-in-law's guilt or innocence.

"Yeah, I 'member you from Maia's party."

"I wanted to call and tell you how sorry I am for your loss. It's been a horrible week."

"*Mahalo*. No kidding. I got Lani's kids here. They're in shock."

"We're all in shock." I let it hang, hoping she'd weigh in on Doug's plight.

"You train over at Doug's place, don't you?"

"I do." The conversation was growing more awkward with each passing second.

"These poor *keiki* are gonna be like orphans, you know? I mean, if Doug did what he said he did he's goin' to prison forever and a day. So these kids got nobody, eh."

Time to pull off the Band-Aid. "Do you think he did it?"

"Don't matter what I think. What matters is the truth."

"I'm trying to get to the truth, Kaili. Would you mind if I came over and talked to the kids?"

An uncomfortable pause was followed by Kaili clearing her throat. "Why you think you can do better'n the cops? That's their job, not yours."

"I realize that, but I'm worried about Doug's confession."

"What about it? You think they forced him to say stuff?"

"Look, I'm only about ten minutes away. Can I come over so we can talk about this? I'd really appreciate getting your take on things."

She reluctantly agreed to see me and I sprinted out to my car.

Kaili's property was only a few blocks from Farrah and Ono's place. I wondered if Kaili had ever seen the cane worker ghost or if the dude only haunted believers like Farrah. The neighborhood had a rural feel, with knee-high grass separating the street from the most of the small plantation-style homes. Every now and then, I saw a cow or a goat in a front yard trying its best to keep the vegetation in check. But from the looks of things, flora was getting the better of fauna in almost all instances.

I checked the house number on the mailbox and pulled into the gravel driveway. As I approached the house, I gasped and an eerie sense of déjà vu caused my hands to grow slippery on the steering wheel. A much fatter version of Leilani Kanekoa, Doug's wife, was standing in the driveway. She gestured for me to park near the free-standing garage.

I parked and got out.

"*Aloha*," I said tentatively.

"*Aloha*, I'm Kaili." She stuck out her hand.

We shook. "Are you Lani's twin? You look so much like her."

"Yeah. I thought you knew. This makes it real hard for me, you know? It's like we shared everything. When we were *keiki*, our mom dressed us the same to fool people. But it didn't work. I always been bigger than her, eh?"

"Again, I'm so sorry for your loss. Your sister was a wonderful person."

She nodded. "I know. She was always way nicer than me. I got the *ali'i* body and she got the skinny. I pro'bly got a little hard feelings about that."

She didn't make a move to go into the house. "I met you here because there's somethin' you need to know."

"Okay."

"I haven't told the kids about Doug saying he did it."

"But it's been all over the news."

"Yeah well, we don't have cable or nuthin'.. And I made them turn off their phones. I told 'em we don't get cell coverage out here, which is sorta true since service is pretty bad. But mostly I don't want them getting worked up over stuff they might see."

"I understand."

"So when you see them, don't say nuthin' about what's goin' on."

"I won't. Would you like me to tell you what I want to talk to them about?"

She narrowed her eyes. "Yeah, I would."

"I just want their take on how things were at the house last weekend. I'd like to know if they saw or heard anything unusual or troubling."

"That's it?"

"That's all I plan to ask. My pretense for being here is to offer condolences and ask if there's anything I can do to help. You know, pick up their homework at school or whatever."

"What if they ask about their dad? They know you're his friend."

"How've you handled it so far?"

"I told 'em he's taking it real hard and needed some time alone. And I said he was getting stuff ready for the funeral."

"When is the funeral?"

She shook her head. "Beats me. The cops haven't released her body. And I guess we're all kinda waitin' to see what happens with Doug."

At that point, DJ came out of the front door. He stood on the porch, arms crossed, glaring down at us.

I waved. "*Aloha*, DJ. It's me, Pali."

"I know who you are."

"I came by to say how sorry I am, and to ask if you needed anything."

His face clouded. "I need somebody to take me serious."

"Excuse me?"

"I said, I need somebody to listen and stop treating me like a dumb-ass kid."

He clattered down the porch steps and stomped over to us in four long strides.

"Okay, I'm listening."

"It's my fault my mom's dead." His face twisted into a mask of despair and he fell against me with such force it took everything I had to stay upright.

17

Kaili patted DJ's back as we half-dragged, half-pushed him up the porch stairs. His loud shuddering sobs echoed through the stillness of the pastoral neighborhood like ricocheting gunshots. I'm not a big fan of emotional displays of any sort and this was the most raucous I'd witnessed in a very long time.

"Can I get him anything?" I said to Kaili, hoping she'd send me on an errand that would last long enough for DJ to get a grip. "Maybe a glass of water or something?"

"Don't go," he wailed. "I need to tell you."

We plopped him down on a wooden glider, the kind that can hold two people if one of them isn't a three-hundred pound *bruddah*. Luckily, DJ was one of those wiry kids who looked like his adolescent growth spurt had focused more on height than girth.

Kaili released her grasp of his shoulder. "You sit here with him. I'll get the water."

As the screen door banged shut, DJ sat up straighter and the sobbing ebbed as he gulped air like a mahi-mahi flopping around on the deck of a boat.

"I don't want my auntie to hear this," he gasped. "She'll never forgive me."

"Go ahead. Tell me." My terse tone shocked even me. Maybe it was divine providence I wasn't destined to have kids. I'm not exactly mother-of-the-year material, especially when it comes to dealing with touchy-feely stuff.

"My mom and dad were fighting on Sunday," he said. "All because of me."

He expelled a loud breath and continued, "On Saturday my friend, Snags, was at our house and I told him my dad had been an Army Ranger."

"Snags?" It came out unbidden. I'd meant to keep quiet and let DJ tell his story, but the idea of someone naming a child "Snags" got the better of me. I guess I have a weird fixation on the whole baby naming thing.

"Yeah, that's not his real name. I think his actual name is Sam or Stan, or something like that, but all us kids call him Snags."

"Okay, sorry for the interruption. Go on."

"Anyway, Snags called me a liar. He said if I didn't prove it he'd tell everyone I was a lying sack of, uh, well, you know."

"The dude sounds like a real jerk."

"He's more than a jerk, he's a...well, I'm not supposed to say words like that in front of an auntie like you." He smiled and I saw Doug all over his face.

I smiled back. "It's okay. I get what you mean. What happened then?"

"My dad was out back and I asked him if he'd show us his gun. The one he got when he was an Army Ranger."

I gave enough of a nod for him to continue.

"He said it was locked up but since I was fifteen now he thought it was time for me to learn about firearm safety. He went inside and got the gun and brought it out to show us."

He took a shuddering breath and went on. "When my mom saw us out there with the gun she went ballistic. I mean, she totally freaked. She started screaming at my dad and me and then she told Snags to go home and never come back. Stuff like that."

He pressed his lips tightly together as he apparently relived the shock and embarrassment. I took it as an opportunity to jump in. "Was this something your mom did a lot?"

"What? You mean, freak out?"

"Yeah."

"She never used to. She was always pretty nice, you know? My dad was the one you didn't want to get mad. He has this look he gives you..."

I'd seen the look. I nodded in solidarity.

"Anyway, lately my mom had been losing it more and more. Like she was tired of being our mom or something. About a week ago she got real mad at my sister and she cut up Maia's favorite bathing suit into little pieces. Then she started laughing real scary-like. She sounded like a witch or something. It was totally nuts. Dad came home and told us not to tell anybody about it. It was like he was embarrassed for her."

Again he paused as if reflecting on the situation. I let the pause drag on until it was clear he wasn't going to say anything more.

"Okay, I get that your mom was really mad at your dad about the gun. But how does that make what happened your fault?"

His face screwed up like a toddler about to launch into a crying jag. "Don't you see? I'm the one who got my dad to take the gun out of the safe. If I hadn't been bragging to Snags about my old man being a Ranger then my dad's gun would've been locked up and that intruder guy wouldn't have been able to shoot my mom."

He took a heaving breath. Then, in a tiny voice he said, "You don't think my dad shot my mom, do you? Nobody's telling us anything but I can't help wonder. He was real pissed at her. In fact, he asked our neighbor if me and Maia could stay at their place that night. He told her he needed some alone time with my mom."

I looked over and saw Kaili standing on the other side of the screen door, water glass in hand. I couldn't be certain of how long she'd been there or how much she'd overheard, but I was pretty sure even if she'd only heard the last few sentences she was probably thinking the same thing I was thinking.

Kaili came outside and handed DJ the water. Then she told him he could go inside and play Xbox games.

"Doesn't sound good, does it?" she said once he was out of earshot.

I contemplated telling her about Doug's jailhouse request and getting her take on what might be in that drawer, but decided to wait. My planned break-in was something I didn't want spread far and wide. It was bad enough I'd blabbed to Doug's lawyer.

"When did you pick up the kids?"

"Early Monday morning. Doug called and said they were at the neighbor's but she didn't want to keep them any longer. Thank God they weren't home when their mother was killed."

"Do you know Doug's neighbor?"

"You mean Ami Tanaka? I know her a little. She's good friends with my sister even though her kids are grown and gone."

"I'd like to talk to her."

She shot me a wry smile. "Don't know how much good it'd do. I'm sure the cops have already grilled her six ways to Sunday."

"I'm sure they have. But I have a couple things I'd like to clear up."

I drove to Pukalani to see if Ami Tanaka was at home and if she'd talk to me. The small brown house looked forlorn with closed drapes and no car in the driveway. Bright yellow crime tape still fluttered outside Doug and Lani's next door. I hoped Ami was home but I was prepared to leave a note if she wasn't. I'd considered calling, but decided against it. It's harder to blow someone off when they're standing right in front of you.

I knocked and a tall, thin woman with gray hair pulled into a tight ponytail answered the door. She looked to be fifty, maybe sixty, but I'm not good at judging the age of women who adhere to the hippie lifestyle this woman appeared to embrace. At the door I saw an assortment of plastic Croc shoes in what Steve would've referred to as "clown colors," bright lime green, fuchsia and neon orange. She wore a calf-length skirt made from Indian print material that reminded me of the coverlet on Farrah's bed. On top she wore a thin used-to-be-red T-shirt that clearly advertised her disdain for undergarments. I flashed on that old joke about the woman who said when she was young she got a rose tattoo on her breast and now it's long-stemmed.

"*Aloha*. Can I help you?" she said in a voice that echoed my dear Auntie Mana's soft volume and cadence.

"*Aloha*, auntie." I wasn't being presumptuous. In Hawaii we tend to address kindly-looking older women as "auntie," regardless of familial relationship. In the past couple of years I've even been called it a couple of times. I must admit it's kind of startling the first time you're called it, since it signals a certain age difference, but at thirty-six I couldn't deny I was decidedly on the cusp of "auntieness."

"I'm a friend of Doug and Lani Kanekoa." I nodded toward the house next door.

The woman's eyes flashed a note of distress.

"I just talked with DJ and he told me he and Maia stayed here on Sunday night, but their aunt picked them up the next morning. Can you tell me why they were only here the one night?"

I've never been good with couching things in politically correct language. In fact, I've been called blunt, abrasive, and occasionally even rude. I've worked on it since it's a handicap in my line of work, but I still struggle with using euphemisms like "passed away" or "crossed over" to describe death. I mean, dead is dead, right?

She didn't appear to take offense. "Ah, you'll have to ask my sister-in-law about that. She lives here. I'm Shirley, over from Honolulu. We got the whole 'ohana here for Ami's birthday on Monday. Ami had to go to the store, but she'll be back in a while."

"Have you heard what happened next door?"

She bowed her head. "Very sad. Ami doesn't seem to want to talk about it much. I know she was close to the family."

"So, she hasn't discussed it with you?"

"Not much. It happened on her birthday, you know? But I know she's upset with the police."

I screwed up my face in an attempt to encourage her to elaborate. "Yeah, she says they've got it all wrong. She's an early riser and she claims she saw the woman that very morning."

"Did she also see the husband?"

"Not sure about that. You'll have to ask her."

18

Over a dinner of Steve's go-to dish, veggie stir-fry, I told him what I'd learned that day from DJ and Doug's neighbor's sister-in-law. I recounted how DJ had cajoled his dad into showing his friend his handgun, and how DJ felt responsible for his mother's death as a result of it. Then I recalled how the kids had been shuttled off to the neighbor's house so Doug and Lani could hash out whatever was going on between them and then how, the next morning, the neighbor recalled seeing Lani before she died.

"Do you know what Doug told the police?"

"I don't have the full story. James said Doug told him they were fighting that morning and he followed her out to the garage and shot her."

"Because..?"

"Who knows?"

"It seems to me you've got to get to the bottom of that first. I mean, you told me yourself Doug's extremely disciplined. What would cause a guy like that to just lose it?"

"I've been wrangling with that since it happened. I know Doug was suspicious that something was going on with Lani, and he even followed her to see if she was having an affair, but when I asked him about it later he brushed it off."

"Did he say what he found out when he followed her?"

"Not really."

He took a second helping of rice and passed the bowl over to me. "Maybe you should start there."

"But what about the broken window in the back door? And the contents of Doug's stash drawer? There are so many loose ends."

"Yeah, but isn't securing loose ends your specialty?"

I shot him a puzzled look.

"You know, like tying the knot."

I groaned at the bad pun but had to admit being a wedding planner had trained me to be pretty good at minding the details. At this point, though, it wasn't so much about keeping track of the details as parsing which ones were relevant and which weren't.

* * *

On Friday morning I got to my shop around nine. I didn't have much to do before heading out to Farrah's house blessing, so I sat at my desk daydreaming about how I could break into the PoP. All at once it hit me. Why not just ask Ho when he planned to unseal it?

I could frame the question so it wouldn't sound suspicious. My daily schedule involved working out there and having the *guan* locked for an indeterminate time was a physical hardship for me and everyone else who trained there. Besides, it didn't make sense for Ho to keep it locked indefinitely. Was he expecting evidence to suddenly appear out of nowhere?

I called the police station and asked to speak to him.

"Detective Ho is away until Monday," said the clerk.

I waited for further details but she didn't offer any.

"Do you know if anyone else there might be able to help me? I need to ask about releasing a crime scene. The police have sealed the gym where I work out there and I'm kind of anxious to get back before I forget my routine—or I give up and gain back the hundred pounds I've lost." I chuckled as if I'd tried for funny, but we both knew it was more lame than funny.

"Detective Wong is taking Detective Ho's emergency calls. Do you consider this an emergency?"

No way I'd go down that road. "No *mahalo*, I was just hoping for information."

I hung up and continued to kick around break-in scenarios. One involved me standing on the alley dumpster and shimmying through one of the skinny clerestory windows, but aside from realizing only a six-year-old could to fit through one of those windows there was also the tricky eight foot drop to the cement practice room floor.

At ten I gave up trying to solve the problem creatively and decided to go direct. I hopped in the Mini and made my way down to the Kahului Police Station. At the front desk I asked to speak with Detective Wong.

Wong came out, lifting an eyebrow as he recognized me as the "citizen" who was there to see him.

"Ah, Ms. Moon. I should've taken bets in the break room that it would be you. Why am I not surprised?"

"Maybe because you know the Palace of Pain is my home *guan*, and having it locked up presents a problem for me."

"Or maybe it's because, once again, you've insinuated yourself into a police matter that's none of your business."

I looked over at the clerk who was pointedly trying to pretend she wasn't eavesdropping. Wong also appeared to be assessing the situation.

"We'll be in Interview Two," he said. "Hold my calls."

Wong closed the door to the interview room and told me to take a seat. I really wanted to get cheeky and plop down in the chair on the "police side," the one closer to the door, but batted down the urge. After all, I was there to ask a favor.

I made my way around the table and got as comfortable as possible in the hard-backed chair. I've never understood the reasoning behind the lack of amenities in police interrogation rooms. It seems to me if you're going to hold someone in an airless, windowless room for hours on end trying to extract information they don't want to give, it would behoove you to make the place seem more like the Merrie Monarch Suite at the Grand Wailea than the Seventh Circle of Hell. I'm just saying. The way I see it, a little *quid pro quo* could go a long way toward making both police work and snitching a lot more rewarding on both sides of the table.

"So, what can I do for you today, Ms. Moon?"

"I'm here to ask when the Palace of Pain in Pa'ia will be reopened."

"I guess that answer rests with whatever succession planning your friend, Douglas Kanekoa, has made. As you know, he's been charged with second-degree murder."

"What I meant was, when we'll be able to get in there and work out."

He twisted his mouth into a puzzled expression. "I don't see why you couldn't get in there today. If you have a key, that is. We locked it after our search on Monday, but as far as I know, it's not a crime scene."

"I was there on Wednesday and Detective Ho sealed the door."

He shrugged. "First I've heard of it."

We stared at each other for longer than is comfortable and then I spoke up. "So what do I do?"

"What do you want to do?"

"I want to get in there and work out."

"Look, Ms. Moon, this isn't my case. If the door is sealed then you'll have to wait until Detective Ho returns and ask him when it will be unsealed. I don't know what you expect me to do."

I pondered my next move since it could go one of two ways. "Detective, you and I haven't always seen eye to eye on my involvement in matters like this, but—"

He cut me off with a snort. "That's certainly an understatement."

"...but you have to admit I've actually helped, rather than hindered, more than a few times."

He leaned his chair back onto two legs and looked up at the ceiling. I wasn't sure if it was a sign of his agreement or if he was simply contemplating where to go for lunch.

I went on. "Remember that rich high-tech guy who murdered his friend over selling their company? Or how about the federal agent who got abducted by the narcos? Helping on that one landed me in witness protection. You want me to go on?"

"Please don't."

"Okay, but I think it's safe to say you owe me."

He crashed the chair back down to all four legs. "That's the most ridiculous thing I've ever heard. And believe me, Ms. Moon, I've had to slough off more than my share of ridiculous when it comes to you."

"What is it with you, Wong? Is it sexism? Or does it just bug you that I've got great instincts but since I'm not wearing a badge you think you can disrespect me?"

We locked eyes again in a game of first to blink loses.

"Ms. Moon, I'll be the first to commend you on your extremely rigorous sense of civic duty. And I'll acknowledge that once or twice your ideas have proven to be helpful to this department. But I refuse to be coerced into doing whatever it may be that you want me to do out of some misguided notion on your part that I *owe* you anything. Do you understand?"

I puzzled over his comment. Was he posturing for the video that was no doubt recording the meeting? Or was he so pig-headed that he truly felt that although I'd helped him numerous times he had no obligation to reciprocate? I took the high road and assumed it was the former.

"Point taken. Then let's not call this a favor but rather an opportunity for you to assist in averting a miscarriage of justice."

He scowled but didn't object.

"I know you're not the lead on the Kanekoa case, but I think the investigation has been seriously compromised."

"I'm listening."

"Doug Kanekoa has allegedly confessed to killing his wife but I have serious doubts about the truth of that confession."

Wong blew out a breath. "Okay, here it comes. The old 'we forced a confession out of him' ploy. Haven't we both been around the block enough times to know that one's not going to survive the smell test? One thing this badge offers is a front row seat to every dirtbag stunt out there."

He went on. "The forced confession scam goes something like this. We pick up a guy and he's still hot from committing some heinous act so he confesses. He knows he did it. We know he did it. God knows he did it. Then the guy lawyers up and, guess what? Pretty soon the lawyer convinces him maybe he didn't do it. Or maybe he had a darn good reason for doing it. Next thing you know, the confession's recanted and Larry Lawyer's pacing in front of the jury box with tears in his eyes bad-mouthing the integrity of the cop who took Señor Dirtbag's confession."

I paused to absorb the enormity of Wong's cynicism. "I understand that probably happens, but in this case I really think the confession's a lie."

"You do realize how lame that sounds, right?"

"I know. But let me explain. Doug's not trying to get away with anything. In fact, I think it's quite the opposite. I believe he's trying to take the fall for someone else."

"By confessing."

"Exactly. Doug knows who killed his wife and he's protecting them."

"Okay, I'll play along. Who do you think did it?"

"I don't know. But I think as long as the police focus solely on Doug's confession, the real killer will never be found."

"Are you insinuating we aren't doing our job, Ms. Moon?"

"I'm not insinuating anything. I'm asking for your help. Would you consider working with me to find out what really happened?"

"A parallel investigation to Ho's?"

"I guess. If you want to call it that."

"Let me see if I've got this straight. You want me to go against direct orders, not to mention alienating my colleagues in the homicide squad, to look for a second suspect when we've already locked up a confessed perp? To put my good name, not to mention my career, on the line so I can go on a wild goose chase with you?"

"Well, when you put it like that it sounds stupid."

"That's because it *is* stupid. And *you're* stupid if you think I'd consider it."

"Okay, I understand this could be risky for you. But aren't you even a little bit curious to know the truth? I mean, you went to school with Doug Kanekoa. You know he's not the kind of guy who'd do something like this."

He furrowed his brow. "You know, Ms. Moon, the one thing this job has taught me is *anybody's* capable of *anything*. Especially when sex is involved."

I straightened in my chair. I'd rarely heard Wong be so candid, not to mention outright blunt. "You think this was sexually motivated?"

"Not for me to say. But point blank range tends to point to a crime of passion. And when the victim and perp are intimate partners, we take that into consideration. Lots of things happen behind closed doors. Things friends and family members never see."

I chewed on that for a moment. Could Wong be right and my highly-disciplined *sifu* was capable of turning into a raging out-of-control killer when he discovered he'd been cheated on? While I considered that possibility in a man I'd known for over ten years, Wong stood up.

"I have no reason to believe Doug Kanekoa's confession is anything but the straight-up truth," he said. "But I'll tell you what. If you bring me even a shred of evidence to the contrary, I'll look into it."

The contents of the stash drawer came to mind. "But what if I need your help to get my hands on the evidence?"

"Sorry. Like I said, it isn't my case. If you insist on making it yours, I'm afraid you're on your own."

I got up to leave.

"Oh, and one more thing, Ms. Moon. If you get slapped with obstruction of justice, don't expect me to come to your defense. As far as I'm concerned, this conversation never happened."

19

I left the police station with new resolve to once again get into Doug's stash drawer. Maybe there was more than just crusty food containers and manila envelopes in there. I hoped there was, because I took Wong at his word about helping me if I could come up with something. Maybe nothing in there had anything to do with Lani's death. Maybe Doug really was just worried about being caught with a substantial quantity of pot.

I checked the time and hustled back to Pa'ia. After all the hassle I'd already endured over Farrah's blessing ceremony I didn't want to be late. I rushed into the Gadda to see if she was ready to go.

"Hey, girl, wha's up?" she said as if surprised to see me.

"It's nearly one. Don't you have somewhere you're supposed to be this afternoon?"

She cast her eyes toward the back room and sidled up close. "It's rad you stopped by 'cuz my man's even taking a pass on driving me home. I'm gonna need a ride."

"So, Ono's really not going to the ceremony? I thought he'd change his mind."

"Nope, he's stayin' here at the store. I'm down with that 'cuz I think him being there could mess up what the *kahu* will be trying to do."

"What about the twins?"

"Steve's comin' by in a few minutes to get 'em. He said he's gonna fix 'em dinner and bring 'em home later."

I puzzled over Steve not mentioning his part in helping Farrah with her *kahu* blessing but let it go. I often imagined myself the center of my friends' universe. I regularly had my comeuppance when they got together for social or work-related events and left me completely out of the loop.

"So, who all will be there?"

"Pretty much just me and you. I think it's better this way. Easy-peasy, with no *keiki* running around and no bad *juju* from my man wrecking the vibe."

Steve showed up a few minutes later and swept the kids up in a hail of promised treats and forbidden TV. Farrah seemed so intent on getting them out the door she failed to launch into her usual, but largely ignored, litany of approved foodstuffs and educational entertainment choices.

When they'd left I said, "You know he's going to let them eat sugary stuff."

"True. But I'm cool with that. Remember, like Maukani said, 'Maui's history is written in sugar.'"

I smiled at her reference to our Hawaii State History teacher, Mr. Maukani. That line about our history being "written in sugar" used to crack us up. Our class had a comeback we'd all softly whisper so he couldn't hear, "...and the *haoles* got the rotten teeth to prove it." I always squirmed at the mention of *haoles*, since ethnically I was one. But when you're island born and raised you get cut some slack even if you've got hazel eyes and light brown hair.

"You ready?"

She wiped a hand across her sweaty brow. "Gimme a minute to wash up. Like I tol' you, the dude's a babe."

Maybe Ono's bad vibe wasn't the only reason Farrah didn't want him there.

* * *

Ono and Farrah's house in Haiku is truly a small patch of heaven on earth. A leafy drive leads to a small plantation-style house set back from the main road just far enough to make it safe for the kids to play in either the front or back yard with minimal adult supervision. When we were kids we played outside for hours on end with little or no parental oversight, but times have changed, even in rural Maui.

The house is one-level, painted dark green with white trim. Its simple square footprint includes a living room, tiny dining area, kitchen and two bedrooms, with the master bedroom only a foot or two larger on each side than the other. There's only one bathroom. The twins share the second bedroom but, according to Ono, plans are already underway to expand the house and add a third bed and second bath.

"That is, if I can get my loving wife to stop spending money like it grows on trees," he's said more than enough times that we all chime in and finish the sentence whenever it comes up.

In true plantation house style, the house has a few wooden steps up to the front door and a nice wide porch, or *lanai*, to sit out on to watch the world go by. But in Farrah and Ono's case, the world goes by behind the thick hedge and explosion of greenery between house and road so sitting on their front lanai is like being in Eden. Nothing but green, and only the sound of trade winds and the occasional bird to break the silence.

"Guess he's not here yet," Farrah said as I parked in front of the house. The driveway was empty.

"Not unless he walked from the airport."

"What if he got lost?"

"Hard to do that with GPS. And besides, doesn't he have your phone number?"

She pulled out her phone and stared at it with a fervor she usually saves for summoning answers from her Ouija board.

"It's only just two-thirty now," I said. "What time was his plane due in?"

"I think around one-thirty."

"There are about a half-dozen flights from the mainland that come in around then. The rental car place is probably a madhouse."

Farrah seemed to accept my explanation, but she knew I knew what I was talking about. I worked airport security both on and off planes long enough to have learned the ebb and flow at OGG, the Kahului Airport. I didn't last at that job but it had nothing to do with an inability to spot patterns in how things worked both on the ground and in the air. During peak arrival times it can take twice as long to retrieve your luggage and get a rental car compared to non-peak times. Trouble is, with Maui tourism on the upswing, there aren't many non-peak times anymore.

She twisted her hands. "I'm gonna make us some sun tea."

I flopped into the string hammock Ono had strung across the lanai, breathing in the clean air scented with the spicy fragrance of a blooming vine or flower I couldn't spot in the riot of green surrounding the house.

"See anything?" Farrah yelled from inside the house.

I shifted my weight, careful not to dump myself unceremoniously out of the hammock, and peered down the driveway. "Not yet."

She brought out two sweating glasses of deep brown tea. Each glass held a few shards of what looked like month-old ice. "Sorry 'bout the ice. I told Ono to flip the wire thingy but he must've spaced it. I had to use the stuff in the tray."

I rolled out of the hammock and took a seat in an ancient plastic chair. I was thirsty and took a deep mouthful. In true Farrah fashion, the heavily-steeped tea hadn't been sweetened. She eschewed sugar as the "opiate of the masses" and refused artificial sweeteners as "gateway chemicals" foisted on us by Big Pharma. But boy, that tea was harsh.

Since there were no side tables I placed the glass at my feet. No way I would give in to my thirst and take another swig of the bitter brew.

"It's getting near three," Farrah said. "Where is he?"

"Maybe Big Island people think 'island time' is any time during the same day. Or maybe he missed his flight. Why don't you call him?" I was growing tired of coming up with excuses for the guy.

She brightened at my suggestion as if it were a surefire solution. "Why didn't I think of that? I'll fetch the number."

She went inside and a half-minute later I heard her talking. I was eager to get this thing over with. First of all, I thought a thousand bucks for a half hour of chanting was pretty steep. And second, I was itching to get back to the Palace of Pain and see if I could find a way in. I was desperate to locate something that would persuade the police to look beyond Doug's confession.

Farrah came outside, the screen door slapping shut behind her. "I had to leave a message."

"He probably forgot to turn his phone back on when he landed." I couldn't believe I was still coming up with excuses.

"Whatever. I hope to get eyes on him soon."

I was about to make a snarky comment about her choice of words, but the panicked look on her face made me bite it back.

We waited. She offered more tea but I declined. I went inside under the pretense of using the bathroom but what I really wanted was a plain glass of water. No ice, no problem. I was parched.

When I came back out, Farrah was on the phone. Her scrunched-up expression reminded me of Hatchie's when she's fighting the bedtime edict. "Hold on a sec. Can I put you on speaker so you can tell my bestie here what you just tol' me?"

Farrah punched her phone screen in a punishing way and a strident female voice bellowed from the tiny speaker. "Yeah, like I just said, my no-good, lying ex musta given you my number. It's not his, that's for damn sure. He probably doesn't even have a phone no more, he's such a deadbeat. Anyhow, he's calling himself a *kahuna* or whatever? That's a total joke. The dude's a bum. Nothin' but a lazy, no good, bum. You got scammed girl. But at least *you* didn't marry him."

Farrah thanked her for her time and hung up.

I blew out a breath. "Now what?"

"Now I gotta think what I'm gonna do."

"You're going to tell Ono, right?"

Farrah snorted a rueful laugh. "Girl, on a scale of one to ten, that's like a minus two. That's the over-my-dead-body last thing I'm gonna do."

"But he's going to ask you about it."

"I don't think so. I mean, he thinks this whole thing's bogus, right? So, if he asks, I'll just say it went good. You with me?"

"You want me to lie? You know what a lousy liar I am."

"Don't sweat it. Just say it was groovy. No details."

"I hate getting in the middle of this."

"Whaddaya mean? You got yourself in the middle when you gave me the moolah."

What's that saying about *no good deed goes unpunished*? I was so done with good deeds.

* * *

Farrah spent the next half-hour wailing over losing the thousand dollars and promising to pay me back. Once she'd beat that dead horse to hamburger she started in on how the ghost was going to really amp up the scary tactics since he'd no doubt witnessed her effort to get rid of him.

"The ghost knows your guy didn't show up?"

"Oh, totally. It's not like I could fake him out, you know."

"But you're willing to lie to your husband?"

"Mango in the left hand, pineapple in the right," she said. In Farrah talk that was the same as mainlanders saying, "apples and oranges" meaning one thing was nothing like the other.

I commiserated with her until almost four-thirty when we both acknowledged it was time to move on.

"You mind stopping by the store and telling Ono we're done?"

"Me? Why don't you just call him?"

"I'm gonna make him a nice dinner. Maybe even mac and cheese. He'll forget all about *kahus* and lost money when he's sitting behind a big ol' mountain of fermented cow milk and high-gluten pasta."

She'd failed to answer the question, but I knew better than to point it out. We hugged good-bye and I drove back to the shop. I hesitated to go next door and face Ono, knowing the only thing I had to offer were lies. But putting stuff like that off only makes it worse, so I sucked in a breath and got to it.

"Hey, Ono, howsit?" His face told me he wasn't delighted to see me, but I made like I didn't notice.

"Could be better. Business is slow. How'd the blessing go?"

"Good."

"How long was the guy there?"

When I hesitated, he went on, "He isn't still there, is he?"

Relieved to be able to tell the truth, I jumped on it. "Nope. Long gone."

"What exactly did he do?"

I floundered for a weasely answer that wouldn't throw up red flags if he asked Farrah the same thing when he got home. "Oh, the usual stuff, I guess. He and Farrah were much more into it than I was."

Ono's brow creased. "Into what? Into each other?"

"No, no, no. Nothing remotely like that. I mean, I'm not as into this paranormal stuff as she is so I'm not the best person to ask, I guess. Oh, and a little bird told me you're going to be eating mac and cheese tonight."

I hoped the reference to his vegan wife setting aside her usual disdain of all animal foodstuffs to make him a much-loved meal would steer him away from inquiring further about the blessing. The way to a man's heart, and all that.

"Sounds good. But I want to know more about this blessing dude. I mean, what exactly does a guy like that *do* for a thousand bucks?"

"Farrah said some of the cost was to cover his airfare from the Big Island."

"She couldn't find one here on Maui?"

"Don't know. She said he came highly recommended."

"Which brings me back to my point. What's a guy like that do that's worth more than I make in a week?"

I mumbled something akin to "Oh, look at the time" and took off. I didn't even stop in at my shop, but instead drove to the PoP to survey the scene. I'd locked the car and was heading down the alley door when my phone chimed. I jumped at the sudden intrusion into my thoughts.

"Aloha?" I hoped my pounding pulse wasn't evident in the sound of my voice.

"Aloha, Pali. It's James Kanekoa."

"My phone showed a different number than yours."

"Yeah, I'm calling from my sister's house."

"Kaili's?"

"Yeah. I need to talk to you. Can you meet me at my office in ten minutes?"

"Is something wrong?"

"Look, yes or no? Can you meet?" His tone told me something was definitely wrong.

"Sure. I'll be there."

When I got to James' office the door was locked. I waited outside, wishing I'd stuck around the *guan* for a few more minutes. I had to find a way to peel that sticker off the door. I was digging in my beach bag purse, searching for a nail file or other sharp tool that I'd be able to use later when a voice boomed, "Thinking of picking the lock on my office?"

I jumped. "Geez, and you wonder why people don't like lawyers."

He ushered me inside and gestured for me to sit. "My nephew says you questioned him at my sister's."

"That's not true. I went to talk to Kaili and DJ came out and said he wanted to tell me something."

"Yeah, well, that's the problem. You should have directed him to me. I'm his father's lawyer."

"James, the kid was upset. He needed to talk to somebody. I didn't think it'd hurt to hear him out."

The pause that followed let me know James didn't agree.

"Pali, I appreciate you going with me to the jail the other day and all, but now this needs to remain solely in my hands. Doug's represented by counsel and any and all communication to him or about him should be directed to me. No one else. Got it?"

I had no idea why James was chewing me out. "Did DJ tell you what he was upset about?"

"Actually, no. He said he was done talking about it. I called you in here to tell me what I should've gotten first hand."

A few beats of dead air passed between us. I shifted in my chair, organizing my thoughts on how to best bring James up to speed without violating DJ's trust.

James slammed his palms down on his desk. "Look, Pali. Don't make me beg. I've had a lousy week, okay? My brother refused to enter a plea at his arraignment so I did it for him. Obviously, I went with 'not guilty' and now he's not talking to me. Then this afternoon I find out you've been skulking around interrogating my *'ohana* members without telling me. I'm not in the best of moods, so how about you just spit out what my nephew said without making me say 'pretty please?'"

Touchy. But I could see his point. Things certainly weren't going his way.

"Okay. In a nutshell, DJ's upset because he feels responsible for his mom getting shot."

"How so?"

"Seems he had a friend over on Sunday and DJ bragged about Doug being an Army Ranger. The other kid didn't believe him, so to prove it he asked his dad to show them the sidearm he was issued by Special Forces. DJ said when Lani saw them with the gun she went nuts. She and Doug had a huge fight and the kids were sent to stay next door. DJ thinks in all the excitement the gun probably didn't get locked up and it was later used to kill Lani."

"DJ thinks his dad killed his mom?"

"No, he's sticking with the intruder angle."

"I see. You have any idea of the caliber of the gun?"

My Homeland Security training kicked in. "I'm pretty sure it's an M9 Berretta—nine millimeter. That's what Rangers carry."

"Same type of slug found in Lani."

I leaned back in my chair. "There's something in DJ's story I can't quite reconcile."

"Yeah?"

"He said it was Doug who went to the neighbors to see if the kids could stay there."

James nodded. "Yeah. I talked with the neighbor and she's willing to testify."

"So, does that sound right to you? I mean, is that how it normally works?"

"What do you mean?"

"When kids go for a sleepover or to the neighbors' for dinner or whatever, who normally sets those things up?"

"Don't know about other people, but at my house my wife pretty much handles that kind of stuff."

"So, no one except Doug saw Lani after the kids left for the neighbors' place?"

James tapped his chin. "I guess."

"Are you thinking what I'm thinking?"

"I wish I wasn't."

20

I returned to my shop, dazed by the realization that Doug might be guilty after all. Things were sure pointing that way. I wanted to get into the *guan* in the worst way, but if I got caught breaking the seal my cover would be blown. There was still one person I wanted to see before taking that drastic step, Doug's cousin. How much had Doug told him when he'd asked to borrow his truck? And what had he said when he backed out on doing it?

I called Piko Kanekoa in Makawao and was pleased when he answered. It was getting late, so I'd hoped he was home from work.

"*Aloha*, Piko," I said. "This is Pali Moon, a friend of your cousin Doug's."

"Hey, yeah, I know you. I came to your house for a party a couple years ago, eh? That was some blow-out. Best ribs ever." Leave it to a three-hundred pound guy to associate me with the food and not the reason for the occasion.

"Listen, Piko, can I come by your place in a few minutes? I need to talk to you about this thing going down with Doug."

"Ah, that's some *bugga*, yeah? I mean, I love that *bruddah*, but now he do this?"

"Is it okay if I come over?"

A pause. "Yeah, it's cool. But my lady got dinner cookin'. You want you stay for grinds?"

"*Mahalo*, but I only need to ask a couple of questions and I'll let you eat in peace."

I asked for his address. "Great. I can be there in ten."

I scrambled out to my car and hot-footed it up Baldwin to Makawao. I'd never been to Piko's place, but found it with the help of GPS. The GPS lady can't pronounce Hawaiian words with anything even approaching accuracy so I ignore her sad attempt at street names. Mostly I just listen for the directions, such as "in five hundred feet, turn right." She always gets me where I'm going so why quibble?

Piko came out to meet me and gave me a big hug, even though I'm sure if pressed he'd never be able to pick me out of a line-up.

"Eh, Pali. Howsit?"

"I'm good. How about you?"

"Can't complain. But it's bad what's going on with my *cuz*, yeah?"

"Yeah. I want to ask you about Doug borrowing your truck."

"He tol' me he need it for a day or two but he brought it back after only a couple hours."

"What? He *did* borrow the truck?"

"Yeah. Like I said. But he was only gone two, maybe three, hours."

"When was this?"

He shrugged. "'Bout a week ago. Yeah, on Friday. I figured he needed it to help a friend move or sumpthin'."

"What'd he say when he brought it back?"

"Said '*mahalo*' and tol' me he got done early."

"And you never asked him what he was doing or where he went?"

"Why ask? He's my *cuz*. I got a truck, he needed a truck. No stink there."

"Well, in light of what's happened, I was hoping you might be able to give me some information. You see, he told me he was going to use your truck to figure out where Lani was going during the day. He was worried about her but didn't want her to see him following."

"Huh? He didn't tell me nuthin' 'bout that."

"On Friday afternoon I went by his *guan* and he said he hadn't borrowed the truck after all."

"Why he lie?"

"I don't know."

Piko shifted his gaze to the freshly-washed Toyota truck in his driveway. "Hey, you wanna know where he went? Only take a minute."

We walked over to the vehicle and Piko slipped into the driver's seat. "I got all the bells and whistles on this baby."

It was true. I'd never seen a civilian truck with so much extraneous hardware. Radar detector, full-screen

GPS, even what appeared to be a CB radio or onboard walkie-talkie complete with handset and exterior whip antenna.

I shook my head. "Why have you got all this stuff?"

"Since I lost my job at the sugar mill I been doing commercial deliveries. Get paid by the mile. I punch in the starting place like this..." He demonstrated setting the GPS. "...And when I get back I turn it off like this. It shows where I went, what route I took, and how many miles I drove. The company I work for wants to see it all. I guess they t'ink some guys take the long way to get mo' money."

I smiled. "But you'd never do that, right?"

"Not with this stuff breathing down my neck."

"Can you see where Doug went on Friday? Or didn't he use the GPS?"

"Don' matter. I set it before he come over. I figured if he didn't bring it back before I needed it, I'd be able to check online and see where he was. You wanna check it out?"

A jolt of anxiety shot through me. It was completely disrespectful of me to be spying on my *sifu*, a man who'd not only trained me to defend myself against tough opponents but also had instilled in me a reverence for authority. The more I learned about the events of the past week, however, the closer I came to losing faith in that same man. He'd gone from a guy who'd flatly refused to lie, cheat, or steal to one who was clearly doing at least one of those things now.

I sucked in a breath. "Yeah, let's see where he went."

Piko pressed a few buttons and the screen lit up with 07/19, 08:38am. He tapped the screen and 37.8 mi appeared. He tapped again and an address on Mahalani Street in Wailuku filled the display.

"There you have it."

"Do you recognize the address?" I asked.

"Not really. Let's look at the map." He tapped the screen yet again and a map of the area came up. "Looky here. It's next to the hospital."

As Piko walked me back to my car. I thanked him and again he asked if I wanted to stay for dinner.

"*Mahalo*, but you've already given me plenty to chew on."

He grinned as if pleased with himself he'd figured out my little pun. I waved as I pulled away.

* * *

It was getting dark but I wouldn't have been able to sleep at all that night if I'd neglected to drive to the address on Mahalani Street. It turned out to be a medical clinic with an array of specialist offices—dermatology, urology, oncology, cardiology, gynecology. Seemed just about all of the "ology's" were represented. But which one had Lani seen? And why had Doug lied to me about following her?

I went to bed promising myself I'd get into the PoP one way or another the next morning. It would be Saturday, which meant more people in town, more people around to witness me flagrantly breaking the law. But I didn't care. I had to get back in that stash drawer.

I awoke at four and was about to roll over and punch my pillow into a cozier shape when I bolted upright. This would be the perfect time to go to the PoP. I had a key, so if a cop rolled down the alley I could always flash the key and say I didn't see the crime scene sticker in the dark. I slipped into dark cropped pants and a black t-shirt, mentally patting myself on the back for my brilliant idea.

I tiptoed through the kitchen and was about to quietly slip out the back door when the room was abruptly flooded with light.

"I was hoping that was you," said Steve.

I squinted as my eyes adjusted. He was dressed in board shorts and a long-sleeved Lycra shirt.

"What are you doing up this early?" I said.

"I always get up around now to surf. What's your excuse?"

In all the time Steve had lived with me I never recalled asking him when he got up. I knew he went to Ho'okipa Bay most mornings to windsurf and hang around with what he called, "my regular guys" but I never dreamed he routinely left the house hours before sunrise.

"I'm going down to the PoP."

"Did they take the crime scene sticker off the door?"

"No."

His eyes widened.

"That's right. I've been reduced to a common criminal. But I've got to find whatever it is Sifu Doug sent me to get."

"I'll go with you," Steve said. "Being a criminal accomplice is on my bucket list."

I tried to talk him out of it but he was adamant. He even insisted we take his car rather than mine, since his wouldn't be immediately recognizable by Wong or Ho or anyone who trained at the Palace of Pain.

"You don't have to get involved in this, you know. You could just drop me off."

"What? And let you have all the fun? No way. Besides, I'm in the mood for some good old-fashioned burglary."

"I won't be stealing anything. Doug asked me to retrieve something for him, so I'm just the messenger."

"What are you looking for?"

"Not sure. But I'm hoping I'll know when I see it."

"Fine, but I'm not letting you do the perp walk alone. If you get caught, we're both going down."

Steve parked on the street, which was a good idea since anyone patrolling the alley would be immediately alerted if they saw a strange car. We carefully made our way around to the back, using the flashlight app on Steve's cell phone.

"It's never this dark at the beach," Steve muttered. "It's like all the light in this alley has been sucked out and replaced by a creepy vibe."

He was right about the vibe. It may have been my reluctance to break the law—or more honestly my fear of getting caught—or the enormity of the horror of the past week, but as we moved through the inky black to the Palace of Pain I felt like I was in a familiar nightmare. In the dream I step off a steep cliff and fall and fall until I jerk awake just before hitting bottom.

"You okay?" Steve stage-whispered. "You're huffing and puffing like you've run a marathon."

He shined the light on the door. The warning on the sticker not only indicated this was a crime scene, but also gave chapter and verse of the law we'd be breaking if we tampered with it. It ended with "Minimum fine $852, and/or 30 days in jail."

Steve flicked off the light. "They really don't want you messing around here. I mean, it's not eight hundred bucks, or even eight-hundred fifty. It's a precise eight fifty-two. They mean business."

"Yeah."

After a few seconds he said, "But hey, if you're willing to do the month in jail, I'll spot you the eight-hundred fifty-two bucks. Under the circumstances, I'm betting they won't go for more than the minimum. Whaddaya say?"

A thirty-day stint in the Kahului jail was nothing compared to the life sentence Doug was facing, but it was no day at the beach, either.

I blew out a breath. "I'm ready. Do you think we should just rip it off?"

"Where's the fun in that? Hold the light for me and I'll demonstrate how I got beer money in college."

While I held the light, he began to painstakingly pick at the edge of the sticker until, millimeter by millimeter, it began to peel away from the door jamb. After a few minutes my arm grew weary and the phone started to shake.

"Hold still," he said. "I'm getting to the tricky part."

He grasped the six-inch long sticker by the top edges and pulled it off in one seamless piece.

"How did mastering adhesives get you beer money?" I asked.

"Not proud of this, you understand. But I'd go to a high-end store and switch price tags. I'd go back later and claim I'd gotten whatever it was as a gift and they'd give me money back. They'd give me the original price, not the one I paid, and I pocketed the difference. I generally made between twenty and fifty bucks on each switch."

"And they never figured out what you were doing?"

"Well, I never went to the same store more than once a year. But in LA there are a zillion luxury stores. I'm not proud of taking advantage of their faith in humanity, but I was desperate for cash."

"I need to get inside."

"Right. Well, here's the sticker. You can put it back on when you're done."

"Do you think it'll still stick?"

"My dear, you're working with a pro. Just make sure you put it back in the same spot."

I handed him back his phone. "You can't tell anyone about this."

"Give me a little credit, girl."

"I'm sorry, but you talk story with your friends. Everyone knows you're the go-to guy for Pa'ia gossip."

In the thick predawn gloom I couldn't make out his face well enough to determine how he'd taken my blunt, but accurate, assessment.

After a few beats he cleared his throat. "You should know I've deep-sixed a lot of stuff that wasn't appropriate for public consumption. And, just so we're clear, in most cases *you* were the primary focus."

If I hadn't been so anxious to get inside the *guan* I would've asked for details, but duty won out.

"*Mahalo*, for helping with this, Steve. I'll let you know how it goes." I gave him quick hug and he turned and disappeared into the darkness.

Once inside, I tacked one small edge of the sticker to the door jamb. I'd try to reattach it when I was finished, but that wasn't uppermost in my mind.

I was mere minutes away from getting my hands on what my *sifu* had sent me to find.

21

I locked the door to Doug's office before turning on the light. I wished he had something other than the blazing fluorescent ceiling light, but my *sifu* wasn't into office décor which meant no desk lamp. I'd need to work quickly to avoid someone seeing ambient light seeping from the high clerestory windows in the practice room. I pulled the pink-capped key from my pocket and unlocked the drawer.

The key turned without resistance. The drawer had been unlocked.

I allowed myself only a second or two of alarm. Had Detective Ho found what I'd been interrupted from finding? If so, Wong's promise to assist me had probably just been a stalling tactic. Perhaps the police already had irrefutable evidence of Doug's innocence but they'd buried it.

The contents of the drawer looked just as jumbled as last time. Plastic containers, mouth guards, and equipment catalogs. Along with the two manila envelopes.

The first envelope held two white belts, made of cotton fabric, folded into sixths. Doug kept those on hand to exchange a belt for the first month's fees when new people signed up. The second contained a half-sheaf of blank promotion certificates. Doug's wife, Lani, had taken a calligraphy class and when students were promoted to a new level she'd painstakingly letter their name on their certificate. I bit my lip as I recalled how when I made black belt she'd fashioned the "P" in my name with lots of curlicues using two colors of ink.

I dug through the debris, dumping the contents on top of the desk. The only thing I was sure was missing was Doug's plastic bag of *pakalolo*. Maybe Ho had had second thoughts about slapping on the illegal drug charge after all.

But how had he unlocked the drawer? As far as I knew, the pink-capped key was the only way in and I'd had that in my possession the entire time. I inspected the lock and it didn't appear tampered with. How had Ho managed to remove the bag of pot?

I slumped in Doug's chair, staring into the drawer as if glaring at it would make it give up its secrets. The drawer was empty, with only a tattered piece of corrugated cardboard fitted to the bottom. In a last act of desperation I jiggled the cardboard free and pulled it out. Underneath was a white business-size envelope folded in half.

I unfolded the envelope. The front of it was covered with a spatter of dark brown blotches. The stains weren't transparent like coffee or tea stains, but a thicker consistency. More along the lines of poster paint.

I sniffed the envelope and an earthy metallic tang caught in my throat. Some odors are immediately recognizable, and blood is definitely on the short list. Even through the dense blood-spatter I was able to make out a single word, "Darling," followed by a heart-shaped symbol, like a love letter.

My pulse raced as I turned the envelope over. The glue on the flap had pulled away, indicating it had once been sealed but later opened. I took a breath and sat back in the chair, even though my brain screamed at me to rip out the contents and get on with it.

A *déjà vu* feeling came over me and I recalled a time when I'd gazed down at a murder victim, knowing I'd never get that image out of my head for as long as I lived. Did I really want to know my beloved *sifu* wasn't the man I'd held him up to be? That he was, in fact, a cold-blooded murderer who caught his wife *in flagrante delicto* and killed her out of anger and spite? And what about her trip to the clinic next to the hospital? Could Lani have sought the advice of a doctor willing to help her erase her shame, like a sexually-transmitted disease specialist or even a gynecologist willing to perform a discreet abortion?

My hands shook. Whether it was from anger over a woman trying to rid herself of an unwanted child when I wanted one so badly, or fear of learning Sifu Doug was as weak and undisciplined as the rest of us, I'm not sure. But I had to take a moment.

I got up and walked out of the office. Through the high windows in the practice room the sky had turned a dusky mauve. A new day was coming on.

* * *

I hadn't heard from Finn since his message on Monday, five days earlier. In all the uproar over Lani's murder I'd put my own looming disaster in my back pocket. But it wouldn't stay quiet. Maybe it was my questioning whether Lani had sought help to deal with the consequences of her infidelity or something else, but as I stood in the practice room pondering whether to examine the contents of the bloody envelope or hand it over sight-unseen to James Kanekoa, I mentally drifted back to the day Finn and I got married.

He'd been the new kid on the block, fresh from a long stint in Australia and given a plum assignment on O'ahu as a reward. I was aware he worked for the U.S. military in some form of cyber warfare, but even after seven months of marriage I still wasn't sure what his day-to-day work life entailed. Was he manipulating bomb-dropping drones, or was he merely a desk jockey commanding nothing more lethal than a mouse to harass and annoy the enemy?

I was a deep in thought when my cell began to chime. I checked the clock. A few minutes after five a.m. I didn't recognize the number but it was local, eight-oh-eight.

"*Aloha*, this is Pali." My pulse raced as I waited for someone at the police department to confirm they knew right where I was and what I'd been doing.

"Hello, *ku'uipo*. Hope I didn't wake you. I finally got cleared for a call."

Finn.

"Hi." I mentally scrambled for more but was shut down by the coincidence of him calling at exactly the same moment I'd been thinking of him. Especially since I'd hardly given him five minutes' thought throughout the past week.

"I've been wanting to call but couldn't."

Probably because you haven't had time to find a divorce attorney, I thought.

"How is it going?" I said in as calm a voice as I could muster.

"Long days. Tough assignment. Look, I'm due back on Monday. Can you take the day off? I've got something important to talk to you about."

The nerve. Like I'm supposed to "pencil him in" so he can dump me.

"Steve's staying at the house for a while."

"What?"

"He and Allen broke up. He's looking for a permanent place but until he finds something I told him he could stay at my place." Okay, calling it "my place" rather than "our place" was pissy, but maybe I wanted him to know I was prepared for what he was planning to drop on me.

"Okay. But could you ask him to give us some space? I need—" At that I heard a loud urgent voice in the background, like someone barking orders through a loudspeaker. "Uh-oh, gotta run. See you Monday." He clicked off without so much as a ta-tah.

The silent phone brought me back to the here and now, staring at the bloody envelope. I set my phone to airplane mode. I didn't want to risk getting another call until I'd decided what I'd do about it.

* * *

When I first gathered the courage to check out the Palace of Pain I'd just turned twenty-three. Fresh from college on O'ahu with a degree in Criminology and Abnormal Psychology. Looking back, I don't think I ever seriously considered working in typical law enforcement. In fact, I'd been heavily recruited to take a juvenile probation officer position in Honolulu and I'd turned it down. They desperately needed women to join the ranks. I assume my being a flinty-eyed criminologist rather than a smiley-faced social worker really got their juices up. Certain neighborhoods in Honolulu are rife with drugs, gangs and underage sex workers and no amount of "Tell me how that made you feel" will ever adequately address the problem.

But Maui was home so I came back. Right away I applied to U.S. Homeland Security to serve as an air marshal on any of a host of international flights that leave Kahului Airport every week.

I went to my initial interview and found out working for the feds was strictly a one-sided affair. I was questioned and tested and back-ground checked even before they'd admit whether they had any jobs available. I figure they do this for security reasons—it seems everything they don't want to talk about is chalked up to "national security"—but still it rankled.

They appear to do a fair amount of "profiling" at these early meet and greets. The irony of government work is that they're required to maintain a delicate balance when it comes to employing people of different genders, ages, and races, but they're the last people who will come clean about it. In Hawaii, we don't tend to have much of a problem with prejudice. That's perhaps because we use family as the marker to bestow favors or articulate bias. And since we even have our own word for family, *'ohana*, it comes across as appropriate, even charming, in our culture to turn a blind eye to nepotism and cronyism. "*Ah, yeah, the mayor's new technology director doesn't even know how to turn on a computer, but she's his niece, so what you gonna do?*"

Not that I'm bitter. But with my *haole* looks and my orphan status, I really needed to do well at the initial interview or my chances would be slim to none.

"We're looking for recruits in top condition," the interviewer told me.

At five-six and a hundred and twenty-five pounds, I was pretty sure I wasn't the worst physical specimen he'd ever laid eyes on, but I was still carrying a bit of the freshman fifteen I'd been unable to shake. I'd dabbled in martial arts in college, getting to brown belt in *kung fu* before literally throwing in the towel in favor of hitting the books.

"I understand. In fact I've recently begun training at a *guan* here on Maui," I'd said.

"A what?"

"A *guan*. A martial arts gym."

"You do *karate*?"

"No, I'm a serious about it. I practice *kung fu*." I'd meant it as a nod to the rivalry between the various martial arts, but apparently his knowledge of *kung fu* was limited to taking his kids to "Kung Fu Panda" movies. He shot me a skeptical look.

I went on. "It's a centuries old hand-to-hand combat technique perfected by the Chinese. It's considered the basis of all martial arts. In fact, the word *kung*, or *gong* as the Chinese say it, means 'work' or 'achievement.' For early Chinese warriors it was the bedrock of their training, in other words, their 'work.'"

He smiled indulgently as if I was a cute kid who'd rattled off the Periodic Table of Elements in a single breath.

"Interesting. So, tell me about this *guan* you've joined."

"Well, to begin with, the name is Palace of Pain."

* * *

I lifted the flap on the bloody envelope. The envelope held a single sheet of paper folded in thirds. A single bloody fingerprint was visible at the top edge of the page. I shuddered as I considered how many times I'd shook the hand of the person who'd undoubtedly be linked to that print.

I put the paper down and gave myself one more chance to walk away. My phone was within reach. All it would take would be a quick call to James. I wouldn't even have to look up the number; he was in my contacts.

I recalled Doug's request: "Tea stash, pink key. Empty it." This had to be what he'd sent me for. This was his way of explaining what'd happened. He must've known I'd share it with his attorney, and then ultimately the police, but it still wasn't clear why he'd chosen me instead of James. Maybe he didn't want to put his brother in the no-win position of uncovering evidence that would lead to a surefire guilty verdict. Or, worse yet, risk his brother's disbarment for withholding it.

Outside, the sky had turned a bright cerulean blue. Once Doug was convicted, he'd only see that sky for an hour or two every day. A thought nibbled at my conscience. Perhaps Doug hoped I'd never show the paper to anyone else. Maybe he considered me the one person he trusted with keeping the foul truth from ever seeing the light of day.

I unfolded the page.

The words weren't written in Doug's untidy print. In fact, the handwriting was in cursive, like a schoolteacher writing on the chalkboard for Parent's Night. The only person I knew who still wrote in cursive was Lani, educated by nuns determined to keep grade-school education totally old-school. Elegantly formed capital letters were followed by carefully shaped vowels and consonants, flowing in a neat hand as if the meticulous execution of the penmanship signaled the gravity of the message.

It took me less than a minute to read. But it would take me days to figure out what to do about it.

22

I knew I should call James immediately, but I also knew Doug wouldn't want me to. Since my loyalty was clearly with my *sifu*, I tucked the letter back into the bloody envelope and slipped it in my purse. I closed and locked the *guan* door and carefully replaced the crime scene sticker over the door jamb. But who was I kidding? The sticker was damaged, even after Steve's meticulous removal process. One edge had folded over on itself and the whole thing was crisscrossed with wrinkles impossible to flatten out.

I parked behind the Gadda but didn't trust myself with what I might blurt out if I went in, so instead, I unlocked my shop door and went in. My brain was turning cartwheels over what to do next. I'd been trained my entire life to tell the truth, regardless of the consequences. But I'd never faced consequences of this magnitude.

My desk phone rang, startling me.

"Where have you been?" Steve demanded. "I've been calling your cell for half an hour."

I dug my cell phone out of my purse. It was still on airplane mode.

"Sorry. What's up?"

"You tell me. What'd you find at the PoP?"

I hesitated. "It turned out to be nothing."

"Nothing? I risked a month of being some three-hundred pound *bruddah's* 'jailhouse wife' for nothing?"

I stuck to the truth as closely as possible. "Sorry. I was hoping I'd find something in the manila envelopes but it turned out to just be PoP stuff. Doug's pot stash was gone so I'm thinking Detective Ho must've taken it and maybe some other things when he put the sticker on the door."

"What're you going to do?"

"Not much I can do. James will have to tell Doug I couldn't find what he sent me for."

There was a pause and Steve said, "Okay. It's me, remember? I'm the guy who's got your back. Whatever's going on, you don't have to hide it from me."

"Really, there's nothing going on."

"Right. And I've got a bridge to Moloka'i I'd like to sell you."

Steve hung up under protest but I couldn't possibly tell the biggest blabbermouth in Pa'ia about the contents of the bloody envelope. I needed to think.

* * *

I spent the rest of the morning holed up in my shop. I cleaned the place, top to bottom. I even dusted along the baseboards, which opened up the nearly healed blister on my foot. Once the shop was dust-free and reeking of a fake lemon smell that didn't come close to resembling any aroma found in nature, I started in on my computer. I updated my website, swapping new photos for ones that had graced it for half a decade. I even wrote a lengthy blog post about selecting the perfect wedding venue on Maui.

I managed to push all thoughts about the bloody envelope aside until my stomach let go with a terrific growl and I looked at the clock. It was nearly one-thirty and I hadn't eaten all day.

I was about to lock up and go next door for some food when Farrah burst in. Her pale face and wide eyes caused me to automatically reach for the phone set, poised to call nine-one-one.

"What is it?"

"He's here."

"Who?"

"The *kahu*."

"He's at the store?"

"No, the house."

"Then let's get over there before he leaves."

"Too late."

"What? He already left?"

"Nope. I'm not that lucky."

I shot her a confused frown.

"Ono's home today," she said. "He's the one who called to tell me the guy was there."

On the way to Haiku we brainstormed ways to explain why we'd lied about the *kahu* already doing the blessing. It was frightening how facile Farrah was at coming up with elaborate scenarios and senseless excuses.

"Okay, how 'bout this? I'll say I had a vision. You know, like a crazy hallucination or a rapture or somethin'. You say you went along so's I wouldn't completely embrace the dark side and freak out on my *keiki*. You know, like you had to play along about the *kahu* showing up or I might go 'Cuckoo's Nest' and 'Sophie's Choice' rolled into one."

"Farrah, Ono asked me point blank how the blessing went. How does that explain why didn't I tell him the truth? You weren't even there."

"Okay, okay. How about we say *you* were the one who flipped out? I could say you scorched me and said you'd kidnap one of the *keiki* until I forked over the thousand bucks. I could say we hassled over it and I sent you home before he got there."

I didn't even comment on that one.

Farrah cleared her throat. "Besides, that's kind of what I told him."

"What?"

"I didn't tell Ono the dude didn't show. I said I changed my mind and told him not to come."

"What? You told me to tell him it'd gone fine."

"I know. I choked."

"So, now Ono thinks I'm a serious liar."

"Better you than me."

We drove to Haiku in morose silence. The bloody envelope was still in my purse but there was no way I'd say anything to Farrah about it. My trust level with her had tipped into the red zone.

Ono and the *kahu* were out on the front porch when we pulled up. They were smiling and joking like a couple of old army buddies recalling fond memories of eluding the MP's after curfew.

I'd planned to drop Farrah off and hightail it out of there, but Ono rushed the car like a crazed fan hoping to take a trophy selfie. "Hey, Pali. Look who's here. *Two days in a row.*"

The sarcasm didn't suit him.

"Okay, I was covering for Farrah. She was worried you'd flip out if you thought the *kahu* had scammed her."

"Yeah, so I guess you figured lying was your best option."

"Hey, all's well that ends well, right? I mean, the guy's here now and the house will get blessed."

He glowered. "You and I have been friends for what, almost three years now?"

I saw where this was going. "Yeah, but I've been best friends with your wife for ten times longer than that."

"Great. Now I know where I stand. When we first met, I remember you giving me some song and dance about how you were a lousy liar. Said you'd been brought up to tell the truth and you were pretty much stuck in your ways. Well, congratulations. Seems you've mastered a whole new skill set."

"Look, Ono, I—"

He cut me off. "No, *you* look. I won't get between you and my wife because that wouldn't be fair to her. But let me be clear. I have zero trust in you anymore. As far as

I'm concerned, everything that comes out of your mouth is BS. And when Finn gets back I'll consider it my brotherly duty to clue him in on what went down here."

I barked a quick staccato laugh. "As if he'd care."

"Oh, he'll care plenty. Believe me."

By now, Farrah and the *kahu* were openly eavesdropping so I didn't want to divulge I knew Finn was looking to hire a divorce lawyer.

"Fine. Do what you will." I popped the transmission into reverse. "Have fun at the blessing ceremony." I jerked the car into gear and roared down the driveway. I'd have enjoyed making my tires squeal an "amen," but with the combination of the tiny Mini Cooper engine and the soft dirt driveway I had to settle for a noiseless dust cloud.

I called it a day and drove up to Hali'imaile. Steve wasn't home when I pulled in but that wasn't unusual since Saturday's a big day for photo events. I puttered around, doing a few loads of wash and even cleaning out the screen in the stovetop fan to avoid looking at the contents of the bloody envelope for the umpteenth time.

At dinnertime, Steve called and said he had a dinner date and might be "staying over." I choked back an Auntie Pali admonition to not drink and drive, practice safe sex, and a half-dozen other motherly clichés that he didn't need to hear and I didn't need to parrot like some spinster older sister. I hung up feeling bereft. I must've been looking forward to sharing the letter and all its implications with Steve more than I'd acknowledged earlier.

Sure he was a blabbermouth. And sure he ran in a different social circle than mine. But in the past few years I'd counted on three guys to steady me when life got rough: Sifu Doug, Finn, and Steve. (Actually, there'd been a fourth guy, but that's a whole different story.) Now Doug was in jail and Finn was overseas, planning to give me the heave-ho at the first possible opportunity. Steve was my last hope at getting a man's perspective, but he was so focused on repealing and replacing the guy he'd swore was his "forever partner" he was never around to help me out.

I drank a bottle of flat beer I found in the back of the fridge and halfheartedly munched a bag of microwave popcorn while watching the evening news. Needless to say, no relief there.

At seven-thirty I gave up and went to bed. I'd been up before the sun, and now I was going down along with it. I'd had plenty of time to consider what I should do about the letter. But I didn't need time. I needed guidance.

23

Sunday morning dawned under cloudy skies. It was warm, but dreary in a way that never makes it into Hawaii tourism brochures or Facebook cover photos. It suited my mood.

Since finding the bloody envelope my world view had become a bundle of contradictions. Anger at Farrah for selling me out to Ono, but understanding why she did. Not looking forward to Finn coming home, yet anxious to see him. I liked the déjà vu normalcy of sharing my house with Steve, but once again I found myself fretting over his safety and whereabouts.

The implications of the letter I'd found also had me racked with uncertainty. There were two paths I could take, like the proverbial fork in the road. Once I picked one there'd be no turning back. No do-overs. No never minds.

Whichever way I'd ultimately go, it wouldn't happen until Monday. The people I needed to involve were week-day workers entitled to their day of rest. Anyway, that's how I justified putting it off. In retrospect, though, I'm pretty sure any one of them would've preferred learning the truth sooner rather than later.

To keep myself from obsessing over the letter I put it away. More specifically, I slipped it between the pages of the latest edition of "Hawaii Bride" I'd left on the nightstand. No way Steve would inadvertently toss it out with the trash since one of our house rules was no entering the others' bedroom unless something's on fire or there's no response after three attempts at knocking.

Time passed slowly as I ticked off long-procrastinated items off my to-do list. I washed my car and bundled what seemed like a year's worth of "The Maui News" to recycle at the dump. I cleaned out the refrigerator, which only took a few minutes given our Mother Hubbard-like inventory of fresh food, then I gave my shower a good scrubbing. I considered re-sealing the grout but enough was enough.

Steve came home at four-thirty. After a few moments of pleasantries followed by his artful dodge of answering questions regarding his activities on the night before, he yawned and claimed he was overdue for a nap.

"Finn's coming back tomorrow," I yelled to his back as he beat a hasty retreat up the stairs.

He turned. "He is? Where's he been, anyway?"

"No idea. Some kind of black ops cyber thing."

"You want me to give you guys a little space? It's cool, 'cuz I've got a place I can crash if you need me gone."

I started to object, then stopped. The last thing I wanted was a blow-by-blow account of Finn's farewell speech circulating around town. I'd already gained the somewhat sketchy reputation as a woman who couldn't hold on to a man. Getting dumped six months after getting back from my honeymoon certainly wasn't something any sane wedding coordinator would proudly slap on her resumé.

"That'd be great. Just a day or two."

"What've you got planned for his homecoming?"

Steve is the kind of romantic for whom everything requires a celebration. A new love, a break-up, getting-back-together, a betrayal, hiring a hit man—okay, he hasn't done that yet, to my knowledge—but every occasion merits lots of planning and over-the-top food and décor.

"I'm playing it low-key," I said. "I'm taking tomorrow off and we'll probably just hang out."

He came back down the stairs and took my face in his hands. "Look at me. Your man's been gone for more than a week. And in that time you've been mourning the loss of Lani while worrying about the fate of your *sifu*, who's been fingered for her murder. This is not a time for 'hanging out.' This situation demands action. And by that, I mean a pull-out-all-the-stops welcome home lovefest to get your mind off things."

If he only knew.

"*Mahalo*, but I've got it handled."

"Champagne?"

"I think I've still got a few bottles left over from our wedding."

"You mean in that box in the garage?"

"Yes."

"Oops. I did you the favor of making sure those fine specimens of viticulture didn't get 'corked' while they waited for you to flaunt your fun side."

"You mean you drank all of it?"

"Not all by myself! Give me a little credit. Remember when Allen came over and we moved my rowing machine over to his place?"

"*That* called for champagne?"

He sniffed. "Well, we *were* in the early throes of blissful two-someness. Everything called for a celebration back then."

"Okay, but then the answer is, no, I don't have any champagne."

He flicked a hand as if waving away a fly. "Consider it handled. I'll make sure you have a chilled bottle on ice before I skedaddle out of here."

"*Mahalo.*" I gave him my best poker face, but I couldn't help thinking how a good bottle of bubbly could go a long way in softening the blow Finn was poised to inflict.

Steve narrowed his eyes. "And how about food? You know, not to sound cruel, but you're a seriously sustenance-challenged person. I'll bet you don't have a speck of brie, Vermont cheddar, or even, *shudder,* Colby cheese on hand. Let alone a cracker that's less soggy than the sponge I use to wash my car. I'll pick up some decent cheese, a cluster of grapes, and new a box of those super-thin French crackers while I'm at it."

"Steve, please don't go to so much trouble. It's just Finn. And he—"

"*Just* Finn? My dear, he's *just* the love of your life. *Just* your lawfully-wedded husband. And he's *just* returned from Kill-you-as-soon-as-look-at-you-stan. Let's get a little perspective here, girl."

I toyed with the notion of bringing Steve up to date on Finn's asking Ono to find him a divorce lawyer but let it go. There'd be plenty of time to stomp through that rubble once Finn had moved out. As Auntie Mana used to say, "Don't borrow trouble. The interest payments are a *buggah*."

Later that night Steve made dinner. While I cleaned up the kitchen he drove off to the store to stock us up on what he refers to as "smile food." When he returned he toted in bag after bag of spendy cheeses, sliced deli meats, aromatic breads, and about five kinds of olives, each in its own little plastic container.

"You can never have too many olives," he crowed. "Those little workhorses can grace a pizza, a salad, or a tiny sliver of baguette. Not to mention being the crowning glory in the perfect martini."

I doubted if Finn and I would be shaking up martinis. But then, I might be swilling gin straight from the bottle after he left and perhaps a little olive chaser would be nice.

"Okay, I've put all the yummy eats away," Steve said. "But before I go, I want you to tell me what's eating you."

"What do you mean?"

"Oh honey, I've lived with you, what, almost four years now? You don't think I can tell when you're about to burst into spontaneous combustion? Spill."

There'd be no getting rid of Steve until I told him something. But what? I wasn't ready to delve into my rocky marriage, and I still hadn't decided which way to go on the letter I'd found in Doug's office.

I pointed to the front porch. "Let's grab a glass of wine and sit outside."

"Don't *even* think that a glass of your less-than-stellar wine will make me leave without learning what's going on with you."

"I know. It's just that it's such a nice night and I'd like your opinion on something." I could always count on asking Steve's opinion to distract him from demanding full disclosure.

"Ah, so that's it. You were reluctant to ask for my advice because you're honoring my recent heartbreak."

I'd forgotten I can also count on him to think everything's about him.

As we sat in the ancient wicker porch chairs that I'd thought would've collapsed years ago and drank mediocre wine I told him about Farrah's troubles with the *kahu*. Steve whistled when I mentioned the guy charged a thousand dollars to bless her house.

"Seems kind of steep. I mean, she wasn't asking him to re-roof it at the same time, was she?"

I explained that she'd had run-ins with what seemed to be a malevolent ghost and maybe he charged more for ghostbuster services. I went on to say when the *kahu* didn't show, she sent me to tell Ono things had gone great. She didn't want him to know they'd been scammed.

"So, what did you say?"

"I said everything went fine."

"You couldn't come up with anything better than that?"

"Like?"

"Like, 'I got a call from work right about the time he was supposed to show. I suppose it went okay, but I'm not sure'."

"You know I'm no good at lying."

"You're no good at *creative* lying. Telling him the guy showed up was a total lie, and worse yet, it was completely unimaginative."

"Okay. Point taken. But now Ono's labeled me a liar and it's damaged our relationship. He's even threatened to tell Finn about it."

"Where do I fit in here? I thought you wanted my advice."

"I do. How do you think I should handle this with Farrah? I mean, I'm really ticked she threw me under the bus with Ono, but I completely understand why she did it."

"I still don't see what you want from me."

"I want your opinion. Should I be mad at her or not?"

In the gathering dark he leaned over and squinted at me. "I'm not even going to honor that with a comment.

But just so we're clear, when you're ready to tell me what's *really* eating you, I'm ready to listen."

24

In the dead of night between Sunday and Monday my phone beeped to let me know I'd gotten a text. I tried to pull myself awake to get it, but as soon as I rolled over I fell back to sleep. When I finally woke up for good at five, I lunged for the phone first thing.

It was Finn. "Arr Maui @ 8."

I blew out a breath. Only three hours before I'd have to face reality. For the past couple of days, I'd talked myself down from a ledge by acknowledging our marriage had been impulsive. Some might call it reckless. Only a few months had transpired between the "meet/cute" and the "I do." Given I'd met Finn only a few weeks after my break-up from a long-term relationship, and given he'd just arrived in Hawaii after years overseas, we should've taken it slow. Allowed ourselves a leisurely engagement.

But now he wanted a divorce? Lots of couples experience rough patches. And more than a few have fertility issues. Why does adversity make some marriages stronger while others fail?

I got up and showered, dabbing on a bit of plumeria cologne. I'm not normally a person who goes for anything more than the scent of shampoo and soap, but one day when Finn and I were idly browsing an ABC Store in Lahaina, he'd spied a tester bottle festooned with a plumeria flower and he'd spritzed some on his wrist.

"This stuff smells like you," he said.

"What?"

"Yeah, it's you. See?" He'd thrust a sinewy wrist under my nose.

I sniffed the cloying scent; sure that he'd eaten or drunk something that'd messed with his olfactory nerve.

"This is pretty sweet."

"So are you."

I flushed at the compliment. I'd steered clear of girly-girl stuff since middle school, when I first recognized there were two ways for women to go. Demand to be treated as an equal, and don't expect to be cut any slack. Or, use feminine wiles to cajole and manipulate your way to success. I went with the former. Not only was my personality more suited to straight-up competition, my face and body would've had to undergo a radical transformation for me to garner significant male attention.

The memory of Finn's comment made me sigh. It was still a mystery why my radically handsome husband had singled me out. Maybe he'd finally asked himself the same question.

I went to the kitchen and was pleased to see Steve had already made coffee. I poured myself a cup.

"Big day, huh?" Steve popped out of the walk-in pantry and I jumped.

"I thought you'd left already."

"Nah, sorry to rain on your parade, but the guy who offered his couch said I couldn't come over until this morning. I guess he fared better at the B and C than I did last night."

The Ball and Chain was Steve's bar of choice down in Kihei. It's a place that swings both ways: family-friendly deli during the day and pretty much only rainbow coalition folks after dark.

"When are you picking up Finn?"

"Eight o'clock. I guess I'll go down to the shop for a bit before heading out to the airport."

"I thought you said you were taking the day off."

"I am. It's just that I've got a couple of hours to kill so I might as well make the most of it."

He eyed me like a wife who knows her husband is feeding her a line but she's not quite ready to call his bluff.

"Okay. Well, the lovefest rations are in the fridge and the champagne's in there, too. Call me if you run out of caviar. I'm just down the road a ways."

Steve was notorious for demanding specifics from everyone else while remaining casually vague about his own circumstances. I attribute it to his decades of being in the closet with a hand on the trap door at all times.

I tidied up the kitchen and then went in to change the sheets on my bed. Something about going through the motions of my normal welcome home ritual comforted me. It was a good thing I never bought the home blood pressure cuff my doctor recommended just before I got put in witness protection because that morning I'd have been tempted to check it out. I didn't need a cuff to know my BP was off the chart.

My pulse thudded in my ears as I made my way out to the car. I sent up a quick prayer to clear all pets and children from the street as I drove out of my neighborhood. I was running on fear and adrenaline. Even when I'd faced off with formidable tournament opponents I had no chance with, I always kept my cool. But on the ride to my shop I had to tighten my grip on the wheel to still my hands.

Why was Finn's rejection so fear-inducing? I'd been tossed aside before. Maybe that was it. Maybe it was like being allergic to bee stings. The first time or two you swell up around the sting. It hurts, sure, but nothing earth-shaking. But after a few more stings things get serious. The body says, "I'm gonna throw everything I've got at this," and the next thing you know your throat is swelling shut and you're in full anaphylactic shock. Only a spendy Epi-Pen or a quick response by paramedics is going keep you from paddling your last race.

I got to the shop and went inside. Finn had left a voicemail on my shop phone.

"Hey, hope you're planning to pick me up Monday morning, but no worries. If you're not there I'll grab an Uber." His voice was casual, like calling a work buddy who owes you a favor.

I fidgeted, arranging and re-arranging the stuff on my desk before giving up and going over to the Gadda. I wasn't really looking forward to dealing with more of Ono's liar, liar, pants on fire accusations, but I did want to check out how Farrah was doing now that her house had been properly blessed.

"Hey," she called. She was in the back, fiddling with the mister hose in the produce section. "You mind pulling that other end? I think there's a kink in here somewhere."

I picked up the hose where it was attached to the wall. Sure enough, after Farrah gave it a good tug the spray went from puny to full-out blast. Tiny droplets blew back in her face, clinging to her mass of espresso-brown curls and giving her a sparkling angelic halo.

"I'm getting all wet here," she said, releasing the lever. The water shut off.

She dropped the nozzle and came over to me. Without a word, she encircled me in a tight hug. "My bad for making you drink the green Kool-Aid with Ono about the *kahu*. Are you mad at me?"

My mind flashed back to the dozens of times she'd drunk the Kool-Aid to protect me. One time she'd even endured a brutal beating rather than let the bad guys get me. Ono being perturbed at me was nothing. Besides, with Finn giving me the heave-ho, I'd need Farrah's love and support more than ever.

"No worries. We'll get past this. We always do."

"Ya know, Ono's not really mad at you. He's just totally gonged about how deep a hole we're in, debt-wise. He even asked if I'd be willing to sell the Gadda."

"You can't do that. Besides, who'd buy it?"

She held out her hands, palms up. "Crazy thing is, I get offers all the time. Go figure."

I couldn't deal with the thought. "I'm on my way to pick up Finn."

"You gonna be okay? You want me or Ono to trip down there with you?"

Oh yeah, that's all I needed. A witness to the bloodletting. "Mahalo, but I'm fine. I think we need to some alone time."

"Not a good word, 'alone.' Seems you and your man been spending way too much time alone lately. That's what's brought this on."

I hugged her good-bye and headed to the airport. Farrah was right. Since we'd come back from our honeymoon it seemed Finn and I had been apart more than we'd been together. Would it really be that much different if we split for good?

I parked in the short-term lot and took my time getting across the street to the meeting area at the bottom of the escalators. I watched the people coming down, most everyone grinning and chattering, excited to start their long-awaited vacation. By contrast, the people lining up at TSA to go up the escalator and back to the mainland looked positively morose. Lots of tanned faces but not many smiles.

At last Finn came into sight. My breath always hitched when I saw him. The man was flat-out handsome and I'm not the only one who thinks so. The moving stairs slowly inched down to street level and I sniffed my wrists to see if I could still catch a hint of plumeria. On the stair right below Finn a flight attendant turned and said something to him, her face lighting up when he responded.

They got to the bottom and Finn raised a hand when he glimpsed me in the crowd. He made a last remark to the flight attendant and she looked over at me. For a brief moment I panicked that he'd spent the last few hours regaling her with his plans to end his short marriage. I felt a pinprick of anger at his betrayal but forced my face to stay passive.

"Hey," he said as he threw an arm around my shoulders. "Glad you could make it."

I looked up at him. Was he being sarcastic?

"Where else would I be?"

"No idea. You haven't been answering my calls so I wasn't sure if you'd show."

"It's not like I could call you back."

"Right. But still. No way for me to know what was going on with you."

This wasn't going well. "Hey, but you're here now and I'm glad to see you."

"You as well. Where are you parked?"

His offhand attitude made me feel like a limo driver with a sign. Like I was picking up a total stranger for a hotel drop-off.

"What's going on? You don't seem very happy to be home."

"Oh, I'm happy. If you'd been where I've been and done what I've been doing for the past week you'd be happy, too. I'm just totally trashed with jet-lag."

"Can you tell me anything now that you're back?"

"Not much. But even if I could, it probably wouldn't make much sense until I get a few hours' sleep."

We trudged out to the car and Finn threw his small duffle into the back hatch. He waited at the passenger door, his eyes searching the parking lot as if looking for snipers, while I unlocked the car.

The ride to Hali'imaile was eerily reminiscent of the ride home from the fertility clinic a few weeks earlier. Each of us lost in our private reverie. I assume Finn's jet lag didn't help the situation, but I was eager to get on with it. I hadn't counted on him being tired. Most times he came back raring to go. One more chink in the wall of what a few weeks ago had felt like a solid relationship.

We got home and Finn dragged himself into the bedroom and shut the door. I sat out on the porch for a while but when neighbors began trickling out to meet the kindergarten bus at eleven-thirty I went inside. I didn't want to dodge questions about where Finn had been the past week, and I wasn't in the mood to smile and talk story about their kid's latest cute antic or commiserate with gripes about the county not filling the Upcountry potholes.

At noon Finn got up and rambled into the kitchen. I was sitting alone at the table, trying to decide whether to slap together sandwiches for lunch or make do with the "party food" Steve had left.

Finn went to the sink. "I need some water. Flying all night takes the piss and vinegar right outta you."

I couldn't speak to the piss, but from where I was sitting it seemed he'd displayed plenty of vinegar from the moment I'd picked him up.

I leaned back in my chair. "Are you ready to talk?"

He scowled. "Look. I haven't eaten anything since take-off."

I had no idea where or when take-off had occurred, but chose not to point that out.

He peered into the refrigerator. "Looks like you're stocked up for a party. Wine, beer, fancy olives. Hope I didn't spoil your plans."

That was it. Hungry or not, I wasn't willing to drag the inevitable out any longer.

"Look, Finn. I know why you didn't call. And why you're being like this."

"Like what?"

I threw up a palm. "Like this. Crabby, pissy, even. You want me to pick a fight so you can blow up and stomp out of here. Then you can feel justified in ending our marriage."

He shot me a sour smile. "Look, I don't need to justify anything. I'm way past that."

I couldn't respond. My arms tingled as if I'd narrowly escaped a physical peril. Like when a car coming the other direction swerves at the last minute, avoiding a head-on. My pulse thudded, drowning out Finn's next few words.

"—so what's the point?"

I scrambled to pretend I hadn't spaced out. "The point of what?"

"The point of messing around like this." He sat down across from me. "Look, Pali. I had no idea, okay? I'd never have put us through this if I'd known. I think we should just go our separate ways. Fair dinkum. No harm, no foul."

His handsome face turned ashen, as if he'd opened a vein. He appeared about to collapse.

My brain scrambled to catch up to what was going on. I ticked through a laundry list of possibilities. Maybe Ono had convinced him he could do better than a lying conniving wedding planner, or perhaps during his hush-hush deployment Finn had realized we'd rushed into marriage and he wanted an annulment. What's that old saying, "Marry in haste, repent at leisure"?

He could be rethinking his entire life. Perhaps living in Hawaii didn't agree with him, after all. Finn wasn't built for same ol', same ol'. He craved novelty and adventure as much as, or maybe more than, his older brother. Traveling the world, working a clandestine and seemingly dangerous job didn't jibe with setting up housekeeping on a sleepy backwater island with a woman whose day-to-day chores included sobering up pimply-faced grooms and refereeing cat fights between mothers-of-the-bride and their ex-husband's latest fling.

The clock on the kitchen wall ticked menacingly in the ensuing silence.

He took my hand in both of his and leaned in. "Remember in high school civics when the founding fathers claimed a slave only counted as three-fives of a man?"

What? The abrupt change of subject rattled me as if he'd left and slammed the door behind him.

"I don't remember that."

"Maybe they didn't dwell on it in Hawaii schools. But I was raised in the South where it was a big deal."

I shook my head. I had no idea where he was going with this and wasn't eager to get into a civil rights discussion while the love of my life was about to kick me to the curb.

"Well, that's how I feel, Pali."

I snapped to attention. Had I heard correctly? Was this actually about us?

"What're you saying?"

"I'm saying my failure to give you children is a burden you shouldn't have to bear. It makes me less than a man. And you deserve a whole man. So, I'm prepared to give you a divorce. I considered annulment but the lawyer I talked to said divorce is actually easier."

"You want a divorce?"

"Not really. But I don't want you resenting me, either. Face it. I've seen how you look at Farrah's kids. In the long run, it's best we part ways before it's too late."

"Best for who?"

His mouth twitched into a boyish grin. "I believe the correct word is 'whom.'"

"Seriously? You're correcting my grammar while you break my heart?"

"That's not my intention. But we can't go on like this. Believe me, you'll thank me down the road."

I swiped a hand across my cheek and was startled it came away wet.

He stood and came around the table, placing his hands on my shoulders. "I've got a meeting in Lahaina at two. You don't need to hire a lawyer unless you feel you need to. I'm proposing we just go back to the way things were."

I snuffed up a trickle that had nearly made it from nose to lip. "Sit down, Finn."

"What for?"

"I heard you out. The least you can do is provide me the same courtesy."

He shambled back to the other side of the table and pulled out the chair, angling it so he wouldn't have to look me in the eye.

Again, I swiped at my face, but it was like trying to hold back the tide. "I appreciate how you feel. But I'm stunned by your cave man solution."

"I just think—"

"No, your turn's over. Now you listen."

He slumped lower in the chair, but kept quiet.

"We took vows, remember? In sickness and health, right? We haven't even talked about this. You've spent the past few years in Australia, a place where men sweat and women 'glow,' but give me a break. I'm not sure I even want kids. I thought *you* did. That's why I went to the clinic with you. But if that's not going to happen, are you telling me the only reason you married me was to have kids?"

"Of course not."

"Then, why did you?"

He crossed his arms. "You know why."

"I thought I did. Now I'm not so sure. Give me three reasons you asked me to marry you."

He shrugged. I felt like I was back in hostage negotiation class.

The clock ticked but I refused to look away.

"Um. Okay. Well, I thought you were lovely." The Aussie accent was back, big-time. "And we have fun together. I mean, it seemed you'd be fun to grow old with." He cleared his throat. "What's with this cross examination? This is stupid. If we can't be a family, what's the point?"

This time I got up and went around the table. I knelt at his side, but he kept his face turned away. "We *are* a family, Finn. We're more than that. We're *'ohana*. We've got Farrah's kids in our lives. I'm their god-mother and you're their favorite uncle."

"Yeah, but—"

"I'm sorry you won't get the chance to be a dad, 'cuz you'd be a great one. But we have a great life and I'm going to fight for it. Go ahead with your meeting in Lahaina.

But tell that lawyer of yours that getting a divorce from me won't be a slam dunk. No way I'm going to make it easy."

He turned and met my gaze. Bloodshot eyes, pale cheeks and sweaty upper lip. Good. I'd have been a lot more nervous if he'd appeared calm and composed.

"Really?"

"'til death do us part, dude. No do-overs."

He went to the living room to call and cancel his meeting. As I strained to eavesdrop, it occurred to me neither of us had mentioned the word "love."

25

I'm pleased to report Steve would've considered the afternoon a proper welcome home lovefest. We spent most of it in bed. Every now and then Finn would pad to the kitchen to retrieve something from the refrigerator. He hauled back a small wheel of brie we ate with our fingers, followed by a container of almond-stuffed olives and a box of seriously under-salted crackers we used to make tiny cold cut sandwiches with greasy mortadella and dry salami from the Gadda deli.

By five p.m. the bed looked like a high school cafeteria after a food fight. Little dabs of cheese littered the covers, along with fragrant oil smudges on the sheets and bits of cracker everywhere. I got up to use the bathroom and Finn laughed at my retreating form.

"Check it out when you get in there. You've got an entire cracker stuck to your back."

I didn't care about any of it. The messy bed, my tender but happy "lady parts," or our still unresolved—or at least unspoken—decision on how we'd go forward. Nothing mattered except Finn was home and our marriage no longer in peril.

At about six we took a shower together. It was tight in the shower-over-tub contraption in the master bath. The shower curtain kept sucking in and sticking to us as we took turns standing under the stream. Finn gently lathered me, and I returned the favor. When the hot water cooled to tepid we still didn't get out, instead clinging to each other as if we finally became aware of how close we'd come to never enjoying this again.

Once out of the shower we dallied, not even bothering to get dressed until I remembered Steve could come home at any moment.

"Sorry, but I didn't get a precise ETA from him. Hopefully he'll call before barging in, but you never know."

"It's okay. I'm pretty much over the jet lag. I think I'll throw on some shorts and go see Ono. He must be dying to know how things went."

I leaned against his naked chest, suddenly possessive. "Don't go."

"I'll only be gone a few minutes."

"I know. But not yet, okay?"

I leaned back to look at him and he shot me a slow smile. "Okay. But you're asking a lot of a guy who's just flown four thousand miles."

I stared into his lapis blue eyes. The whites were still bloodshot from his long flight but the color never failed to startle me. I recalled when I'd first met him and I'd wondered if he was wearing colorized contact lenses. Smiling at my originally passing him off as a vain "pretty boy" I gave him a quick kiss.

"Ready to tell me where you've been bunking this past week?"

He shrugged. "You know the line."

"If you tell me, you gotta kill me?"

"Something like that."

"Well, at least I'd go in peace." I kept the smile going for a few more seconds, then sucked in a breath. "It's not easy staying behind. I worry, you know."

"Believe me, it's no picnic for me, either."

"There's life after government service. I'm living proof."

"And so you are." He wrapped his solid arms around me and squeezed. "So, Ms. Private Sector, may I have your permission to take a quick trip to Pa'ia to give my regards to my worried brother?"

"Of course." My pulse hitched. "But don't believe everything he says, okay?"

He put his hands on my shoulders and stepped back as if appraising me. "Funny. That's what he said about you."

* * *

Finn came back an hour later. I'd used the time to tidy up the bedroom and make myself presentable. When he pulled in I was on the front porch, in an ancient ladder-back rocker Steve had picked up at a yard sale. The inky night sported only the first twinkling of a few stars.

"How'd it go?"

He pulled me into a warm embrace. "About how you'd expect. What's the deal about you getting in the middle of this witch doctor thing?"

"It was a misunderstanding. And the guy isn't a witch doctor. He's a *kahu*. When Ono and Farrah moved into their house they forgot to get it blessed. Then Farrah started seeing a ghost in the back yard and she freaked out. I helped them hire the guy."

Finn plopped down in a chair next to the rocker and I resumed my seat. "I hear the dude didn't come cheap."

"A thousand bucks."

"I also hear that not only didn't he come cheap, he didn't come at all."

I hung my head. "He finally showed up. But it was after I'd lied to Ono."

"Hey, you did the right thing. Maybe not the lying part, but I prob'ly would've done the same thing under the circumstances. But we've got to get on the same page with this money lending stuff, don't you think?"

"I know. I'm sorry about throwing away money like that. But you were gone and Farrah was so worried about the kids. I couldn't say 'no.'"

"Yeah, that's number four."

"What?"

"Remember when you asked me to give you three reasons I wanted to marry you? Well, your soft heart is number four, followed by number five which is your inability to say 'no.'"

"I say 'no' all the time."

He grinned. "Not to me, you don't."

He leaned in and gave me a soft kiss.

I took his hand. "We're going to get through this not having kids thing, aren't we?"

"I hope so. I also hope you won't resent it when I hit middle age and want to buy a red sports car."

"No problem. As long as you make sure to get two sets of keys."

I let a few seconds of silence go by. "You know, you never said you married me because you love me."

He slowly turned toward me. "Right. Well, that sort of goes without saying, don't you think?"

"I think I need to hear it now and then."

"Duly noted. As do I."

"I love you, Finn."

"And I love you, Pali. But here's the rub. I think love is a decision, not a feeling. Way after all the squishy stuff is gone, I'll love you. Every day I'll wake up and make the choice to love you until I draw my last breath. You can count on it. If you need me to remind you I will. But trust me, I don't need to remind myself."

We watched the moon slide toward the looming bulk of Haleakala. More stars appeared, first one at a time and then clusters, like popcorn popping over an open flame. I felt enveloped in the velvety warmth of a Maui mid-summer night.

"You hungry?"

"For food? No. Are you?"

"Not really."

After what could've been as little as ten minutes or as much as half an hour, the quiet was broken by my phone chiming inside the house.

"You need to get that?"

"I'll check it later."

Finn reached over and laid a hand on my thigh. "You want to talk about what's going on with Doug Kanekoa? Ono caught me up on what happened and I couldn't believe you hadn't said anything about it."

"I'm sorry. I guess I've been so worried about our marriage blowing up, I had to set aside my feelings about Lani's death."

"Is it true Doug's the primary suspect?"

I blew out a breath. "Yeah, at this point he's the *only* suspect. But that may change. I want to show you something I found in his office."

* * *

I retrieved the bloody envelope from where I'd hidden it in the magazine. We sat at the kitchen table. The overhead light seemed too bright after the comforting darkness of the porch, but I wanted Finn to get the full impact of the letter's message without having to strain to read it.

My attempts at covering up my racing pulse and churning stomach were dashed when my hand shook as I pulled the single piece of paper from the creased and mottled envelope.

Finn grimaced and pointed to the rust-colored spatter. "What's that?"

"Blood."

"I was afraid you were going to say that."

I glanced at the writing, but handed it over before reading it one more time. It'd be rude to keep him waiting, and besides, I'd practically memorized the whole thing. I couldn't keep myself from re-reading it over his shoulder, though. The note was on plain white paper, the kind you buy by the ream for a copy machine. The precise handwriting was in blue ballpoint pen.

Ku'uipo,

> *Forgive me for leaving so soon. And forgive my decision. I made it look like a break-in to make it easy on you. I can't do this anymore. Sorry for the mess.*

> *I love you. I know you are mad at me, but I need your help. Don't tell DJ and Maia what happened. I love them and don't want them to think bad of me. I'm committing a mortal sin and I will face God for it but please don't burden our keiki. I don't want them to think I didn't love them enough. Pray for me. When we got married, you promised to love and honor me forever. Please honor me now.*

Your Leilani

Finn turned his head and looked at me. "Oh. My. God."

"Yeah."

"She killed herself?"

My voice was thick. "Looks that way."

"How?"

"It seems she shot herself."

"And he's taking the fall?"

"Yep."

"Why?"

"Why what? Why'd she kill herself, or why did he confess?"

He held up his palms. "Well, both."

I pulled out a chair and sat down. "Here's my theory so far. I think Lani must've had some kind of medical problem. A *serious* medical problem. Doug mentioned she'd been regularly disappearing and then lying about it. He followed her one day and the GPS showed she went to that clinic by the hospital."

"The GPS? I wouldn't think Doug's old Jeep would have that."

"It doesn't. But when I visited him in jail I—"

"Whoa, wait right there. You went to the jail?"

"Yeah, with James, Doug's brother. He's a lawyer and he's representing him."

Finn shook his head as if trying to dislodge water from his ear. "Okay, okay. You need to start at the beginning. Sheesh. I leave for a few days and all hell breaks loose."

I filled him in, backtracking to when Doug told me he thought Lani was having an affair and his plans to secretly surveil her. I recapped how he'd acted nonchalant the next day, as if he'd changed his mind, and how on the weekend of Lani's death they'd fought and he'd farmed the kids out to the neighbor.

Finn crossed his arms. "Wait a sec. They had a fight? Maybe this letter is bogus. Maybe Doug killed her and concocted this letter to cover it up."

"Have you ever seen Sifu Doug's handwriting?"

"No."

"Well, I have. The guy can barely print. Even his signature is undecipherable."

"So? Maybe he had someone else write it for him."

"Remember that old saw about two people can keep a secret if one of them is dead? And besides, Doug would never ask someone to do something like this to save his own skin."

"Maybe you don't know the guy as well as you think."

I bit back a harsh retort. After years of unbridled loyalty to my *sifu*, my go-to response was to always shield him from attack. But Finn had a point. Maybe this suicide note was part of an elaborate scheme. And I was being played.

"I don't know what to think. But this looks like Lani's handwriting. And she loves her kids so much it's understandable she wouldn't want them to think she killed herself. You know, kids don't get over stuff like that."

Finn looked at the kitchen clock. "You wanna hit the sack?"

"You're ready for another round?"

He laughed. "Nah, you're safe there. But I'm tired and I've got a feeling we'll both be awake long before daybreak."

26

Finn was right, of course. It wasn't so much that I woke up early as I never went to sleep in the first place. The time I spent tossing and turning became a long series of what-ifs; my mind playing various scenarios like movie trailers, complete with the booming voice of that guy who always starts by saying, "In a world where..."

Did Lani end her own life or did she ask Doug to shoot her? Or, God forbid, had he murdered her and then fabricated the note he'd ordered me to find in his office? One place to start would be to find out which doctor's office Lani had visited the day Doug followed her. I'd have to come up with a plan. No use going door-to-door at the clinic asking if she was a patient. Thanks to federal HIPAA laws I'd be greeted with a blank stare or a pointed finger ordering me to leave the premises.

One small consolation was the alleged suicide note had put to rest the theory that Lani had been killed during a bungled home invasion. The note referenced Lani and Doug's children by name, not to mention it was nearly a full page long. Not typical of a drug-addled burglar trying to cover his tracks. But had she shot herself, or convinced him to do it for her?

As much as it pained me to admit my *sifu* could be so cold-blooded, I had to add a third possibility to the mix. In the heat of yet another vicious fight, had Doug shot Lani and then concocted a suicide note to cover it up? His everyday scribbling could be hiding the fact that although he'd had the same nun-based education she'd had, he'd chosen to put it behind him. Until now.

Which led me back to my wanting to find out where she'd gone the day he followed her. I had a feeling in order to get to the bottom of the how and why Lani had died, I'd need to determine motive. If Lani's final trip to Kahului had been to a gynecologist to be treated for a sexually-transmitted disease it'd throw a whole different light on things than if she'd been told she had a heart defect.

Before I headed out I left a note for Finn, signed with a little heart. Okay, that's not my usual MO, signing stuff with hearts, but I was in a mushy mood. I'd spent the last week fretting about being dumped by the man I loved so I figured a little schoolgirl sentimentality was in order.

I drove down to my shop. I considered going next door to fill Farrah in on the latest developments but figured I wasn't ready for it to be all over town. Farrah was always quick with a "pinkie-swear," but she was equally quick to break it if Ono played the spouse card.

I fiddled around at the shop until eight o'clock when I called James. Not revealing this bombshell to Doug's lawyer was unfair, even though I was still unsure how much I was willing to share.

"I finally got a chance to clean out Doug's drawer," I said.

"And?"

"I found what appears to be a suicide note."

"What?" He yelled so loud I had to pull the phone away from my ear. "How long have you known this?"

"It took me a while to find it." I mentally patted myself on the back for the quick, and relatively truthful, save.

"But Doug sent you there almost a week ago. Don't tell me it's taken *six days*."

"As you know, there were complications. I didn't see it at first, and then—"

He cut me off. "Enough with the excuses. Where is it?"

"I've got it here in my shop."

"Great. You find material evidence of Doug's innocence that should've been turned over to me immediately, and you're keeping it in an insecure location where it could get damaged or stolen at any moment. Tell me, Pali, are you nuts or just stupid?"

I chose not to respond.

"Who else has seen it?"

"Uh, pretty much nobody."

He blew out a breath. "Doug trusted you. He even trusted you over me, his attorney. And now you pull a stunt like this? You better hope the court will allow the note into evidence."

"But Doug doesn't want it made public." I was already regretting my decision to bring James up to speed.

"Too bad. My job is to defend my client. Stay right where you are, Pali. I'll be there in ten minutes."

The phone went dead. I'm sure he was wishing we'd been talking on a landline so he could've slammed the receiver down with a bang.

I hurried over to the Gadda. Farrah had put in a little business corner up front with a fax, a high-tech copier and scanner. I had an ancient copier at my shop but the note was too important to trust to last-century technology.

I slipped in the front door and headed straight to the copier. Farrah was in back, deeply involved in "talking story" with a regular, so I hoped I'd be able to get in and out without being seen.

No luck.

"Hey, Pali. How you doin'?" Timo, a big local guy who worked at the Pa'ia Fish Market came in and lumbered over. He leaned in, making no attempt to conceal his effort to read over my shoulder. I'm sure he would've comped me a fish sandwich if I'd willingly offered to let him see the note.

I flashed him a quick smile but kept quiet.

"So, what you got there?"

"Just a client contract. They need it right away."

"Why don't you email it?

"It's signed in blue ink. Besides, I don't have a scanner at my place."

He pondered my reply for a few seconds. "You know, you can jus' take a pic with your phone and send it. Works the same."

In that moment I wished I'd thought of that. If word got out about the note, Doug's control over its contents would be history.

"Say, Timo, what's this I hear about your mom winning that banana bread contest?" Luckily, I remembered a photo I'd seen in the *Maui News* of his generously-proportioned mother beaming as she held a brick-size banana bread with a ribbon stuck to it.

"Oh yeah. Tha' was ages ago. For Mom's Day, eh? She was way proud of dat. Her sister not talk to her since."

I chuckled. "Sounds like a little sibling rivalry."

"Nuthin' *little* 'bout it. You hear 'bout that show, 'Cake Wars'? Well, in our *'ohana* we got 'Banana Bread Wars.' Those two been talkin' trash for years."

I patted his beefy arm and was rewarded with a wide smile.

"See ya around," he said. He shuffled back to the candy and cookie aisle, leaving me free to resume my secretarial duties.

"Hey, girl. I didn't see you come in." Farrah had sneaked up behind me.

I whirled around, slamming the lid on the copier.

"Hey, take it easy on the gear, girl. The repair dude was jus' out here."

"Is it broken?"

"Wasn't a minute ago..." She reached over to lift the lid but I flattened my palm against it.

"What're you doin? I jus' want to make sure it's okay."

"It's fine. I'm kind of in a hurry, Farrah."

"What's the matter with you? You still got beef with me 'cuz of the *kahu* thing? I already told you it's my bad. I was in a tight place with Ono, eh."

"Sorry. I'm late for a meeting with James, Sifu Doug's lawyer."

"Yeah, what's happenin' with that?"

"Not much. He's hoping I found something at the *guan*, but I'm afraid he's going to be disappointed."

She scowled at the copier, then said, "Talkin' about bummed out, how'd it go you're your man Finn?"

"It's good."

"Fo' real?"

"Yeah. We're good."

"What'd he say about asking Ono about a divorce lawyer?"

"Ah, that. It was a misunderstanding. I guess a guy who works with Finn is having wife troubles."

"The guy live here on Maui? What's his name?" Farrah's got an equal opportunity gossip policy. Even if she's barely heard of you, your personal life is fair game.

"Finn didn't say, but I don't think it's anybody we know."

"How you know that? I got a ton a' people comin' in day in and day out." She looked perturbed.

This is why I hate lying. It takes a lot of energy to keep the lie going, and I'm not very creative in coming up with believable stuff. Besides, James was probably already outside my door, expecting me to hand over the note that was trapped under the lid of the scanner.

"Would you do me a favor? I haven't had a thing to eat this morning and I'm starving. Would you mind grabbing me a mango yogurt while I finish up here? Like I said, I'm really late."

Farrah flashed me a "you owe me" look before heading back to the dairy case. I swiftly fed quarters into the machine and pushed the Copy button. After much grinding and whirring the machine spit out two pieces of paper which I snatched up, folded, and stuffed in my beach bag purse.

I paid for my yogurt and went out the back door. Time for show and tell.

* * *

Once I was back at my shop I pulled out my phone and took two fast snaps of the note before unlocking the front door. Sure enough, James was standing there with a surly look on his face.

"Isn't it bad enough you're withholding evidence? Now you keep me waiting for nearly ten minutes. My time is valuable, you know. At my hourly rate you just burned through about fifty bucks."

I apologized and offered to make a fresh pot of coffee. He declined, taking a seat across from my desk.

"This isn't a social call, Ms. Moon."

I slid the creased suicide note across the desk and waited while he read it.

He blew out a breath. "I'm speechless. And that's not something we lawyers easily admit. How long have you had this in your possession?"

"Not long."

"Could you be more specific?"

"I'd rather not. But I haven't shared this with anyone but you and my husband."

"Your husband? Where does he figure in this?"

"He doesn't. But I needed to talk to a neutral party. And he's about as neutral as they come."

"Please tell me he's not a reporter or a cop."

"He's not. He works for the government, in military intelligence."

James barked a staccato laugh. "An oxymoron if I ever heard one."

I didn't join in his mirth. "He has a top secret clearance, and he just got home from working overseas messing with the cyber capabilities of our enemies. So laugh all you want. The guy's an unsung hero as far as I'm concerned."

James pulled back his grin. "Yeah, well, bully for him. But that still doesn't take away from the fact that you should've handed this over to me as soon as you found it. By the way, I'm assuming this came from that stash drawer Doug wanted you to clean out."

"It did."

James stood. "I need to get this in front of the judge. If Leilani committed suicide, they'll have to release him."

I stood. "Whoa, not so fast. Don't you think you should talk with Doug?"

He glanced at the note, then at me. "Why? This is clearly a suicide note. It needs to be shared with the cops and the judge. As soon as this gets authenticated, it'll be game over."

"But don't you see the problem? Doug doesn't want you to take it to the judge. He's honoring her wish that no one learns she killed herself, especially her kids."

"Frankly, I don't care what either one of them wants. This is a question of justice. If Leilani Kanekoa took her own life, there's no way I'm going to sit back and let him take the fall. We're talking a life sentence here, Pali. No hope of parole."

"I know. But it's Doug's life, not yours. What about attorney-client privilege?"

"What about it? My brother isn't thinking straight. I appreciate him wanting to go along with his dead wife's request, but this is too much. Besides, if I don't place this evidence before the court I'll be guilty of obstruction of justice. That's a fast road to disbarment."

"Look, all I'm asking is that you talk to Doug before you do anything."

He looked down. When he looked up again, he shook his head. "Sorry. No can do. Every minute I stall I dig the hole a little deeper. Pretty soon, there'll be no way to crawl out."

"Just give me a day, James. Schedule a time for us to see Doug in jail and I'll take it from there."

"Look, I know you mean well, but you're way off base, Pali. I gotta go." He started for the door.

I crossed my arms. "James, do yourself a favor and don't take that note to the judge."

He waved the note at me. "Sorry. There's nothing you can say that will change my mind."

"I'm pretty sure there is."

He squinted at me like a dog waiting for his master to throw the Frisbee.

I stepped between him and the door. "What you've got there will never be authenticated."

"Says you."

"No, says the state-of-the-art color copier it came out of."

27

James stomped out in a whirl of fury. Before his departure he spent a few minutes threatening, then cajoling, me to hand over the original note but I stood fast. At one point I was a bit concerned he was about to resort to physical violence, but one of the upsides of having a black belt in martial arts is I'm supremely confident I can take almost anyone. As long as they don't have a weapon. If they're armed, my confidence shrinks to simply betting I'll be able to escape.

I went out back and hopped in the Mini. Next stop, Walmart. I'm not a loyal Walmart customer since I have mixed feelings about the big box behemoth they built in Kahului. On one hand, the store has brought low prices for thousands of things that were either unavailable or ridiculously expensive in our little corner of the world. On the other hand, it's put more than a few local retail outlets out of business. Thus, I pick and choose what I will and will not purchase there.

One thing nearly every local buys at Walmart is prescriptions. The prices are so much lower than anywhere else on the island it's laughable. I don't take a lot of pills besides a few supplements now and then, but when Farrah was pregnant with the twins she told me her prenatal vitamins were half the cost at the big retailer compared to the drugstores in Makawao or Wailuku.

I got in line at the Walmart pharmacy drop off window and waited while the woman in front of me tried to wheedle a refill on painkillers. There's a six-foot "privacy space" between the customer being served and the next person in line, but six feet is simply not adequate when the customer is bellowing at the top of her lungs at the weary clerk perched behind the sliding glass window.

"But I'm in *pain*! Can't you see? My doctor told me if I came here you'd fix me up."

I thought that last part sounded suspiciously like a clean-cut tourist trying to coax a reluctant *pakalolo* dealer to sell him some weed, but I averted my eyes and kept my mouth shut. After all, I was in the "privacy space" and wasn't supposed to have overheard any of it.

The clerk finally handed the woman off to the pharmacist at the "consultation" window. She probably figured since his professional status meant he made five times what she did she'd let him earn it.

I stepped up to the window. The clerk shot me a thin smile as if hoping I wouldn't turn out to be another junkie trying to con her out of narcotics.

"*Aloha.* I hope you can help me," I began.

The smile dimmed.

I soldiered on. "I picked up a prescription here a couple of weeks ago and lost my receipt. I was wondering if I could get a copy."

She squinted as if trying to recall my face.

"For insurance purposes," I said. "If I don't provide a receipt, they won't pay me back for it."

She seemed to take that at face value. "What's the name of the drug?"

"I'm afraid I can't recall. Besides, you've got to have a degree in chemistry to pronounce most of these things, right?"

She appeared to be warming to my dilemma. "Okay, then what's your name?"

"Leilani Kanekoa." I was about to provide Lani's Pukalani address, but held back. Hopefully, the clerk wasn't a big local news fan, but even casual watchers might recall the name if they'd heard anything about the murder in Pukalani.

"Birthday?"

I rattled off Lani's birthday. It was easy to remember since it fell on the Fourth of July, and she and Sifu Doug were born the same year. The clerk typed the information in her computer, peering at the screen as if trying to find Waldo in a cartoon drawing of a crowd.

"Oh, wow," she said. "I can see why you'd want to put a claim in on this one."

I nodded in solidarity, even though I had no idea what she was referring to.

Behind her, a dot-matrix printer began spitting out paper. "Hold on. I'm afraid it's got to do the whole thing. It won't let me just print a receipt."

I waited. After nearly half a minute, she gathered up the pages, tore them along the perforated edges and stapled them together. Then she folded the thick sheaf in half and slid it across the window ledge with a tepid smile.

"*Mahalo* for shopping at Walmart," she said. In a softer voice she added, "And God bless."

I thanked her and slipped the papers into my bag. I didn't want to appear eager to peruse the documents since supposedly I already knew what they said.

I speed-walked out of the store and didn't allow myself to take a deep breath until I was in my car with the doors locked.

* * *

My Walmart run had provided me with everything I needed to move forward. I went back to my shop and got to work on the computer. It took seconds to look up the name of the doctor on Lani's prescription and his medical specialty. Another few seconds yielded the uses and side effects of the extremely expensive drug she'd been prescribed.

Armed with this new information, the rest of the puzzle began to fall neatly in place. Now the question was what I should do about it.

One of Sifu Doug's favorite quotes was from Albert Einstein. "Those who have the privilege to know have the duty to act." Doug was referring to our responsibility as trained fighters to not allow bullying or criminal acts to go unanswered. But how would he feel about this?

My morning of snooping had left me with a pretty good idea what'd gone on in the Kanekoa's garage a week earlier, including how and why it happened. I also knew Doug loved his wife in a way most women could only imagine. From the looks of things he was willing to lie and take the fall for her desperate final decision even beyond "'til death do us part."

I'd been taught to value truth above all else. And yet, now my *sifu*, the father of two young motherless kids, was facing the rest of his life in prison.

28

Visiting an inmate at the Wailuku jail isn't a simple walk-in process. Late in the day I called to make an appointment for Wednesday and was advised only family members and legal representatives were allowed in for the first thirty days or until an inmate fills out a visitation list. Then the clerk advised me that no, Douglas Kanekoa hadn't made such a list.

That left me with a dilemma. Should I call James and beg him to reinstate me as his paralegal? If I did, I'd have to tell him what I knew. The result would be disastrous. But I couldn't move forward until I had a chance to talk with Sifu Doug and since I wasn't a family member—even I draw the line at trying to single-handedly lie my way into a locked facility—the only way I was going to be able to talk to him was to go with James.

I pondered a possible negotiation. James was still angry with me so I had to hope he was more concerned about freeing his client than teaching me a lesson.

I called his office and his secretary put me through. "James, it's Pali Moon. Don't hang up." No sound came from the other end.

"Okay, I realize you're probably still pretty ticked with me, and I want to apologize. I wasn't intentionally keeping information from you. I was just trying to figure out what it all meant and what I should do."

"It's *my* job to figure out how to produce evidence to the court, not yours."

"Yeah, well about that." I went on to explain my idea. James and I would meet with Doug to see what he wanted me to do with the suicide note. I was pretty sure I knew the answer, but there was no way to know if perhaps a week in jail had faded Doug's resolve.

"I don't care what he wants," James said. "There's no way I'm going to let a client of mine go down for a murder he didn't commit. We've got a bona fide suicide note."

It was a good thing we were talking by phone and not in person. James wouldn't have appreciated my eye roll at his use of the word, "We."

"But it's still unclear who pulled the trigger."

No comment.

"Look, James. I've got something you want, and you've got something I want. How about we work out a deal? Can I come over?"

He agreed and I drove to his office. It was late in the day. When I walked in, his assistant was packing up her purse looking eager to head home.

She scowled at me, then went to his office door. "You need me to stay, Mr. Kanekoa?"

"Mahalo, Irene, but no. Go home. And tell that no-good husband of yours I'm all in for the Warriors by six against Boise State this year."

Fat chance, I thought. The University of Hawaii Rainbow Warriors football team fought hard for every point but often came up short. Especially against a powerhouse rival like the Boise State University Broncos.

James waved me in and I took a seat. He offered me coffee or a soft drink as if this were a casual consultation but I could spot a "tell" when I saw one. He was nervous.

"So, Pali. What brings you here?" As if we hadn't spoken less than ten minutes earlier.

"Save the idle talk story chit-chat for your paying clients, James. You knew perfectly well why I'm here."

"Fine then. You go first."

In my Homeland Security hostage negotiation class the number one rule was to never mediate an unknown. That is, don't offer anything until the suspect tells you what he or she wants. The reason is simple: if you offer a million bucks and a plane to Cuba and all the suspect wants is immunity from the death penalty, you lose. Big time.

"Okay, let's discuss the situation," I said. "I've got a piece of evidence that will certainly clear your client. All I want in return is a few minutes of face-to-face time with him."

"But the suicide note isn't irrefutable proof of who pulled the trigger."

"True. But it shines a whole new light on motive."

James shot me a sardonic smile. "You missed your calling, Ms. Moon. You should've gone to law school." His reverting back to using my surname signaled he wasn't going to make this easy.

"I have a degree in Criminology, so I tend to look at things from the other side of the courtroom than you do, Mr. Kanekoa. If I'd gone to law school I'd have become a prosecutor."

"Nothing wrong with that. I love a good fight."

We stared at each other for a few seconds. He blinked first.

"Look, Pali, I've got to get home. My wife's got dinner ready. So why don't you just tell me what it's going to take to get you to hand over the original note."

"I never said I'd hand it over. I said I needed a few minutes with Doug in order to decide what to do with it."

His eyes narrowed. "I've had just about enough of your games. You know I could go to the police right now and show them the copy. One call to a judge and you'd be relinquishing the original or facing obstruction charges."

"Yeah, but what about your client? Are you willing to risk your brother hating you for the rest of your life for betraying his confidence?"

He leaned back in his chair. "This feels a lot like extortion."

"Nothing of the kind. All I'm asking for is ten minutes."

He swiveled his chair to gaze out his office window. "First thing tomorrow. Same rules as last time." He paused a moment and said, "And shut the door on your way out."

It was the first time James and I hadn't shaken hands or hugged upon parting. But then, I'd gotten my "get into jail free" card so I wasn't about to stand on ceremony.

* * *

Finn listened patiently as I recalled the scenario over dinner. He'd picked up a pizza and I nibbled on a piece as I did my best to remember James' exact words.

"This is no piece of piss, is it?" Finn often fell back on Aussie slang when the situation warranted. What he'd said was the dilemma I faced was complicated.

"Yeah, it's tough. If Doug sticks to his guns I've got to respect it. But what he's doing is wrong."

He looked pensive. "You think she shot herself or she asked him to do it?"

"Does it matter? Either way she's dead."

"I think it matters a lot," he said. "If she took her own life and he had nothing to do with it, then he's completely innocent. If he popped her, then he's probably at least guilty of manslaughter."

I chewed on that thought for a moment. "True. But how will I find out what really happened?"

"Can't help you there, love. But one thing I know is if anyone can get to the bottom of it, it's you."

When we went to bed that night Finn dropped off to sleep as soon as his head hit the pillow. I, on the other hand, spent more hours than I'd like to admit fretting over what I'd say to Doug in the morning. Although it was good to know Finn had faith in me, it ratcheted up my stress level. Was he right? Was I seriously the only person standing between Doug and a life in prison? If I failed, chances were I'd never get a good night's sleep again.

29

James pulled up in front of my office and I dashed out the door to meet him. No sense making him park and come in since I was already banking on him being in a cranky mood.

As I slid into the passenger seat he growled, "You're not even going to offer me a cup of coffee?"

"Oh, sorry. Would you like me to make some? I thought you'd want to get this over with."

"That's the problem with you, Ms. Moon. You think too much."

I let that roll around in my head for a moment but didn't reply.

The ride to Wailuku seemed to take forever since neither of us spoke. The traffic was bad. Every now and then James would mutter curse words under his breath at left-hand turners who held up the line, or a motorcycle who'd zipped in and out between the cars like an annoying housefly.

We parked and he got out, pulling his briefcase from the back seat before locking the car.

"You can't take that in with you, you know," I said.

He glared. "How'd I ever manage to practice law before you came into my life?"

"I didn't mean to nit-pick. I just thought maybe you'd forgotten."

"There you go thinking again."

I straightened my shoulders and followed him inside. We went through the tedious admittance process: handing over ID, stashing our belongings, getting patted down and walking through a metal detector, before being escorted to a room painted the color of pea soup.

James gestured toward a chair on the near side of the metal table and I sat.

"Do you think they purposely chose this color?" I pointed at the wall. "Or do you think they just threw a bunch of old paint together to save money?"

The look he shot me could've etched glass.

Luckily, a metal door on the opposite side clanked open and a guard escorted Sifu Doug inside. He was wearing hand-cuffs and leg irons, which seemed excessive to me given the circumstances. He kept his gaze lowered, either in deference or humiliation, as the guard put a hand on his shoulder to lower him into the chair opposite us.

The guard barked a few rules, which were clearly posted on a sign inside the room, and then left.

"*Aloha*, Sifu," I said.

Doug brought his head up. The look on his face seemed to say he was surprised to see me.

"*Aloha*, Pali."

"I asked James to bring me here today so I could talk to you."

Doug shifted his gaze briefly to James, but then settled it back on me.

"Did you do what I asked?"

"I did. That's why I'm here."

"Have you shared it with anyone else?" Doug seemed to be patently avoiding his brother's presence.

"Only James and Finn. And I have Finn's word it will go no further."

He glanced back and forth from James to me. "Which of you has the item in question in their possession?"

"I do, Sifu."

"Good. I want it to stay that way."

James scowled but kept quiet.

Doug turned his attention to his brother. "I'd like a few minutes alone with Pali."

"We've been through this before, bro. I'm the attorney of record. If I leave, she leaves."

Doug hung his head as if considering his options. "Fine. But from this point on, I'm speaking to you as my brother and not my lawyer. Are we clear?"

James nodded.

"You read Lani's letter, so you probably have a good idea of what happened."

This time we both nodded.

"I love her as much as anyone can love someone, you know that, right? Her last wish was that the kids never know what she did so this is how I want it handled."

James leaned in. "But what about DJ and Maia? They're barely teenagers. They need you."

"I've thought of that. And that's why I'm going to have you draw up a custody agreement for me. I want them to live with Kaili."

"That's not how it works, man. If you're incarcerated the court will decide where they live, not you. And there's a good chance they'll be put in foster care. They'll be split up and bounced around the system like three-day-old fish. They'll think their dad killed their mom and how do you think that'll go down? My money's on DJ becoming a thug and Maia sleeping with any dude who'll give her a little attention."

Doug's expression hardened. James was laying it on a little thick, but I had to agree.

In a softer voice, James said, "You're not in charge here, bro. If you don't listen to me, your entire 'ohana will blow up. You in prison, your kids in foster homes, your sisters and brothers conveniently forgetting to visit you or include your kids in 'ohana events like birthdays or Christmas. This lie isn't worth it, man."

Doug chewed his bottom lip. "But I want to do right by her."

"I know you do."

We sat in silence for a few seconds before the guard poked his head in and barked, "It's time for my break. You done in here?"

Doug sent me a pleading look.

"I can't see any way around this, Sifu," I said. "You're going to have to let me give it to them."

"Correction," said James. "Tell her to give it to me."

Doug hung his head and gave a barely perceptible shake. "Sorry, bro. I can't."

The guard entered and stood behind Sifu Doug. "Time's up. Any last words?"

Doug got up from the table, chains clinking. As he shuffled out, he didn't look back.

* * *

"That certainly screws the pooch," James growled as we pulled out of the jail parking lot. "But here's the deal. I took an oath to uphold the laws of the state of Hawaii and to provide the best legal counsel I can. There was no mention of going along with every stupid thing a client wants me to do."

"What are you saying?"

"I'm saying my brother doesn't get the last word on withholding evidence." He paused and looked over at me. "And neither do you."

"Didn't we already have this conversation?"

"We did. But there's no way I'm going along with this."

"We both know Doug pretty well. If you go against him, he'll never forgive you. Your 'ohana will be forced to choose sides."

"So be it. I lose either way."

For the rest of the ride back to Pa'ia we said little, each lost in our own thoughts and what-ifs. He pulled in front of my shop and stopped. As I got out I said, "Can you give me until tomorrow?"

"What for? It's not gonna get any easier. In fact, the cops and the court are already going to censure me for not being forthcoming. I seriously don't need it to slide into 'obstruction' territory."

"It'll be on me, not you. I'll testify I didn't find the note until today. Or better yet, I'll have you draft me an affidavit to sign."

"Great. We can add 'endorsing perjury' to my disbarment violations."

"Just one more day, James. If I don't have something for you by tomorrow morning, I'll hand it over. I'll claim I came across the suicide note after talking to Doug today."

"You know, it's days like this that get me dreamin' of buying a food truck. Spend my days stokin' a grill and cookin' up a mess of *huli huli* chicken. I'd park down by the beach." His face softened as he stared listlessly out the windshield.

"I know there's a way to make this work," I said. "I just need a little more time."

I went inside but walked right through and out the back. The answer I was looking for wouldn't be found within the four walls of a bridal shop. As Einstein would say, I had a duty to act.

30

I called Steve's cell while driving home. My car has BlueTooth so I wasn't breaking any laws, but it was still distracting.

"I'm in the car so this needs to be quick. Where are you?"

"At the house. I'm just about to leave, though. I'm supposed to shoot some golfers down at the Blue Course in Wailea."

"Can you call and postpone it for half an hour?"

"What's up?"

"It's a matter of life and death. Well, not exactly death, but the next thing to it."

"What's going on, Pali?"

"Half an hour. That's all I'm asking."

He agreed and my next call was to Detective Glen Wong. I had to leave a message, but he called back a few minutes later. He was much more agreeable than the last time we spoke.

My third call was to Kaili, Doug's sister-in-law.

"*Aloha*. This is Pali Moon. I came to your house last week and talked to DJ."

"Sure, I 'member you."

"Can I come by your house in an hour or so? I've got something I think you'll want to hear."

"Why don't you just tell me?"

"No, not on the phone. I'll bring lunch for you and the *keiki*. What do you like?"

"Don't matter what I like. The *keiki* all like plate lunch with chicken from that drive-in place down in Kahului. Tell them double mac salad. I got five *keiki* here, you know."

"Let's make it noon. It'll take me a few more minutes to get from Kahului to your place."

I figured chicken plate lunch was more Kaili's choice than the kids, but kept it to myself. Any woman wrangling five kids under the age of fourteen over summer vacation deserved to be indulged.

I made one final call. It was the most important call of all, but unless everything else fell into place it would amount to nothing.

The Mini flew up the rises and hollows of Hali'imaile Road, bottoming out on a couple of the steeper dips. I hoped this wasn't one of the few days each year the Maui Police set up speed traps Upcountry. I didn't need any more points on my driving record and today of all days I couldn't afford the time it would take to try and talk my way out of it.

Steve waved from the front porch when I pulled up. The tires *skritched* as I brought the car to a quick stop and bailed out.

I clomped up the stairs and Steve handed me a glass of tropical ice tea. "You just rob a bank or something?"

"No, but I need your help. Your friend Glen Wong said he'd join us in a few minutes. I think I may have come up with a plan to save Doug Kanekoa."

"Okay. Fire away."

"No, if you don't mind I'd like to wait for Wong. If he won't go along, I'll need to consider Plan B."

"Which is?"

'Which is not the one I want to go with."

At that moment Wong arrived in his big Ford sedan. It's a standard-issue cop car without the bells and whistles. Literally. The thing is an unadorned white Crown Vic with no light rack, no exterior markings whatsoever, and the ugliest excuses for wheel covers ever devised by a major automotive company. Rumor was Maui county officials bought the cars at a fleet auction when a big-city mainland police department upgraded to newer models.

To his credit, Wong popped out of the car quickly. But then, if I had to drive that thing I'd hastily put as much distance between myself and it whenever possible. I stared out at the sad-looking car and recalled my own years of suffering from vehicular embarrassment. For almost five years I drove an ancient Geo Metro, a brand and model that didn't last much longer than that Samsung phone that burst into flames on airplanes. It was a sickly green color and even when I washed and waxed it, which was happened about as often as a solar eclipse, it looked grubby and forlorn. It was one happy day when I was finally able to drive my new red Mini Cooper off the lot.

"I hope this doesn't turn out to be one of your famous wild goose chases, Ms. Moon," Wong said by way of greeting.

I ignored the snarky comment. "I appreciate you getting here so fast."

He looked at his watch. "I've got somewhere I need to be in exactly forty minutes."

"Hi Glen," said Steve.

Steve and Glen share a similar, albeit discreet, lifestyle. Anyway, Wong is discreet. Steve wears his LGBT status like a rainbow badge of honor. But although social acceptance of differing lifestyles and viewpoints is a much-cherished Hawaiian norm here in the islands, there are still some hold-outs. And certain individuals, especially those in public service, often prefer a clear separation between their personal and professional lives.

The two men shook hands and Steve offered to get him water or ice tea. The detective chose the tea, and once Steve had cleared the door Wong turned to me.

"You're down to thirty-eight minutes."

I nodded. "You told me to find some evidence and I did." I handed him the second copy of the suicide note.

As he read, Wong scrunched up his face like a little kid trying to phonetically work out a string of unfamiliar words. "This for real?"

"I'm pretty sure it is."

"Why hasn't Kanekoa's lawyer brought this in?"

"He doesn't have it. I do."

"Why're you holding on to this? I thought you and James Kanekoa were friends. And from what I hear you're almost *'ohana* with his client, Doug."

"That's true."

Wong checked his watch again. "Thirty-five minutes."

"James knows about it but I'm keeping the original because, as you can see, Doug's wife didn't want her kids to know she'd committed suicide."

"So? She's dead. I think her voting rights terminated when, or maybe I should say, *if,* she wrote this note and then pulled the trigger. This needs to be brought to the attention of Detective Ho."

"This isn't the only thing I've got."

A beat passed between us, and Wong checked his watch one more time. "Do I need to keep reminding you that time is passing?"

"No, sorry. It's just that I'm trying to figure out the best way to phrase this."

"Spit it out, Ms. Moon. Remember, the Kanekoa case isn't even mine. I'm pretty sure there'll be plenty of time for wordsmithing once the evidence is all out in the open."

Steve came out with Wong's drink. "Sorry it took so long. I had to make a fresh pot of tea. What'd I miss?"

I recounted my trip to Walmart where I'd learned Lani had been prescribed a series of drugs associated with late-stage cancer.

"But you have no corroborating evidence from a doctor?" Wong said.

"Not yet."

"I'm willing to overlook the obvious procurement of information under false pretenses, namely you masquerading as the victim, but the court will not. It's called 'fruit of the poisonous tree,' Ms. Moon. Before I'm willing to bring any of this to the attention of Detective Ho or anyone else you better come up with something that'll hold up."

"I'm working on it."

"Good." He stood. "Then I guess I better be going."

I reached out and touched his forearm. He pulled back as if I'd zapped him with a jolt of electricity.

"Can I ask you a favor, detective?"

He blew out an exasperated breath. "What now?"

I made my request and he said he'd think about it. He skidded out of the driveway throwing up a fury of dirt and gravel. As soon as the dust settled I hopped in my car and careened down the highway toward Kahului.

31

Kaili shuffled quickly out to my car as I pulled into her driveway. It was more activity than she'd displayed during my last visit, but then, this time I was bringing lunch. She was wearing the same red and black *mu'u mu'u* she'd had on before.

"Here, let me help with that," she said, snatching two large white bags from my arms.

She opened one of the bags and sniffed the homey fragrance of plate lunch: *shoyu*-bathed meat and tangy mayonnaise. "You got chicken, right?"

I assured her I did and we went inside. The place was oddly calm for a small plantation-style house with five rambunctious kids. Quiet and empty.

"Where are the *keiki*?"

"I sent 'em down to the beach."

"But I have lunch for them."

"Don' worry, they not starve. I made sandwich." She said it like "sammach" and it definitely sounded singular, rather than plural.

She took a seat on the dilapidated sofa and began rummaging through the food bags. After half a minute, she looked up.

"Why you stand? Sit down, girl. I gotta eat somethin' befo' we talk story." She took out one of the food containers and then pushed the bag across the scarred coffee table toward me.

I was eager to get to the point of my visit, but from the looks of things, I'd get more co-operation if I let her eat first. She snapped open the carton and shoveled food down so quickly it was like watching a "now you see it, now you don't" magic act.

I picked at my food as I rehearsed my appeal.

"Wha'sa matter? You don' like?" she said.

"Yeah, it's good. I'm just not that hungry right now."

"Look to me like you neva' hungry. You skin and bone."

She finished the last of her mac salad and tossed the Styrofoam carton on the floor. In seconds flat a plump tabby-striped cat materialized out of nowhere and began licking the carton.

"Get outta there." Kaili made a shooing motion, which the cat ignored.

Sensing an opportunity, I pulled another carton from the bag and held it just out of reach.

"You want a little more?"

"I guess. It will jus' get cold before those *keiki* get home, anyway."

"Okay. But first we need to talk. Did you know your sister was ill?"

"You mean sick? Yeah, I knew. She tol' me she din't want Douglas to know. And her *keiki*. She say she din't want to bother them."

"Did you ever go with her to the doctor?"

Kaili's expression darkened. "How you hear that? I tol' those nurses to keep quiet."

"Did the nurses talk to you about what was going on with Lani?"

"They did. But I din't understan' most of it. There was somethin' wrong with her head. She got the cancer in there, that's all I know."

"How about the doctor?"

"What about him? He seem like a nice man. Little *haole* guy, but mos' doctors over here are."

"Did he talk to you?"

"Only when I went in with Lani. He said I could come with her because sometimes she gets stuff mixed up, what with her brain sick like that."

"I need to tell you something that's going to be hard for you to hear."

"Somethin' bad about Leilani?"

"Yeah."

"What could be mo' bad than her being dead?"

She had a point. "Yeah, that's about as bad as it gets. But what I'm about to tell you doesn't make it any better. Especially since I know your family has strong religious beliefs."

I showed her the copy of Lani's suicide note. It took her a long time to read. Maybe she took her time because it comforted her to see her twin sister's handwriting and she was realizing this would be the last communication she'd ever see from her sibling. Or maybe she was just a slow reader.

Finally, she looked up. "You think she killed herself?"

"I do."

"With that gun DJ was talking about?"

"I think so."

"So that means Douglas din't do it?"

"I don't think he did."

"Then why he say he did?"

"He's protecting her memory. He doesn't want DJ and Maia to think badly of their mother. She was worried the kids would think she didn't love them enough to hang on for as long possible."

"And besides, killin' yourself is a sin."

I nodded.

She heaved her weight forward and grabbed the carton out of my hands. "That plate lunch gettin' cold."

I waited while she stuffed mouthful after mouthful into her mouth. When she came up for air, I leaned in and put a hand on her knee.

"I need you to do something for me. I've got an idea of how we can honor Lani's request and still get Doug out of jail. You want his kids to go back home, don't you?"

"Not if they're going to be living with my sister's killer."

"You know that's not what happened."

She hung her head and said in a low voice. "I was worried she might do sumthin' like this. She was out of her head crazy with pain. Even with all those drugs they gave her. But how we gonna tell the truth without the *keiki* finding out what she did?"

"I've got an idea. If you'll help me, I'm hoping together we can do right by everyone in your *'ohana*. Are you willing to go with me to Kahului?"

* * *

I allowed Kaili to finish the rest of the second container of plate lunch. Then, while she cleaned herself up in the bathroom I put away the leftovers. I offered to leave her the rest of my largely untouched meal but she insisted we take it with us.

"I might need a snack while we're on the road," she said.

Kaili went next door to ask the neighbor to keep an eye out for the kids before heading over to join me in the Mini. It was a snug fit for Kaili, but she seemed to enjoy the ride.

"This car's like wearin' tight shoes," she said. "You look good, but they pinch a little. I like the open-up sky, though." She waved a hand out of the sunroof like a girl in a limo during a bachelorette party.

We got to Kahului at about two. I parked in the clinic parking lot and Kaili took a deep breath before heaving her way out of the passenger seat.

"I know this doctor did his best by my sista. But it wasn't good enough."

"You don't blame him, do you?"

"No. But I don't like being here. I was hopin' to never see this place again."

My fourth call that morning had been to make a two o'clock consultation appointment with Lani's oncologist. The appointment nurse had tried to put me off for a couple of weeks but I promised to take only five minutes of the doctor's time. I fibbed and said Leilani Kanekoa's sister had a couple of questions and was extremely distressed. A few words from the doctor would go a long way in allowing her to accept her sister's death.

The nurse grudgingly admitted they'd had a cancellation and told me to be there at two-thirty.

"Don't be late. We don't do island time here. Some of our patients are measuring their lives in days, not years, so every hour matters."

Kaili and I got checked in and seated by two-fifteen. About a minute later, a nurse opened the door that led to the back and said, "Kaili?"

We both stood. The nurse looked at her clipboard. "I'm afraid I'm only showing Kaili's name here. Are you 'ohana or merely a friend?"

I looked at Kaili. On the ride over I'd explained what I wanted from the doctor so I hoped she'd be able to handle it alone, but she looked puzzled.

"No, she comes with me. I'm too sad." With that, she burst into a torrent of tears.

The nurse glanced around the waiting room. A half-dozen patients and caregivers were shooting her major stink eye.

"Fine. Come this way."

We were led to an office with a large window that looked out on an open-air atrium. It featured an artfully-arranged rock garden and a multitude of tropical flowers.

"Tha's pretty," Kaili said after the nurse had closed the door. Her tears had stopped as quickly as they'd started. I was about to remark about her remarkable acting ability when the door swished open and a tidy man in a white lab coat entered. He was short, about five-six, with sad brown eyes and a fringe of light brown hair around a rather shiny pate.

He held out his hand. "Hello, I'm Dr. Randolph. I'm sorry for your loss."

I stood and shook his hand. "Pali Moon. I'm hoping you might be able to help Lani Kanekoa's sister here."

Kaili had assumed an expression akin to the mask of tragedy but stayed silent.

"In what way?" the doctor said.

"She's having a hard time accepting her twin sister's untimely death. I was wondering if you could explain exactly what Leilani Kanekoa was facing, if she had lived."

The doctor squinted and leaned back, crossing his arms. "This is highly unusual. I heard Lani was murdered."

"That was the original assumption, but new facts are coming to light."

"May I ask what facts?"

"Doctor, I've been admonished by the police to keep my mouth shut. But Kaili here is extremely upset over her sister's passing and I'm hoping a few words from you might assist her in understanding her sister's situation, regardless of the unfortunate circumstances surrounding her death."

He kept the squint going. "I'm afraid I'm not following you."

"Would you please tell Kaili the prognosis you gave Lani when she came to this office on Thursday, July twenty-fifth?"

He glanced at the folder in his hands.

I went on. "I believe you'll see that Lani had Kaili, her sister, on her list of HIPAA-approved contacts. She'd appreciate you being straight with her about her sister's prognosis."

And then, like a sudden Upcountry shower on a sunny day, once again Kaili burst into tears.

The doctor bit his lip. "Okay. Let me review my notes."

Kaili kept up the waterworks.

The doctor took a seat behind his desk and silently pushed a box of tissues toward the seemingly distraught woman. "I'm afraid your sister had an incurable situation. She had glioblastoma multiforme, or GBM. Hers was a grade four astrocytoma, which we don't have a cure for at this time."

"And she knew this?" I said.

He nodded. "She did. When she came in on her last visit she was emphatic that she be told the truth. Normally I don't give patients such a blunt prognosis, but she was very clear she wanted to know where things stood."

"And what symptoms was she having?"

Once again he dropped his gaze to the folder. "Severe headaches. Loss of impulse control, loss of memory and even occasional loss of vision. She was having a hard time keeping food down and claimed she was sleeping up to fifteen hours a day."

"What were her treatment options?"

"Realistically, none. In certain circumstances we can slow the tumor growth with chemo or radiation, but in Mrs. Kanekoa's case neither would've been effective. Besides, she'd opted out of treatment. She said she and her husband had discussed it and decided to allow Nature to take its course."

That stopped me short. Had Doug known? I willed my face to not betray my thoughts and went on. "How long did she have, doctor?"

"We don't make predictions like that."

"But, realistically. In your professional opinion, how long would you expect a patient in Lani Kanekoa's condition to hang on?"

He shrugged. Obviously, this was not a subject he was comfortable discussing.

I persisted. "Months?

He shook his head.

"Weeks?"

"Perhaps two to three." He steepled his fingers. "If she was lucky."

32

We left the oncologist's office and I drove Kaili home to Haiku. It was coming up on three-thirty when we arrived at her house. She hesitated before opening the passenger door.

"You wanna come in?"

"No, *mahalo*. I need to finish up a few more things. I appreciate you going with me to the doctor's office."

"No worries. I knew Lani was sick, but I didn't know how sick. The doctor said she was in a lotta pain, eh?"

"There's no way to know for sure, but from the pills she was taking, it must've been brutal."

"You believe she going to hell?"

I shook my head. "I think her hell was here on earth. Imagine the situation she was in. Her meds were costing a fortune and there was no hope she'd ever get better. She was becoming more and more mentally unstable, turning her into a stranger to her husband and kids."

"You think she a quitter?"

"No. I think she was desperate."

"What am I supposed to tell her *keiki*? She didn't want them to know what she did, but if the police show everybody that suicide note, what'll I say?"

"For now, I think it's best to say nothing. I'm still working on it."

"I love her so much, ya know?"

"We all did."

She started to tear up and from the looks of it, this time it was for real.

I patted her fleshy upper arm and let out a sigh. As much as I fancy myself a pretty good candidate for motherhood, I'm not that great at comforting people in emotional distress. It's probably because from an early age I had deal with grief on my own. My auntie was a capable, no-nonsense caregiver who single-handedly raised more than half a dozen kids, most of whom weren't her own. No easy task in Maui's over-heated economy with sky-high rents and five-dollar-a-gallon gas. She made sure there was food on the table and a hug before bedtime and for that I'll be eternally grateful.

Kaili turned her tear-streaked face to me. "Sorry for crying. I been holding it back for the *keiki*. But now that I know how bad things were for my sista, it make me sad I couldn't do nothing."

"None of us could. I think that's why Doug confessed. He thinks going to prison will make up for not being able to fix things for Lani when she was alive."

That brought on an even greater onslaught of tears.

I reached into the back and grabbed the Styrofoam box of plate lunch she'd insisted I take with me. "Here. Maybe a little snack will make you feel better."

"It been out here in the car all this time," she said. "You think it's still okay?"

"Smell it first." That was all Auntie Momi. When anyone showed concern about eating food that'd gone bad she'd advise them to "smell it." It's a wonder none of us died from salmonella poisoning.

* * *

I beat Wong to my shop by only a few minutes. He came in the front, glancing over his shoulder as if he was worried he'd been followed.

I stood. "Everything okay?"

"I can't believe the things I agree to do for you, Ms. Moon. If I got caught leaking info like this I could say *aloha* to my badge and gun."

"I really appreciate this. But it's the right thing to do. Neither of us wants to see an innocent man go down for a murder he didn't commit."

"Yeah, but his innocence hasn't been determined. Take a look."

He handed me a stapled document folded into fourths. I unfolded it. There were three pages total. The first page was marked, *Summary Preliminary Report of Autopsy*.

I quickly read through the findings, ignoring details such as brain weight, what she was wearing and a narrative describing her four small tattoos. I scanned down to the section titled, "Description of Injuries."

In that section, the medical examiner presented a meticulous listing of the damage Lani's body had undergone at the time of her death. It was grisly reading. The report referenced drawings and photos that Wong had kindly not included.

At the bottom of the page were two sections: Cause of Death and Manner of Death. The cause of death described the gunshot wound to the head in minute detail, clarifying the amount of cranial damage and resulting tissue injury. On the Manner of Death line the doctor had written a single word: *Homicide*.

"What about her brain tumor?" I said.

Wong shrugged. "I figure the GSW must've literally blown it away. Can't fault the ME for not finding something that's no longer there."

"But it's important to this case."

Once again, Wong shrugged.

I pressed on. "Has Detective Ho seen this?"

"According to the ME, Ho came by while they were stitching her up and they talked. He was the first to get the written report."

"Can we challenge the findings?"

"We can, but doctors are like judges. They don't like being told they were wrong."

"But I talked to Lani's oncologist. He gave her zero chance of survival."

Wong narrowed his eyes. "Seriously? He said that?"

"Well, not in so many words. But his prognosis was bleak. She was on a boatload of painkillers and antipsychotics. Ever hear of fentanyl?"

"Yeah, it's a killer street drug."

"It is. But it's also prescribed when morphine and less-effective opioids aren't enough."

Wong reached out for the autopsy report. "Mind if I look at that again?"

I waited while he carefully perused the pages. Finally he looked up. "If Leilani Kanekoa was taking all the drugs you say she was, why don't any of them show up on the tox screen?"

"Good question. Detective, would you consider taking me along to check out the crime scene?"

He blew out a breath. "Look, this isn't my case. If I got caught, especially with a civilian in tow, I'd better be ready to request a transfer."

"Not if you have a good reason."

"Such as?"

I mentally flipped through the events of the past two weeks. "How about saying you left something behind when you were out there earlier?"

"Why would I bring you along?"

"Better still. Say I thought I lost something and I asked you to help me find it."

He scowled. "Not very convincing."

"But convincing enough?"

"I guess."

Wong checked his watch. "I need to go. I'll meet you up there at six o'clock tonight. Don't make me wait, Ms. Moon."

Time was running out. I assured him I'd be prompt.

33

Is there anything more frustrating than cooling your heels when you have no time to spare? At six-twenty I called Wong's cell one more time. And, again, it went directly to voicemail.

"I'm at Kanekoa's in Pukalani," I said. "Call or text me with your ETA."

The car was getting stuffy but the last thing I wanted was for a nosy neighbor to catch me loitering outside Doug's house. No doubt the police had asked the neighbors to keep an eye out, and since nothing much happens in the sleepy bedroom community there was little chance I'd go unnoticed.

Then I got an idea. I got out and went to the house next door and tapped on the screen door. The plastic Crocs were no longer on the doorstep, and I hoped that meant her family had returned to O'ahu. A tiny elderly woman with Asian features scuttled to the door as if she'd been lying in wait.

"*Aloha*," I said. "Are you Ami Tanaka?"

She regarded me with a sharp eye. "*Aloha*. And yes, that is my name. How can I help you?"

"May I come in?"

"What? You try to sell me something?"

"No, auntie. I'm sorry to bother you at dinner time. My name is Pali Moon, and I'm not selling anything. I'm a friend of Doug and Lani Kanekoa's.."

She unlatched the screen and stepped back to let me pass.

"That was some kin' of bad, eh?" she said.

"It was. It still is."

We stood there for a few moments without saying anything, lost in our own recollection of the loss. The house didn't smell as if dinner was on the stove. It simply smelled clean, like she'd lemon-oiled the ancient rattan furniture ten minutes earlier.

"What can I do for you?" she asked again.

"I'm trying to get to the bottom of what happened next door."

She narrowed her eyes. "You a reporter?"

"No, auntie. I'm just a friend. Doug is my martial arts *sifu* and Lani was my friend. I don't think the police have got the story straight."

She looked down. "Okay. You come in and we talk story a bit, eh? I just put the water on to boil."

She gestured for me to take a seat while she scurried off to the kitchen in the back. I took in my surroundings and it dawned on me that Ami's house was the mirror image of the Kanekoa's. Front living room with tile floors, dining area and kitchen behind, and a hallway with bedrooms and bath on one side. Although the houses were identical, they didn't appear to be from the street since the builder had apparently taken pains to alter the front exterior so all the houses didn't look alike.

When she returned with the tea tray I'd mentally organized the questions I had for her. We went through the requisite small talk—where I lived, if I was locally born and raised, her recent loss of her husband due to a heart attack—before I was able to pose my first query.

"I heard that Doug came over on the Sunday before and asked if the kids could stay with you. Is that right?"

Her eyes squeezed shut, and I was concerned she might be getting ready to cry. I felt the urge to pull back the question but didn't. It was getting late and I felt tantalizingly close to learning something significant.

"Yeah, he asked me. I had my whole *'ohana* coming that week. It was my birthday, eh? I turn seventy-five and this the first year without my Kaito."

It took me a moment to grasp Kaito must've been her husband's name. For a second, I thought maybe she'd had something surgically removed.

I nodded.

She went on. "So, Doug comes over and I tell him, 'Sorry' but I can only keep the *keiki* one night. Look at this house. Three bedroom, and I got nine *'ohana* from Honolulu coming next day. Where I put everybody?"

She leaned in and poured the tea. "You take sugar?"

"No, *mahalo*."

"Milk?"

"No."

She wrinkled up her nose. "That good. Only baby drink milk, eh?"

She handed me the tea cup and I thanked her with a head bow. I'd sipped tea in Sifu Doug's office enough times to have a nodding acquaintance with proper tea etiquette.

"What did Doug say when he asked about you taking the *keiki*?"

"He say he need some alone time with his wife."

"Did he seem angry? Or upset?"

She gazed off to the right. "No, he seem troubled. That's what I told police. He didn't look mad. He was sad. There's a difference."

Big difference, I thought, but I kept it to myself. I glanced out the front window to see if Wong had arrived, but my car was still the only one out there.

"What did he say when you told him you could only take the kids for one night?"

"He say not to worry. He got a sista-in-law in Haiku who would take them. I guess the *keiki* want to stay here that week so they could be with their friends, but I couldn't help. Now I'm sorry 'bout it."

"I'm sure Doug understands."

"I don' know, but he probably glad they weren't here when it happened."

That answered my next question so I moved on.

"What did you see or hear the day Lani died?"

"I already tell the police this."

"Yes, and I'm sorry to make you go through it again, but some new developments have come up and I want to see if they make sense."

"What new developments?"

"I'm pretty sure Doug didn't kill Lani."

She blew out a quick *phht* and waved a hand. "Course not. That all bullshit."

I blinked at her earthy profanity. "You don't think he did it?"

"No way. It's not possible."

"Why?"

"Because when he left that morning Lani was fine."

"How do you know?"

"I see her. I'm putting out the garbage can in the street, you know? It's Monday and that when the garbage come, and there she is in the front window. She wave at me." Ami dropped her head and covered her eyes. Soon, her back twitched as if she were discreetly holding back sobs.

"I'm so sorry to make you go through this again. But you're helping. You really are."

She nodded and lifted her head. Her cheeks were tear-stained. "I love her like a daughter, you know? She a good girl and a good mother. I know she been sick, but that morning she look so happy. Like an angel." She paused and shook her head. "And next thing I know, she *is* an angel."

"Who do you think killed Lani?"

"Don't know." She bit her lip.

"But you have an idea, don't you?"

She nodded.

"What did you tell the police?"

"I told them I thought it was the robber."

"Because the back door window was broken?"

"Yeah."

"Did you see an intruder over at the Kanekoa's that morning?"

"No. But I can't see their back yard. They got a fence and bushes back there. You go see for yourself. No way to see." She said it as if I'd accused her of not being a good neighbor.

I paused to give her a moment to collect herself.

"Who do you really think killed Lani Kanekoa?"

"I love her so much, you know?" She broke into inconsolable sobs.

"Your sister-in-law told me you think the police have it all wrong."

"They do. No way Doug shot her."

"How can you be certain of that?"

She squeezed her eyes closed as if trying to make a painful decision.

"I know about the suicide note," I said.

Her eyes popped open. "You do?"

I nodded. "Doug sent me to find it in his office."

"Ah, then you know."

"Yes."

She blew out a breath. "I heard the gun that morning. I thought maybe a car had backfired because it was only the one time. But then, I got to thinking I should check it out."

I waited.

"When Doug came home I was pounding on their door."

"What happened then?"

"He told me to stay there and he went inside. When he came out, he showed me the note."

"Did you tell this to the police?"

She gave her head a barely perceptible shake. "No."

"May I ask why?"

"If you read the note you know why."

An ugly white Crown Vic pulled up outside leaving me to ponder the proverbial fork in the road.

34

It was almost seven and starting to get dark. I finished up with Ami, apologetically made my way out, and dashed over to the Kanekoa house. Wong was waiting at the front door, arms crossed, face glowering.

"Didn't I make myself clear about keeping me waiting?"

"But you're an hour late. I was talking with the neighbor."

"I can see that. Now, let's get inside before someone sees us out here and calls the police." In the shadowy porch it was hard to make out Wong's face but I could hear the wry smile in his voice.

"*Mahalo*, but I don't need to go in the house anymore, Detective."

"What? You drag me up here, which means I'm missing dinner, I might add, and now you don't want to go in?"

"Sorry. But I'm ready to make my case. Would you like to sit in your car or mine?"

He glanced at the Mini and mumbled we could use his car. He even opened the car door for me. I was half-expecting him to put a hand on my head as I ducked inside, but thankfully, he didn't.

He held up his wrist and inspected his watch in the glow of the overhead light. "You have five minutes."

I took a few seconds to decide where to begin and then I plunged in.

When I finished, Wong leaned back in his seat and shut his eyes. He stayed like that for what seemed like two or three minutes but was probably much less. I remained quiet.

He finally turned and faced me. "Okay, let me see if I've got this straight. You're telling me the victim had inoperable brain cancer and took her own life."

"That's correct."

"With the alleged perpetrator's handgun."

"Yes."

"And the ME didn't find evidence of the tumor because the GSW obliterated it."

"The autopsy report indicated a point blank gunshot to the head. I can't speak for Lani, but if it was me, I'd probably aim for the place where I was having the most pain."

"What about the broken glass in the rear door?"

"Lani didn't want her family and friends to know what she'd done, so she staged a break-in before she went out to the garage."

"You know we dismissed that intruder theory from day one."

"I was pretty sure you had."

"And you're saying that on the day of her death, the victim called her husband and told him what she was planning to do and he came home and found her dead in the garage?"

"That's a little fuzzy, Detective. At this point there's no way to know what Lani said in that final call. But I firmly believe Doug Kanekoa was either at his place of work or on his way back to his house at the time of her death."

"How do you know he didn't come home and do the deed for her? You know, like a mercy killing."

"Because there's an eye witness."

"To the murder?" His voice rose an octave on the last word.

"No, to the time Doug came home and found his wife's body in the garage."

"The neighbor?"

"Yes." I pointed to Ami's house.

"Why didn't she tell us any of this when we interviewed her?"

"She claims you didn't ask."

Of course that wasn't the whole truth. Ami and Doug had read the suicide note together and Doug had sworn her to honor Lani's wishes. She'd agreed, thinking the fake intruder scene would suffice. When they accused Doug of killing Lani she'd had many sleepless nights, but her loyalty remained with the woman she'd loved like a daughter.

"I'm going to have to file a report on this, Ms. Moon. Detective Ho will want to reevaluate this case as a suicide and there will be a formal inquiry. Your pal Doug will probably get out, but the cause of death will be public record."

"I was afraid you'd say that."

"I don't see any way around it."

"What if I can get her doctor to sign an affidavit of her terminal prognosis?"

He shrugged. "That would go to motive, but a suicide's a suicide. And that's what will be stated as cause of death on the autopsy."

"Can you give me one more day before you pull the trigger?" As soon as it was out of my mouth I regretted my choice of words. "I mean, before you bring this to Ho?"

Wong checked his watch. "You've got until eight pm tomorrow."

* * *

I apologized for calling James during family time, but told him I had information that couldn't wait. I briefly described my meetings with Ami and Wong and asked if we could meet in the morning.

"Are you nuts? Where are you? I'll come wherever you are now."

I fibbed and told him I was at home even though I was only halfway there. He said he'd be there within half an hour and hung up without saying, "goodbye."

Lucky for me, Steve had gone out and Finn had left a message he'd be working until after nine. The house was eerily quiet except for the brisk trade winds rattling the palms like a bagful of chicken bones. I put on a pot of coffee. I chastised myself for craving caffeine when I knew it would keep me up all night, but then ruefully acknowledged that after the events of the day I probably wouldn't sleep anyway.

James arrived looking like a man whose wife usually picked out his work clothes. He wore a stained and faded red t-shirt with a stretched-out neck and cargo shorts that not only had seen better days but probably had been made for a man fifty pounds heavier. As he kicked off his *rubba slippas* at the door, I couldn't help notice one was brown and the other black.

"Sorry I didn't take time to clean up." Gone was the guy who'd treated me like an annoying gnat, replaced by a guy who looked like a kid coming downstairs on Christmas morning. "So, what've you got?"

I reiterated the information I'd just gone over with Wong. When I finished, James asked a few questions, and before long he knew everything I knew.

"So, that's it," he said. "I'll file a motion tomorrow."

"Not so fast. What about Lani's wish to keep her cause of death secret?"

"What about it? I've got a client who's been wrongly accused and enough evidence to back it up. Great work, by the way."

If he thought an offhand "attagirl" was going to dissuade me from pressing him on the cause of death issue, he was sorely mistaken.

"Look, James, Doug was willing to go to prison for the rest of his life over this. I think before we rush in we need to consider the consequences."

He looked beyond annoyed. "I smelled coffee when I came in. Can I talk you out of a cup?"

* * *

We stayed up until long past Finn came in. In fact, James left only a few minutes before Steve showed up at midnight. I was still sitting at the kitchen table when my bleary-eyed housemate stumbled through the back door.

"You shouldn't be drinking and driving," I said.

"I know. I grabbed an Uber." He slurred the word, Uber, making it sound more like, Over.

"You want some coffee?"

We sat in the harsh glare of the overhead light as I shared the plan James and I had crafted and then meticulously gone over at least a dozen times. When I finished, he nodded.

"Happens all the time," Steve said.

"Especially under the circumstances."

"People think having a gun in the house makes them safer, but statistics show it's quite the opposite."

"Especially with people who've never fired a weapon before."

"You sorry you told me?" he said. "I'm kind of known around these parts for having a big mouth."

"I trust you. But I am going to make you do a 'pinkie swear.'"

   We locked little fingers, but when I looked into his half-lidded bloodshot eyes I was pretty sure he wouldn't remember most of it anyway.

35

Of course I first had to sell Detective Wong on the brilliant solution James and I had come up with. Then he had to sell it to Detective Ho, who in turn, had to get buy-off from the prosecuting attorney. I spent a nervous week waiting for phone calls and anticipating emails, but by mid-August it was done.

As is common in Upcountry ʻohana like the Kanekoas, every victory is marked with a "come one, come all" luau, complete with a pig in the ground and two or three kegs of local beer. At the party Finn was off in a side yard talking to a clutch of Kanekoa brothers, including Doug, newly-released from jail but still bearing the somber aspect of a man in mourning.

I was watching a group of *keiki* playing tag when Doug's brother, James, ambled over.

"From what I hear, nobody on this island was looking forward to prosecuting my brother," he said. "I'd already lined up like a hundred character witnesses. And the state's evidence was pretty much circumstantial."

"Why didn't they find any drugs in Lani's system when they did the autopsy?" It was the one nagging question I'd yet to answer.

"Doug says she was totally righteous about drug use. She bought the stuff but never even considered taking it. He said that's why he was so shocked when she killed herself with the gun. He figured if things got real bad she'd take an overdose. He never saw the other thing coming."

"The kids think it was accidental?"

"Yep, that's what everyone thinks. The ME even amended the autopsy report."

"So the story is she was in a lot of pain and went to the garage to get the gun out of the house and she must've stumbled and it went off."

"That's what the neighbor said. In her sworn statement she said she saw Lani that morning after Doug left, and she heard the gunshot before he got home. No mention of the suicide note."

"How is DJ taking it?"

"He's upset, but he seemed to settle down when he had a chance to talk to her doctor. Both the kids now know their mother only had a short time left."

We watched the kids laughing and rolling around on the grass. Even DJ, who probably considered himself too old to be playing children's games, seemed to be caught up in the familiarity of acting like a kid again.

"And how about the note?" I said. I'd given James the original and all the copies. I didn't want the burden of having it and I certainly didn't relish the notion of destroying it.

"Don't worry, Pali. It's right where it should be."

I looked over at the side yard. "And so is Sifu Doug."

EPILOGUE

To this day, Doug and I have never discussed the details of the tragic weeks after he lost his beloved wife. It's strange, because we talk about everything else.

Lani's memorial service was a family affair. The extended 'ohana gathered at Baldwin Beach to reminisce and pledge remembrance before Doug and the kids headed out in a cousin's outrigger to return her ashes to the sea. Out of respect no uninvited mourners attended but Sifu Doug shared a photo taken at the scene which showed a single lei bobbing on the waves. I waited until I was back in my car before allowing the tears to fall.

Finn and I are still trying to create a child. I have no idea how or if it will ever amount to anything, but I must admit I'm enjoying the process.

Farrah and Ono have not been troubled by their cane worker ghost since the *kahu* finally showed up. I still think the guy charged too much, and I question his business judgment. I mean, what if I just blew off a wedding and showed up the next day? But they're happy with the results so who am I to judge?

Steve has recovered from the blow-up of his relationship with Allen. There were a few fits and starts when it looked like they might try to patch it back together, but at this writing it's history and he's still my housemate. Personally, I'm fine with that. Finn still travels a lot and I enjoy Steve's company over loneliness. Besides, he's an excellent cook.

The lesson I learned from Doug and Lani's tragedy is there are still chivalrous men in this world. I might be putting too fine a point on it, but ask yourself, who do you know who would honor their marriage vows to the extent Doug was willing to?

When I asked him about it, he shrugged. "I had no choice. I know I'll see her again and she'll know what I did. She believes she married a man who'd keep his word and, nine times out of ten, my wife is right."

AUTHOR'S NOTE

This story was conceived like a mid-life baby, unwanted at first but cherished all the more because it was a surprise. I thought I was finished with the "Islands of Aloha" series with "Hilo, Goodbye" but Sifu Doug's character kept yammering, "What about me?" and I had to answer. He's a guy you ignore at your own peril.

As always, there are people to thank. *Mahalo* to my first readers, Tom Haberer, Diana Paul, and KC Curtis. What would I do without you? I also want to give a shout-out to Debora Lewis, of Arena Publishing, who creates the print version, taking the manuscript from digital ones and zeros to an actual thing you can hold in your hands. For those of you who tell me you want to read "a real book" rather than an e-book, she's your hero since I couldn't do it if you held a gun to my head (oops, bad reference, sorry).

This book is dedicated to a dear friend, Susan Cook-Goodwin. We share a rather complicated past, but we also share a most treasured future. Sue is my son's stepmom and no one could hope for a better person to entrust their child to every other weekend and Wednesday nights. *Mahalo*, Sue, for all you've done to help "our" child become the best person he could be (and to marry the best young woman on the planet).

For those of you who are asking, will there be another Pali Moon story, I say, "Who knows?" I'm not being coy, it's just that I haven't heard from any of the characters in a while. But if I do, you'll be the first to know.

Titles in the "Islands of Aloha Mystery Series"
—in series order

Maui Widow Waltz
Livin' Lahaina Loca
Lana'i of the Tiger
Kaua'i Me a River
O'ahu Lonesome Tonight?
I'm Kona Love You Forever
Moloka'i Lullaby
Hilo, Goodbye
Isle Be Seeing You

Other books by JoAnn Bassett:

Mai Tai Butterfly
Lucky Beach

"Like" her Facebook page at:
JoAnn Bassett's Author Page

And check out her website:
http://www.joannbassett.com

Made in the USA
San Bernardino, CA
17 September 2017